FOREST OF ECHOES

VIRAL MONSTERS™
BOOK ONE

MICHAEL TODD

I appreciate your love, your
support and acceptance
when you don't have a
clue what I'm talking about!

CHAPTER ONE

Night hung thick among the tall pines. Jackson could sense the damp snap of needles under each step. He paused to broadcast a quick greeting to the camera in his hand. A few watchers had tuned in and tossed chat messages about Bigfoot sightings and urban legends. Mia glanced over his shoulder with an uneasy smirk, flipped her phone to front-facing view, and shone a shaky beam of light ahead. They had planned to fake a creature encounter, but their costumed friend canceled, leaving them alone in Washington's Gifford Pinchot Forest with nothing but a mix of fear and ambition.

Jackson stepped around a knotted trunk and tried to maintain a confident tone for their audience. He teased Mia about jumping at every sound, though he was the one who nearly tripped over an exposed root a moment earlier. The chat feed taunted them with contradictory messages. Is Bigfoot real or a hoax? Mia shrugged at her phone and joked that they were about to find out. She flashed a grin that looked forced around the edges.

They had set out around midnight in hopes that late-night authenticity would catch viewers' attention. The flashlight beam carved odd shadows across branches, and each shape in the distance felt like prying eyes. Mia kept glancing at the comment feed on her screen. Every few seconds she read a snippet from chat and joked that Bigfoot had better hurry if he wanted to make it on time. Jackson tried to keep the camera steady while stepping deeper into the undergrowth.

Earlier that day they had decided to launch their stream from a small clearing near an abandoned logging road. Now they realized how far they had wandered. The forest's nighttime hush felt stifling. Whenever the wind shifted they heard faint rustles or swift scuttling from unseen critters. Each time a twig snapped or a shape flickered in the corner of their vision they froze. Only moments later did they realize that nothing was there.

Mia exhaled and forced a laugh for the camera though her voice shook. "Guess we're jumpy. Good content, right?" Jackson nodded and then panned his phone around with a theatrical flourish. The chat erupted with viewers egging them on and urging them to push deeper. Some watchers claimed they saw movement behind certain trees, likely hoping to build hype.

Mia muttered, "This was so much easier to do when we thought we'd have a fake monster." Her breath left small clouds in the chilly air. Jackson tried to encourage her by whispering that they still had the adrenaline factor and the bold idea of capturing something creepy on film. He stepped around a log and his light illuminated an array of fresh wide footprints in the mud.

"Could be from some hikers," Jackson said, but his tone was uncertain. Mia leaned in and shone her phone's light, which revealed the tracks more clearly. They were oddly spaced as if the maker had an unusually long stride and each toe print was broad. Chat scrolled with guesses from prank to real cryptid. Jackson scowled at some obnoxious jokes then followed the tracks deeper into the trees.

They pressed on, guided by a half-formed plan and curiosity. Mia filled time by describing humorous theories about Bigfoot's internet presence. Her voice wavered whenever a branch creaked in the distance. As they hiked deeper, the vegetation grew tangled. Jackson realized they might be lost but kept that thought to himself. He filmed while scanning the feed for instructions or barbs from viewers.

Several times they heard something move in the distance. The forest never stayed silent long and each rustle set them on edge. Mia stepped on a hidden puddle and soaked one sneaker. She cursed under her breath. Jackson gave the camera a shaky grin and told chat that Bigfoot was messing with them by rearranging puddles. That drew a few laughs from the watchers. He hoped the comedic act would keep them from noticing his sweaty grip on the phone.

They found a narrow deer trail that curved around a large cedar. Mia waved her smartphone to highlight the trunk where an odd spiral was carved into the bark. She moved closer and the symbol revealed smooth deliberate lines. She called Jackson over and he showed it on the livestream. The chat lit up with theories about cults, hidden rituals, or cryptid signposts. Mia said it felt unsettling and he studied the pattern then concluded it was a leftover prank from earlier visitors.

They turned to move on when Mia spotted something. A silhouette loomed beyond a cluster of saplings. She raised her light expecting to see their friend in a gorilla mask. Instead the figure stood taller and broader than she anticipated with an odd protrusion along its shoulders. Mia's heart pounded and she felt her pulse in her throat. She tried to rationalize it and Jackson caught a glimpse on his phone screen then nearly dropped the device.

He recovered and aimed the flashlight. Ordinarily, he would have cracked a joke or tried to rationalize the sight, but only a strangled sound left his lips. Mia's eyes locked on a shape that seemed layered with something bone-like across its spine. When she raised her phone higher, her light revealed a momentary glint along that plating. A sudden stink hit them, a reek of wet fur and decay that made them both recoil. Before she could speak, the shape crouched in a way that suggested sudden movement. The watchers typed frantically, spamming the chat with expletives and demands to see more.

Mia inhaled sharply and took a step back. Her foot tangled in a root and she stumbled into Jackson, jarring the camera. The flashlight swung wildly, capturing a half-second of the creature's face, or at least a stony brow. Jackson's heart hammered. "Run!" he shouted. His voice cracked. He darted sideways and tugged Mia's arm.

They sprinted blindly, stepping across ferns that snapped underfoot. Jackson tried to hold his phone, but his sweaty grip slipped and the device tumbled to the ground. He hesitated as he glanced back, but the heavy snap of branches behind them shot panic through his veins. Then he bolted. The phone streamed audio into the darkness. Mia's breath sounded ragged and their footsteps pounded away from the camera's vantage.

A few yards behind them, something large crashed against the undergrowth. The phone's lens aimed at nothing but twigs, though the feed continued to broadcast the chaos. Thousands of viewers typed question marks and theories, unsure if it was an elaborate trick. The phone's small LED indicator stayed lit, shining across damp leaves.

A bent figure emerged briefly near the fallen phone. He wore a dark hood and gripped a separate camera rig at chest level. He adjusted the angle to capture the phone's position. His posture was calm and calculating. He filmed the scattered leaves then pointed his camera toward where Jackson and Mia had run. He recorded the fleeting echo of their footsteps and a scattering of distant crows. Then he knelt, studying the half-lit phone.

His face twisted in a sinister grin.

He lifted the rig again and recorded a final sweep of the area, letting his lens linger on a tall trunk carved with a spiral. A faint glimmer passed across his eyes. Then he stepped back. The phone's feed continued rolling. Seconds later, he vanished into a patch of brush that blocked the moonlight.

As the moments ticked by, the chat feed on the fallen phone went wild. Viewers typed everything from genuine concern to mocking jeers. Some insisted it was staged. Others panicked, claiming they heard real terror in Mia's scream. A handful demanded the exact location so they could investigate themselves. The phone captured only the rustle of leaves and an occasional faint hiss of wind that carried across the forest floor. Without Jackson's presence, the stream offered no visuals except for the muddy ground, a scattering of crushed ferns, and the distant shapes of looming pines.

A subtle crunch nearby indicated an animal scurrying past. The phone mic picked up a low grunt, possibly from a deer or a startled raccoon. That sound faded, leaving watchers with a feed that drifted between rustling static and the frantic comments scrolling unseen across the screen. A few watchers typed instructions, wishing someone would pick up the phone or show a sign of life.

Meanwhile, a mile east, Jackson and Mia stumbled to catch their breath. Their hearts still pounded, and neither spoke for a minute. Mia leaned against a mossy trunk and her eyes darted back the way they had come. Jackson fumbled for the smaller backup phone in his jacket pocket, but his hands shook too badly to open any map. Each surge of adrenaline kept him from thinking straight. He tried to joke that this incident would make headlines, but his voice cracked again.

She asked, "You saw it too, right?" He swallowed and nodded. Part of him wanted to dismiss it and think someone had worn something on their shoulders, but he could not accept that explanation. Mia attempted to calm herself by repeating that they might be overreacting. Neither fully believed it.

They stayed low, scanning the shadows with the faint glow from Mia's phone. Her battery showed a dangerously low percentage. Jackson said they should walk fast but stay quiet in case the creature remained nearby. Mia's hands trembled and her anxious breathing weighed on her. Each step forward felt like a gamble.

Back at the spot where the original phone lay, the feed continued. An occasional beep signaled new viewers joining, though no one appeared on screen to ease their confusion. The LED glowed against the uprooted fern, and the chat scrolled with demands for answers. A few typed that they heard something crunching in the distance. Others guessed it was all a stunt gone wrong. Nobody had any clarity.

Within a secluded vantage deeper in the forest, the hooded cameraman sorted through his own footage. He tapped the small viewer attached to his rig and checked angles of the bone-plated creature. He replayed a snippet, a glimpse of plating and the shape of a savage outline. His breath wavered as he studied the shot's clarity, then he switched off the screen and lifted his gaze to the dark canopy.

He shifted his attention toward the direction Jackson and Mia had fled, then looked at the new spiral carving on a nearby cedar trunk. Earning the public's gaze was the first step. He turned and walked, each footstep measured, camera held tightly at his side. Soon he disappeared behind tall firs, leaving no trace except the fresh markings in the bark.

Minutes later, the phone's last watchers realized no more movement would appear and started to trickle away. A handful stayed, listening to the hush of the forest. Each departure chipped away at the view count, but the rumor mill was already turning in towns and on message boards across the web. Some posted frantic highlight clips, slowed the footage to spot fleeting details, or argued about hoaxes. Others hammered out disclaimers that, if real, the screams might signal danger.

No one could confirm what had happened to Jackson and Mia, and the chat dissolved into theories and speculation. Meanwhile, the phone's battery indicator neared its final bar. For a moment the audio picked up the wind brushing through undergrowth and the rustle of leaves. Then the stream cut off, leaving thousands to replay those last frantic moments and wonder what else lurked among the towering pines.

CHAPTER TWO

Mara Bishop entered the SRD briefing room early, the overhead fluorescents casting a stark glow across the metal table and wall display. She still felt caffeine pulsing through her veins from a rushed cup of coffee, her mind racing over what she knew of the Bigfoot Attack Video.

Dr. Sato stood at the head of the table, her posture rigid and blazer crisp. Finch sat beside Link with his laptop open, data streams flickering across the screen. He gave Mara a tentative nod before focusing on his display. The air tensed as each person waited for someone to speak.

Mara served as an agent for the Secure Research Division, a clandestine government unit tasked with identifying and neutralizing anomalous threats, especially those amplified by collective belief, to protect the public from nightmares brought to life. This mission, like all others, aimed to contain such horrors before they spiraled out of control.

"Sit." Dr. Sato said in a tone that undercut any casual greeting. Mara took a seat opposite her and placed her palms on the cool surface.

Sato began by summarizing how the forest livestream had

spread overnight, saturating cryptid forums and major social media channels. A faint spiral watermark surfaced in every upload. She switched the display to a paused frame of flickering pixels. The clip showed a shaky view of dense trees before cutting to black.

Mara leaned forward. "What about local law enforcement?" she asked quietly.

Memories of her cousin's ordeal surfaced. This was similar to what had happened back then.

Focus on the job.

Sato said the local sheriff's office remained cautious: the missing phone had not been recovered at the abandoned campsite, and no sign of Jackson or Mia had appeared. Deputies treated the search as if it were a prank gone wrong. Mara frowned, recalling that typical public reaction. People always found reasons to doubt until the threat escalated.

Finch cleared his throat. "I noticed the spiral watermark in multiple downloads." He typed a quick command, and a cluster of still frames appeared on the screen. "Each clip comes from a different user on a different platform, yet the symbol appears in every version." He scratched his jaw as his voice lowered. "Last time we saw anything resembling this pattern, it involved small-scale disruptions. This is far bigger."

She recognized the tension in Finch's gaze. His job was to map these anomalies, but he was never comfortable with how quickly they grew. Mara recalled her first encounter with his reputation: a case in Montana that began as local rumor and escalated when a stray hashtag triggered crowd hysteria. They were seeing the same pattern multiplied, she thought.

Dr. Sato turned to Mara. "You will deploy with our core team. We need eyes on that campsite and any unusual markings. Keep it discreet. The sheriff is wary, and we do not want a press fiasco over federal interference."

Link's voice cut in through a speaker on the table. He was

patched in remotely as usual. "Mara, are you checking these numbers?" he asked, his tone exasperated and energized. Engagement metrics are climbing every hour, and user engagement is significant. If that spiral is truly fueling a manifested form, we might be dealing with something that grows faster than we can scramble.

Mara exhaled. "Any leads on who is pushing it all? The initial footage was from Jackson and Mia, but they are off the grid now. Somebody is amplifying it. That watermark alone suggests intention."

"Not sure yet," Link replied. "I see an account named Vale-Sightings posting about the forest. It might be a cryptid hunter or a bored influencer provoking interest. I will keep monitoring."

Mara drummed her fingers on the table. "Bust this wide open and the crowd swarming that forest will become an even bigger problem. Half the internet wants a piece of the action."

Sato crossed her arms. "Hence your instructions. Keep a low profile, investigate the signs, confirm an anchor if it exists, and figure out how to contain it. Local law enforcement is not entirely convinced, but they are on alert for any real danger. Offer them assistance but do not reveal specifics of our division. That remains standard protocol."

Finch tapped the trackpad and brought up a close-up of the spiral. The lines glowed faintly as if the digital feed itself carried an odd pulse. "Belief metrics are spiking in an unusual pattern. People are resharing this footage like it is the next cryptid phenomenon. If enough people latch onto it, that creature's manifestation can escalate. We might see an entity with bone plating become physically stronger and possibly more aggressive."

Mara's stomach tightened. "Then let us get going. The longer we stand by, the more momentum this thing picks up."

"I agree," Sato said. She adjusted the collar of her blazer and nodded at Mara. "Grab tangible evidence, interview the deputies, and coordinate with Finch and Link for any new sightings. Once we confirm a central anchor, assuming there is a carved sigil or something fueling the cryptid's presence, we will proceed with standard containment steps."

Mara thought about the last time such an operation came down the wire, an urgent effort to break a belief network before it reached critical mass. She could still recall the distant howls in that Oregon case when Finch was only starting to refine the ARGUS system. This situation felt more potent.

Sato turned to Finch, who was tapping on his laptop. "Your data will be essential, Dr. Finch. Keep me updated on any significant surges or new angles on that watermark."

He nodded. "Roger that. If local rumors keep fueling it, we might see an acceleration by midday."

Mara caught in the big screen's reflection a blurred tall shape and a hint of a shoulder ridge. The resolution was too poor to be conclusive, but the watchers online devoured it anyway.

They want it to be real. They always do.

She stood and gathered her notes. "I'll get things under way. Skyhook can get us out there quickly and land near the forest perimeter to avoid prying eyes."

Sato gave a measured nod. "Do that. I'll coordinate with the broader SRD command and see if we can tamp down some of the viral posts. Link, keep digging for that ValeSightings account, and Finch, pack your gear for rendezvous at the hangar."

Mara tried to ignore the knot in her chest and took a steady breath. I will not repeat my cousin's tragedy. That memory still stung, but operational mode demanded she push aside personal baggage. She fixed her gaze on Finch's display one last time. The spiral graphic shimmered, each digital swirl a reminder of how easily rumor became threat.

They parted ways. Finch closed his laptop with a resigned motion and headed to load his analysis equipment, his footsteps echoing in the corridor. Sato lingered a moment and then reminded Mara how crucial timing was. "I know you're good, but it's my job to remind you. No one wants a fiasco," she said, her tone calmer now. "We saw how quickly events can snowball. If you see evidence of purposeful manipulation, note every detail."

Mara swallowed. "Understood." She braced a hand against the door frame as she left. The corridor lights reflected off white walls that led back toward the main reporting station. The building smelled faintly of disinfectant and recycled air, a far cry from the damp forest aroma ahead. She moved on, her footprints clicking on polished tiles.

Down the hall, she found Finch hunched over a secondary console, a data cable draped over one arm as he rummaged through a case of field monitors. She reached him and noticed the tension in his posture. "You good?" she asked.

He glanced up, nodding. "I'm preparing for possible curveballs. This scenario looks bigger than the typical rumor-based anomalies. That video's audience exploded overnight. My readings show a direct correlation between shares, repeated mentions of a bone-plated monster, and that spiral. It's like planting seeds in every new viewer's mind."

"Then we uproot them before they sprout any further." She slung her gear bag over her shoulder. "Grab your gear. We leave for Fort Lewis in twenty minutes."

Finch let out a shaky exhale. "Right. I'll be there." He stared at his screen as data scrolled by, raw numbers showing an upswing. Mara saw how the lines soared when she looked over his shoulder. The shape of that curve suggested a threat that might outpace them if they waited.

She pivoted, headed for the exit, and crossed the threshold of steel-framed double doors that led outside. Early light fell across the SRD facility courtyard. A couple of plain black SUVs sat parked at an angle, waiting for team deployment. She rubbed her palms together and scanned the horizon. Time to head into the field and do our job.

She called Link, who was off-site. His voice came through her SRD earpiece with a burst of static. "Just a heads-up." He said. "Some personality named 'ValeSightings' keeps stirring cryptid mania. It has already posted multiple times this morning, teasing 'raw footage coming soon.' This creep knows how to harness the internet zeitgeist."

"Send me any leads you grab." Mara answered. "We're stepping off. If you see anything location-specific from that user, let me know instantly."

"You got it, Mara." Link replied. The line clicked, leaving her with only the hum of the earpiece.

She strode to the nearest SUV, opened the driver's door, and set her gear bag down. Finances, local politics, and tangential cryptid fanatics meant nothing if the anchor in the forest thrived on belief. She thought about how quickly a few retweets or video shares could amplify nonsense into a near-physical threat. The fact she was living proof of that reality never ceased to unnerve her.

Behind her, Finch approached carrying a black case of digital sensors and a compact drone rig. His face still bore worry from the briefing. He said, "All right. Let's do this. If we get out there soon, we might get a handle on the local chatter. I just hope the sheriff cooperates."

Mara stepped aside so he could secure the case in the back seat. She remembered how local cops typically viewed the SRD as an unwelcome intrusion, though if they discovered real danger they might change their tune. "We'll handle them carefully." She climbed into the driver's seat. Finch took shotgun and fastened his belt. The tension between them was not personal. It was the usual sense of racing an invisible clock.

She turned the key and the engine rumbled to life. Her earpiece buzzed as Dr. Sato's voice chimed in. "Mara, take care. The last frames of that video are inconclusive, but if there is a creature out there, we need to confirm soon. Finch will monitor your location feed. Good luck."

Mara signaled her readiness with a short reply, then nudged the SUV forward. The gates parted ahead, and they rolled out onto the road leading west toward Fort Lewis. She pictured the forest in her mind: tall pines, a missing phone, a swirl of rumor, and possibly a monstrous shape that had seized public fascination. She could almost hear her cousin's voice telling her to keep her guard up.

She followed the main highway for a few minutes, the cityscape thinning out behind them. Finch breathed quietly beside her, eyes fixed on a handheld screen that displayed updating share counts. Every new spike seemed to weigh on him. She tapped the wheel with her thumb. "Once we get the gear loaded onto Skyhook's VTOL, we'll regroup about five miles from the forest boundary. Then we'll move to the campsite." Finch gave a subdued nod. "Understood."

They drove onward, passing through a security checkpoint near the base. Soldiers waved them through, ignoring the inconspicuous black SUV. It was another special operation.

Except now the entire globe was watching phone footage in which every tree shadow offered a clue. She scanned the road, her mind drifting to scented pines and to the possible role of ValeSightings. It felt orchestrated though she still lacked direct evidence.

Soon they reached the final approach to the staging area. The large hangar loomed ahead, a forklift shifting crates while ground crew in green vests walked about. Mara pulled the SUV to a stop. A stiff breeze swept across the tarmac, carrying the distant churn of rotor blades. She cut the engine and glanced at Finch. "We have our marching orders. Let's lock this down before the buzz grows any further." He lifted the black case onto his lap. "Agreed." His voice was quiet but his resolve showed in his expression.

Mara stepped out and slammed the door, scanning the hangar for Skyhook. The pilot was likely inside, prepping the aircraft. A noise from behind signaled cargo being loaded. She inhaled the crisp air, her mind set on the forest and that swirling shape in the video.

No more tragedies. We handle this now.

CHAPTER THREE

At the Fort Lewis Hangar, the pre-dawn air was thick with drizzle and anticipation as Mara and Skyhook loaded the VTOL. Their cargo was a grim manifest of SRD's specialized tools, including EM-coil carbines, cases of sedation darts that felt increasingly inadequate, and the crucial thermite charges intended for any anchor sigil. Link's voice crackled through Mara's earpiece with unsettling updates. Gifford Pinchot had drawn a throng of thrill-seekers with viral footage of Jackson and Mia's disappearance, and their shredded tent and ominous footprints were the only clues found so far. Compounding the chaos, the online persona "ValeSightings," Carter Vale, fanned the flames, teasing more footage and feeding the cryptid frenzy.

Dr. Sato's final instructions underscored the mission's urgency: confirm the presence of a physical sigil, the suspected anchor for this belief-fueled manifestation, and neutralize it while navigating potential friction with Sheriff Thomason. Finch's analysis from the mobile command trailer was equally sobering. He reported that the cryptid's theoretical power had already surged in direct correlation with the online hype. Vale's cryptic mention of "old logging roads" sent Finch scrambling through maps. With each moment amplifying the threat, Mara and Skyhook lifted off in the VTOL and flew through the dim morning toward a discreet landing zone near the forest perimeter, the weight of their clandestine mission pressing on them.

After landing, Mara and Skyhook found the local ranger's office with help from Finch and Link. The morning air smelled of damp pine as Mara stepped onto the gravel outside the ranger station. She noticed the pale sun still struggling to pierce the canopy and casting an unsettling half light.

She pushed open the wooden door and stepped inside with Skyhook close behind. A weary ranger in a wrinkled uniform sat at a modest desk piled with scattered papers and a half-finished cup of coffee. The fluorescent overhead lights gave the room a dull glare that neither soothed his bloodshot eyes nor suggested any comfort.

Mara introduced herself, her voice calm and crisp. "We're with SRD," she said, showing the ID badge on her vest. "We heard you had some unusual sightings in the area. We'd like to hear what you've got." She felt the tension wafting off him as his gaze flicked between her and Skyhook.

He exhaled and rubbed his temple. "I'm not sure what's out there, but something's wrong. I've been hearing about weird prints and that spiral carving. Even the local cryptid fans seem spooked."

Skyhook nodded in encouragement. "We took a look at a campsite not far from here. We want to confirm if the same shapes or prints match what we found."

The ranger scratched a patch of stubble along his jaw and sipped some stale coffee. "Name's Kerr," he said. "I've been patrolling these trails for four years, and I thought I'd seen everything. Then people began talking about new markings, spirals carved into trees and rocks. I thought bored visitors were messing around until the calls started piling up."

Mara felt a small pang of frustration remembering how often

warning signs got ignored once online rumor mills began churning out sensational stories. "How many calls would you estimate?" Mara asked.

"Ten or so in the last week." Kerr replied. "One came from a group who insisted they saw something big creeping near the old ridge. Another claimed they noticed stacked stones forming a spiral pattern on a half-collapsed path. Sure, we get random attention-seekers hoping to find Bigfoot, but this feels organized."

"Organized how?" Mara asked.

Kerr glanced at his half-empty cup and set it aside with a sigh. "The carvings keep popping up in the same region. The footprints, if that is what they are, end up on a trail that I gated off months ago. Signs telling visitors to stay away keep getting yanked down. We even tried roping that area shut, but people tear through every time they mention that spiral they saw online. They mention a watermark in a video."

Mara exchanged a quick look with Skyhook. Finch had been zeroing in on social media signals, and Link kept spotting new posts referencing the same symbol. "We're aware of it." Mara said. "We believe it's connected to the rumors stirring up this forest."

Kerr shifted his weight in the chair and drew a folded map from a side drawer. He spread it across the desk and pointed to a winding trail with faded annotations. "This used to be accessible years ago. Debris from storms made it dangerous, so we officially shut it down. Lately those spiral carvings are popping up right here. We have no staff to patrol it regularly, so it's become a magnet for so-called explorers."

Skyhook leaned over, crossed her arms, and studied the map. "People see a no-entry sign and treat it like an invitation."

Kerr gave a sardonic huff. "Exactly. And when we tell them it's for their safety, they ignore us because they want photos or they think the government is hiding Bigfoot. Some folks claim it's 'the real frontier of cryptid country.'" He let out a tense laugh. "I don't know if they said that ironically, but it sure keeps me up at night."

Mara drummed her fingers on the desk. "We're looking into a disappearance that might connect to these same patterns. Two campers, Jackson and Mia, haven't been found yet. Have you received any information about them passing through?"

Kerr nodded and rummaged through a battered metal filing drawer. "They're in my reports. Locals recognized them from that stream. I guess they made a last run for supplies in town a day before they vanished. The next morning we found scraps of neon tent fabric near a popular clearing."

Mara pictured the bright green shreds she had collected in an evidence bag. "That's consistent with what our team saw." She chose not to mention the claw-like rips or the way the ground had been churned. She preferred not to freak out the ranger any more than necessary.

Kerr lowered his voice as though someone might overhear. "I went out to that clearing myself right after some cryptid hunters started sharing sightings. I heard sounds that made my hair stand on end. Deep, groan-like calls late at night. Not bears. Not cougars. Something else."

Skyhook's expression grew serious. "How recent was that?"

"A couple of nights ago. Then I started hearing from hikers that more of those stones had been rearranged, like someone carefully set them up in patterns. I found some faint spiral carvings on fallen logs too. Some visitors teased me for sounding paranoid but I know the forest. This is new."

Mara appreciated the directness. The ranger's insights lined up with Finch's belief metrics. Carter Vale's viral watermarks had spurred a wave of new believers, which fueled the growing rumor behind the scenes.

"We'd like you to alert us immediately if you see anything else." She said. "Especially if you find fresh carvings."

Kerr nodded then set his map aside. "I'll give you my personal number. The sheriff's office is spread thin with all the out-of-towners showing up. I already tried giving official warnings but a few big groups of enthusiasts keep rolling in. One of them even asked me if I'd heard about a 'spiral broadcast' and some talk about a looming 'forest king.' They mentioned a name: Vale-Sightings."

Mara's mouth tightened at the mention. Carter Vale's alias. She supposed it was a matter of time before locals started hearing that handle tossed around. "We've encountered it." She said. "He's stirring a lot of trouble online."

"Then you know more than I do." Kerr said, tapping his desk. "I've been telling people to stay clear. I don't have the manpower or the authority to block the forest entirely. They think my warnings have no basis."

Skyhook offered a small grimace. "This is bigger than standard rumor control. We'll do what we can to contain it."

The ranger hesitated, staring at the small SRD insignia stitched into Mara's vest. "If you folks are who I think you are, then we're talking about something truly dangerous, right? Should I be telling people we have a lethal predator on the loose?"

Mara glanced around the cramped station, noticing a dusty corkboard pinned with missing pet notices and out-of-date trail closures. No point in softening the details. "We have reason to believe a creature is involved." She said. "It's capable of injuring anyone who gets too close. That might sound unbelievable but we're dealing with the consequences of viral misinformation plus an unknown threat stoking the situation."

Kerr sighed. "I can push out more urgent bulletins but I doubt it'll keep the thrill-seekers away. You might have more luck if your agency can step in on an official level."

She was about to respond when her comms earpiece buzzed lightly. Finch's voice crackled. "Mara, we have a fresh angle. Link's drones spotted a couple of hikers moving toward the restricted zone Kerr mentioned. They're crossing that old trail. ARGUS readings detect a social post tagging the same location. I suggest we hurry."

Mara shifted her weight, feeling the slippery edge of frustration. "You copy all that, Kerr?" she asked, tipping her head toward the earpiece. "We're about to chase down more potential victims if they don't watch themselves."

Kerr folded his arms over his chest. "I can show you a quicker route. The path from here loops around, but there's a shortcut behind the station. You'll save twenty minutes if you cut through the brush line."

She smiled at him gratefully, though the atmosphere felt grim. "Excellent. We'll take it. If possible, notify the sheriff's office that SRD is heading that way, so any spare deputies know where we are."

Kerr rose from his chair, grabbed a battered jacket from a hook by the door, and tentatively offered to guide them. "We can at least walk partway. If I hear those noises again, I'd rather not be alone in that brush."

Mara glanced at Skyhook. "We could use the help," she said, motioning for Kerr to lead the way. They stepped outside and followed the ranger around the side of the building, boots crunching on wet gravel. The forest rose before them, thick with pines whose branches dripped from last night's rainfall. Mist wove through the trunks.

Mara toggled her comm to an open channel. "Link, Finch, do we have a bead on those hikers' exact coordinates?"

A short burst of static, then Link's voice. "Sending them to your comm overlays now. The feed shows them heading deeper along that old path. We're trying to contact them with a local broadcast, but no response."

Mara scanned the tree line. A swirl of worry pooled in her gut. She typed a quick note that read, "Two civilians were unresponsive and appeared to be random explorers. Must intercept."

She dug her flashlight out of her belt and pressed it against her vest. "We'll move carefully. No scaring them off with gear in their faces unless necessary."

Kerr pointed to a narrow gap in the vegetation behind the station, leading to a rough slope. "This is the shortcut. Follow me."

They trudged across mossy ground, stepping over tangled roots and fallen branches. The ranger paused sometimes to pivot his head, apparently alert for the same uncanny noises he had mentioned. Mara found it odd how quiet the forest felt then. Normally she would detect bird calls, but it was as though the local wildlife had retreated.

Skyhook walked just behind Mara, scanning overhead. "Finch, do we know if the cryptid has been sighted this morning?" she asked over comms.

"Nothing definite," Finch said. "ARGUS flagged a spike in cryptid mentions just after sunrise, but no confirmed images. Keep your guard up."

Mara signaled for them to slow as they reached a small ridge dotted with black ferns. "Kerr, how close are we to that old trail intersection?"

He studied a line of conifers to his left. "It should be about a hundred yards that way. You'll see a broken sign near an uprooted stump."

Mara's pulse jumped. She hated the idea of stumbling on half-informed hikers wandering into potential danger. She pressed her earpiece again. "Link, any movement from that drone feed?"

"Not sure," Link answered. "It's patchy under the thick canopy. If they keep going, they might cross that clearing where we found the shredded tent. You'll want to hurry. Also watch for stacked stones. A local forum posted a fresh photo of them about an hour ago."

She swallowed a knot of anxiety. Those stacked stones likely bore that spiral pattern. This area felt loaded with Carter Vale's handiwork as it spread panic through gullible visitors. She focused on the basics: find the hikers and get them out of there, then confirm the location of the new carvings. That was how the SRD would keep this from spiraling further.

They pressed on until they reached a fallen log bridging a shallow ravine. Kerr pointed down a slope where the undergrowth thickened. "The official trail is right below. You'll see the sign if it isn't knocked over."

Mara noticed faint footprints in the damp soil that led deeper into the gloom. She tapped Skyhook's shoulder. "We'll follow these prints." She turned to Kerr. "Thanks for your help. We'll handle it from here if you want to head back."

He hesitated then gave a tired nod. "I'll hang around the station. If you come across anything new, let me know. Otherwise I'll push out the warnings I can." He stepped back and glanced warily at the looming pines. "Good luck."

Mara waited until he disappeared from view then moved forward and scanned the ground. The footprints suggested two sets, possibly the same hikers Link saw. They looked recent. "Let's make this quick." She murmured.

Her earpiece crackled again. "Mara." Finch spoke with unusual urgency. "I picked up fresh chatter in a local social group. They're talking about hearing a low growl near that collapsed trail. One user posted the spiral symbol again and claimed it marks a path to 'the real cryptid lair.' I'm concerned we'll have more amateurs joining them soon."

Mara let out a grim laugh. "That's just what we need." She exhaled. We do not have time for any more reckless onlookers. "We'll sweep the immediate area. Keep the drone overhead and let me know if you spot anyone else approaching."

She and Skyhook trekked for another minute in tense silence. The soft ground showed tracks that were easy to follow. Spruce boughs formed a canopy above and sealed out most of the morning light. The hush felt unnatural and every step made her hyperaware of potential ambush points.

Skyhook nudged her lightly and said, "Got a feeling we'll be doing search and rescue all day if Vale's hype keeps drawing these people in."

Mara tightened her grip on her gear. "We can't cover everything. We have to handle what's in front of us." The layered scents of wet mulch and pine pitch clung to the back of her tongue. She recalled how each droplet of social media chatter expanded the cryptid's power, stoked by Vale's endless antics. If this growth continues, it will soon become unstoppable.

They reached the broken sign. It lay face-down in the dirt, chipped around the edges, with jagged bits of rope attached to what had once been a boundary line. Mara knelt and flipped it over. Paint scrawled across it read KEEP OUT, but someone had scribbled a spiral shape over the warning. She clenched her jaw.

"That's our sign," she muttered. She tapped her earpiece again. "Link, we found more vandalism. Confirm these coordinates. Looks like we're on the right track."

He replied, "Coordinates marked. The hikers are about a hundred meters ahead, best guess. The drone is losing direct visual, but I have partial glimpses."

Mara pictured them stumbling across a carved stone, snapping pictures with no idea what they risked conjuring. She rose and gestured for Skyhook to follow her deeper along the trail. "Let's try to catch them before they cause more trouble."

She stepped past the battered sign and hoped the ranger remained safe at the station. With every new clue, she sensed Carter Vale's network strengthening. They would do their part and gather any intelligence they found. Then they would call Finch for analysis. It was their only plan.

CHAPTER FOUR

Mara paused at the lip of a muddy roadside shoulder. The makeshift barricade ahead looked more like a suggestion than a real blockade. She counted ten cars parked randomly on the gravel, some bearing cryptid decals, others showing homemade Bigfoot silhouettes.

She tugged her tac vest, appreciating its familiar weight. Sheriff Thomason stood by his patrol SUV with his arms crossed, his broad frame and thinning brown hair framing an expression of fatigue and defiance.

"Agent Bishop," he said, glancing at the badge clipped to her vest. "I wish I could say I'm glad to see you."

She stepped forward and her boots crunched on damp gravel. "Good to see you too, Sheriff." She watched deputies wave vehicles through. "Turning people back has been tough."

He nodded. "These visitors ignore warnings. Some think it's just a stunt to attract tourists. Others suspect we're hiding something."

Mara studied his drawn face. "Two campers went missing, so this is more than an inconvenience." She looked past the barricade to the rutted track where strangers wandered with cameras. "News must be spreading fast."

"It's worse than that," he said. "My men are stretched thin. Half are stuck chasing false sightings; folks claiming to record howls or trace monstrous footprints."

Mara tightened her rifle strap. "I understand the frustration. I'm here to trace the source of this hype." She spotted a group of teenagers slipping around an orange cone. "We can shoo them off, but more keep arriving."

Sheriff Thomason rubbed his jaw and gestured at the line of cars. "My department handles lost hikers or petty theft, not a crowd of cryptid enthusiasts. County officials want tourists to keep coming. They hate turning people away from a forest that brings revenue."

She chose her words. "They might leave more willingly if they sensed real danger. I doubt that is your goal."

He gave her a measured look. "So what are we truly facing? I doubt it's just bears or a mountain lion."

"Our unit has tracked a potential threat that normal wildlife doesn't exhibit." Mara swept her gaze across the crowd. "It has injured a couple of witnesses, and we suspect it ties to the online frenzy."

He laughed hollowly. "I'm seeing that frenzy firsthand. Locals relay half-baked rumors from cryptid forums. They point their phones at me, claiming a monster hunt."

A tall man in a camouflage hoodie slipped around the barricade, fiddling with his phone. A deputy tried to block him, but he flashed a laminate reading Field Research Media. Mara sighed.

"You see that nonsense?" Thomason asked. "I've tried citations, but they ignore them. We can't eject them all."

She stepped aside as two onlookers squeezed past, a camera's beep echoing. "Sheriff, you said you have a small search for those missing campers. Any leads?"

"Not many." He answered. "We found the campsite or what's

left. Torn tent, their stuff scattered." He paused and shot her a look of resentment. "I'll be honest. I don't appreciate the hush-hush approach. My people are risking their necks poking around these woods and if this threat is real, I deserve the truth."

She tilted her head. "You do deserve a heads-up and I'll be as open as I can. The culprit here is bigger than a typical animal. We're trying to stop its spread before more folks get hurt." Then she tilted her earpiece slightly and asked, "Link, you reading me?"

Link crackled to life. "Loud and clear. That user, ValeSightings? He's stirring every forum he can find and rallying cryptid lovers to trek out there. The chatter is spiking every hour."

Mara's lips thinned. "He's a content creator who's fueling folk tales about a bizarre creature in these woods. He calls it the 'Bone-Plated King.' Something like that. He's encouraging people to show up and 'witness history.'"

Thomason smacked the side of his SUV in frustration. "Great. World's worst carnival right here on my roads."

She shrugged. "I won't disagree. Our intel suggests he's distributing physical flyers and live streams using some spiral symbol. Seen anything matching that description around here?"

He nodded. "I've heard from a deputy who picked up a weird flyer off the ground. It had a swirling design and asked folks to 'keep watching for the truth.' The deputy brought it back and said it all seemed like a cheap stunt. I tossed it."

Mara frowned. "If you come across more, set them aside. They might be part of how he's driving interest." A gap formed between the milling onlookers and she saw an overgrown trail entrance beyond the barricade. "We'd like to investigate that area. My team has reason to believe our suspect is guiding these fans to the old trailhead."

He tapped his radio and called in a tired-sounding deputy. After a few instructions telling the deputy to maintain watch on any late arrivals, he turned back to Mara. "I want to coordinate but I'm not thrilled that you're keeping details under wraps. From my end, the missing campers come first."

Mara noticed his furrowed brow. "Understood. My team wants them safe too. We'll share anything relevant but we have our protocols."

"Protocols sure." He muttered. Then he straightened as if trying to keep a calm facade in front of passersby. "Get out there and see what you find but if my people are in danger, I expect a heads-up."

"Fair enough." She said. She glanced at the crowd again, uneasy about so many gawkers. Her comm chimed softly. Link's voice whispered in her ear. "UFO watchers in that chunk of the forest are retweeting some new clip. Could be more folks heading in."

Mara shook her head at the relentless attention. Digital onlookers were drawn to every odd spectacle. "Sheriff, I'll let you know what we discover." He nodded and stepped away to bark warnings at the next group of camera-wielding explorers.

She edged around the parked vehicles and found Skyhook leaning against the side of a black SRD SUV, scanning the crowd with steady eyes. The pilot's jacket bore an SRD patch, and her short black hair barely moved in the light breeze. "Atmosphere's downright cheerful." She remarked dryly.

Mara snorted. "It's always a party until something big with claws shows up." Then she lowered her voice. "We might need immediate extraction if things go south in that old trail. Be on standby."

Skyhook casually tapped her earpiece. "Got it. The VTOL is prepped over at the next clearing. Finch said the belief metrics popped again. Probably from Vale's new post."

Mara rubbed the back of her neck. "Link, Finch, and I suspected Vale was behind this surge, but I didn't expect it to spread so fast. People are calling it a Bigfoot festival, or some twisted wilderness challenge."

"Social media can morph anything into a spectacle." Skyhook replied. "Let me know if you want eyes from above."

Mara nodded with the weight of the mission pressing on her. She preferred not to see innocent hikers caught in this mess. She locked her rifle. "I'm heading down the old trail. If I run across anything that roars, I'll call for backup."

Skyhook nodded. "Stay safe."

Mara turned from the SUV and cut through the boundary of onlookers. A few people followed at a cautious distance, but she glowered until they backed off. Some recognized the official gear and kept their distance, though curious eyes lingered. Mud squelched beneath her boots, and the canopy ahead looked dense. Droplets clung to the evergreen branches overhead.

A memory of the campers' shredded tent crossed her mind. She had seen the pictures. This is no casual hoax. Someone's fueling something real, and the price keeps climbing. She stepped over a broken branch on the trail. Up ahead, twisted roots crossed the path like an obstacle. She listened for any sign of movement or stray chatter from deep in the undergrowth.

Her comm crackled again. Finch's voice arrived, sounding tense. "Mara, I've got partial confirmation that Vale was live a few minutes ago, encouraging watchers to 'venture bravely' into an old-growth cluster. Coordinates match your location."

She exhaled. "Appreciate the heads-up. Keep me posted if you see any major spikes in chatter. The sheriff's at the roadblock, so we'll have something resembling control behind me."

"Understood." Finch said. "Stay alert."

She started down the trail again, scanning tree trunks for spiral carvings. In the gloom, she spotted no immediate markings, but she knew Vale never stuck to just one path. At least the crowd noise began to fade behind her, replaced by rustling leaves and the slow drip of water running off branches.

A narrow side path broke from the main route. Wheel tracks suggested someone had driven a small ATV or maneuvered a bike. She knelt to feel the damp soil and found half a shoeprint. The shape was too large for a child and not wide enough for typical boots. It might belong to one of the missing campers or an overzealous cryptid sleuth.

Her radio beeped quietly. "Link here. Sheriff's reporting a small group heading your way, maybe four or five, carrying cameras. Want me to direct him to hold them back?"

She rose and scanned the narrow path ahead. "If they can be deterred, yes. We don't need more amateurs in the line of fire. I want the last known location of those campers to remain as empty of onlookers as possible."

Link's sigh came through. "I'll do what I can. He's not pleased with the crowd but he's short on options. We keep hearing folks mention some 'Bone-Plated King' stream."

Mara gritted her teeth. "That name again. Keep me notified." She pushed onward and felt the underbrush scratch her pants. What if this leads me nowhere but hype and footprints?

She paused to examine a broken branch. The break was fresh and sap still oozed. The ground had no blood or stray fur. Nevertheless something or someone pressed through here recently. She wondered if Carter Vale scouted these trails in person and planted physical clues.

A noisy rustle in the bushes made her tense. She raised her rifle and turned off the safety. A startled deer bolted across the path and disappeared behind a cluster of young pines. She exhaled as adrenaline flared. I'm jumping at any movement. Great sign. She forced her shoulders to relax.

Her mind flicked to the conversation with Thomason. He seemed torn between local obligations and the fear that this federal group was stepping on his territory. She felt sorry for him, forced to juggle political pressure and real danger. But she had no time to sugarcoat the mission.

Ahead the path widened and she could see a slight indentation of a campsite clearing. She overheard voices echoing from somewhere behind, likely persistent onlookers. She moved quickly, determined to stay well ahead of them. The trees around her stood tall and damp and the canopy cut out much of the light.

Her earpiece chirped again. This time Skyhook's voice cut through. "I'm hovering above a side road. Saw a cluster of hikers trying to slip past the next bend. Thomason's deputy is corralling them but more keep arriving. I might land if you need direct support."

Mara shook her head though the pilot couldn't see. "Hold position for now. Let the sheriff do his best. I'm almost at that old campsite area."

She pushed aside a veil of ferns. The ground dipped slightly and led to a small clearing dotted with puddles. A leftover char mark from a long-dead campfire sat in the middle ringed by scattered stones. She walked around the perimeter searching for any sign of the missing campers or new markings.

Discarded snack wrappers poked out from under wet leaves. One bore a stylized Bigfoot silhouette.

Someone is collecting cryptid souvenirs out here.

The litter annoyed her but she was more concerned about evidence of violence or deeper sabotage.

A battered cooler lay half-concealed under a rotting log. Mara crouched and lifted the lid carefully with her forearm. Inside she found empty soda cans and waterlogged sandwich bags. There was no sign of anything serious. She hovered for a moment and examined the log for the spiral sigil but found nothing.

Her radio crackled. "Finch here. Belief metrics are rising. Are you seeing any new signs of Vale's handiwork?"

Mara stood and scanned the tall pines. "Nothing yet. It might be further along." She hesitated. "The sheriff is hoping I will share details but I am holding back because the crowds are intense."

Finch's tone remained level. "Understood. We can't exactly reveal that a viral phenomenon can bring nightmares to life. At least keep him posted on direct threats."

Mara nodded. "I will. He is on edge but we have a fragile cooperation, and we must maintain it." She pressed on, circling the site until she glimpsed weathered footprints near a large cedar. Two distinct impressions showed where someone had stood facing the camp. They might be the campers themselves or a bystander from another day.

She paused to call Link. "Any fresh sightings near me?"

"Just comments from watchers who say they heard strange howls. It could be attention seeking. No one mentions your exact location."

Mara swept the clearing one more time. The hush that enveloped the forest felt tense as if the trees were holding their breath. She knew each rumor and post online magnified the cryptid danger. Vale thrived on that dynamic and encouraged anyone to film these supposed Bigfoot hunts.

She pressed her lips together and pivoted back toward the main trail. It was better to cover more ground before night fell. She walked across thick roots then paused to angle her rifle's muzzle downward as water dripped from overhead branches onto her gear.

She gave the campsite a final glance. There was no sign of Jackson or Mia. The sheriff's halfhearted blockade might keep a few amateurs out but the flood would not end until Vale's stunts stopped. She keyed her comm. "Skyhook, remain ready. If something ugly turns up, I might need swift backup."

"Roger that," Skyhook replied.

A swirl of heavier wind rustled the leaves, and she remembered the wave of cryptid watchers lurking nearby. She pictured Thomason scowling as they marched around his cones. At least he was cooperating enough to share what he found. She pressed on, knowing she would need more than local manpower to curb the mania.

Her final instruction before heading deeper was for Link to coordinate with the sheriff. "If he spots a real threat, he needs to let me know. This entire zone is about to crawl with thrill seekers."

"Got it," Link said. "Stay safe, Mara."

She drew a breath and stared into thick stands of timber. The campers' fate remained unknown, and Carter Vale diverted the crowd's attention in dangerous directions. She felt urgency rise in her chest. Then she waded forward and renewed her promise to contain this crisis.

One step at a time, she moved deeper along the path. If the local authorities had no options left, fine. She had hers and intended to use them.

CHAPTER FIVE

Mara stood at the edge of a small clearing, studying the damp ground and noting how the footprints and shredded fabric told a raw story. She had seen drone footage of the tent and the mountain that Link had sent her but seeing it in person revealed details that the images had missed.

She moved closer to the remnants of a bright green tent that lay in strips across the mossy soil. Water droplets clung to the torn nylon, reflecting a dull sheen in the dim forest light. Twigs snapped under her boots as she crouched, scanning the scene for any sign of blood or forced struggle. Nothing conclusive. She braced one hand on a tree trunk, then spotted the first spiral carving. The gouge looked recent, the exposed wood pale and damp.

She radioed Link. "I've got spiral markings at the campsite." She paused while he entered data into his console. "We're logging them." He said. "I'm also seeing new cryptid-hunter videos posted overnight. Half the internet is fueling this thing's hype." Mara exhaled slowly. "Keep track. Carter Vale might be behind half those uploads."

She surveyed the tent's remains again. The bright color and

scattered food packaging implied the campers had prepared for a leisurely outing. The shredded state of everything suggested the exact opposite. A pungent animal odor lingered in the air, like the thick musk of a large creature. She studied footprints sunk a few inches into the damp soil, large enough that she measured one with her glove. The stride length from one print to the next was unnerving.

She spotted a corner of the tent jammed under a root so she pulled it free and bagged it for forensic analysis. Her attention flicked to a scattering of snack wrappers near a soggy backpack. The items inside looked intact: a flashlight, two charging cables, some clothing. No sign of a phone or camera. She recalled Jackson and Mia's livestream. That phone had captured their frantic last moments before the feed cut off. If the phone still existed, Carter Vale might have snatched it for his own twisted ends.

She rose and let her gaze roam the tree line. Trampled bushes marked a path deeper into the forest. A swirl of footprints, bent bracken, and broken branches suggested that at least two individuals or possibly more had fled in that direction. Mara touched her comms earpiece. "Skyhook, you reading me?" A crackle, then Skyhook's familiar voice came through. "Loud and clear. You need a flyby?" Mara nodded even though no one could see her. "Yes. Scan for any sign of a hideout or a lair. The ground clues suggest they ran that way. If it's safe to land a drone, do it."

A pause followed before Skyhook answered. "Roger that. I'll deploy a small unit from the chopper. One more thing. Sheriff Thomason is inbound to your location." Mara frowned. She had hoped to keep local law enforcement at a safe distance. "Understood," she said, forcing calm. She turned and noticed deeper claw marks etched across a nearby trunk with a spiral carved around them. It seemed like a signature.

She snapped a photo of the trunk with her phone and sent it to Finch via the encrypted feed. Her boots squelched in the mud as she moved around the perimeter, surveying the battered campsite from multiple angles. A small cluster of footprints nearly formed a circle as if the campers had spun around in confusion. She imagined a surge of fear when the presence stomped through. They must have fled.

Link's voice filled her earpiece again. "Mara, I've tracked repeated mentions of Bigfoot, bone plating, and people in the area. The number of hashtags is unusually high." After a brief pause he lowered his voice. "It's definitely increasing the cryptid's hold on reality or however Finch would phrase it. The more people believe in it, the more it materializes in the real world. I would not be surprised if in a few days it begins turning people's most extreme comments into reality." Mara walked toward a half-toppled camping chair and flipped it to see if anything lay underneath. "Then Finch needs to keep crunching that data and let me know if anything points directly to Vale. If he's distributing flyers again or has posted new footage, I want to hear it."

She found no phone near the chair so she set it upright and noticed the distinct smell of stale coffee on the seat, a detail that did not seem like normal camping fuel. It could be Vale's cheap cologne.

She pulled out a small plastic bag and swabbed a faint drip of an unidentified substance with a gloved hand. It smelled acidic, possibly an energy drink.

A twig snapped behind her. She turned to see Sheriff Thomason approaching with two deputies. His stern, weary posture showed his displeasure. She gave him a quick nod. "Sheriff," she said. "The campers are still missing, and we found these footprints. We also found spiral carvings on the trees that might relate to the sightings reported online."

He scanned the carved trunk. "Damn it, that's the same symbol I've been hearing about. The locals can't stop talking about it." He took a moment to inspect the shredded tent. "And you still think this is more than a hoax?" Mara exhaled. "Look at those footprints. That's bigger than a standard black bear. It's not a hoax."

One deputy crouched near the remains of the campfire ring, rummaging with a grim expression. Thomason sighed. "We'll cordon off the area. I have to keep the public out, but you know how it goes. People are already sneaking in for a chance at viral stunts." Mara folded her arms. "We'll do what we can to contain it, but with the internet feeding this, we can't block everyone."

Skyhook's voice cut in. "Drone is airborne. Sending visuals to Link. Stand by." Mara leaned against a tree, adjusting her earpiece. A high-pitched whirr drifted overhead as a small black drone zipped past the clearing. Thomason squinted up toward it. "Ever feel like the forest's turning into one big camera fest? Everyone's recording everything. Shame people can't leave it alone." Mara managed a hint of a grin. "Would've been easier for all of us."

Link piped through again. "Mara, the drone feed shows disturbed brush to the northeast, about a quarter mile from your current position. Could be an animal bed or something bigger." She nodded. "Copy that. Let's keep it in mind." She glanced at Thomason. "We'll check it out after you finish your walk-through here. I also want to see if we can find any leftover gear that might confirm Carter Vale's presence."

The sheriff hesitated, then waved his deputies to separate corners of the campsite. Mara knelt near the footprints again, her gloved fingers tracing the edge of one. Water had pooled in the depression. She used a measuring tape to note its approximate length. She snapped another picture and murmured, "Finch will enjoy plugging these into his models."

She rose, feeling an ache in her knees from crouching. "Sheriff, we'll keep you in the loop. Any new calls from the public, forward them to us immediately." He nodded, glancing at the swirling spiral again. "I'll do that. And I'll tell folks to stay off these trails, though some of them will ignore me." He tilted his hat in a stiff goodbye and busied himself surveying the rest of the mess.

Mara headed back to the shredded tent for one more pass. She reached inside what remained of a side pocket and found a half-sealed box of matches. The label came from a local convenience store near the highway, which suggests they stopped there before heading out. She tucked it into an evidence pouch. One of the deputies gave her a curious glance, but she ignored him and continued checking the ground for any personal items, such as a phone case or an ID. She found nothing.

She stepped over a cluster of snapped branches and paused at the remains of a half-buried cooler. The lid was pried off, and water dripped from the corners. She saw claw-like gouges around the plastic edges. "This must be how they lost part of their food supply," she muttered. The stench made her nose wrinkle. The contents were rotting scraps or worse. She sealed the cooler shut with a piece of tape to keep animals from rummaging further.

Her earpiece chirped again. Link's voice came out clipped. "I found another post referencing the campers' missing phone. A user claims it's live-streaming from deep in the woods." Mara's eyes narrowed. "That's impossible unless Vale reactivated it. Do you have a location on that?" Link swore.

"No direct location. The post is low on details, might be a troll. I'll keep digging." Mara inhaled sharply. "Do it. That phone is key to what happened here."

She surveyed the edges of the clearing one final time. A battered plank of wood propped against a tree read "No Trespassing." It was covered in graffiti. There were scattered footprints around it, possibly left by thrill-seekers ignoring the warnings.

"We're done here." She announced to Thomason, who was finishing his assessment. "Heading northeast to follow those drone leads."

The sheriff frowned. "Stay in contact. My guys will keep an eye on this site, but don't expect big results from forensics. Too much contamination already." Mara nodded, noticing how his shoulders slumped a fraction. "Understood. Thanks anyway."

She turned, feeling a swirl of frustration. The missing campers had left behind countless questions and no straightforward clues. We're stuck chasing leads in circles.

She moved west briefly to scan the perimeter near a thicker cluster of pines. Low branches brushed her shoulders, leaving damp streaks on her gear. A small scatter of footprints branched off, but they soon faded into the undergrowth. She heard the drone whine overhead, invisible behind the canopy. "Anything on thermal, Link?" she asked, stepping over a tree root. A second passed. "Empty. I see nothing warm-blooded except a few deer. No sign of humans in that sector."

She pivoted back toward the main trail. She called to the sheriff and his deputies, "We're heading out." She slung her EM-Coil Carbine over her shoulder, then started weaving through the underbrush toward the direction indicated by Link's drone earlier. Vines snagged at her boots, and the occasional rock threatened to twist an ankle if she didn't watch every step.

She noticed a slight rustle ahead and signaled for silence. She was alone except for the drone overhead. Her ears strained, but the sound vanished. She edged forward and scanned the ground for footprints. The remains of a small campfire lay near a thick trunk, but it looked older than the shredded campsite remains. She stooped and brushed a layer of moist leaves aside. No spirals, no fresh sign of Vale.

Her mind circled back to Jackson and Mia. If you're still in here, I hope you found a safe spot or managed to get out.

She felt a pang of worry for them. Then she tapped her comm again. "Skyhook, we're about a quarter mile from the original site. Anything on your heat cams?" The reply was quick. "Not seeing anything big enough to register as the entity. Just a doe and two fawns heading west."

Mara exhaled. "All right. We'll keep going for a bit, then regroup at the main trail." She pressed on, stepping over a fallen log covered in damp moss. Water droplets clung to her tactical pants. The forest felt oppressive, like it was feeding on every rumor swirling online. The more they hype it, the more real it gets. Her own voice echoed in her mind: We have to contain this soon.

After a few more minutes, she found nothing definitive, only more twisted branches and a faint track that led nowhere but deeper under the canopy. She decided to backtrack and meet up with Sheriff Thomason, who might have gleaned something from the campsite. Thunder rumbled in the distance, which meant the weather could worsen. Mud and rain would soon erase any footprints.

She walked briskly, mindful of her footing. When she reached the clearing, Thomason had already pulled his squad car some distance away, and two deputies lingered near the tent wreckage. Mara told them about the fruitless sweep. The sheriff looked unconvinced. "That's a whole lot of nothing." She shrugged. "We'll run the data with our team. Sometimes the smallest detail breaks the case. Meantime, watch for Carter Vale. He's cunning and probably enjoying every second."

Thomason shoved his hands into his belt. "I've heard rumors of a man distributing cryptid postcards at the local diner. If that's your suspect, I'll keep an eye out." Mara thanked him, then stepped away and called Link to arrange pickup. Skyhook's VTOL was refueling, so they had to hike to a makeshift rendezvous by a logging road. A half mile of forest stood between her and the transport site.

She turned again toward the shredded nylon and dangling bits of the destroyed tent. The odds of Jackson and Mia emerging from those woods unscathed grew slimmer by the minute. The carved spirals, the footprints, and even that strange musky odor pointed to a cryptid growing bolder. Raindrops sprinkled the trees overhead, giving the leaves a light patter. The situation was worsening, but she forced herself onward with comm in hand, determined to find anything that would bring those campers home and shut down Vale's twisted show.

Rain began to fall in earnest, plastering strands of hair to her forehead. Her comm earpiece crackled to life. Link's voice cut through the downpour with new urgency. "Mara, change of plans. Sheriff Thomason said that one of his deputies picked up an injured hiker near the north perimeter, says he was wandering delirious, something about a man with postcards and then... something big. He's stable at the local clinic. Thomason thinks he might have seen something useful." Mara felt adrenaline surge through her weariness. A firsthand witness, someone who might have encountered Vale or the creature itself, was too valuable a lead to ignore. The VTOL rendezvous could wait.

CHAPTER SIX

Rain misted the clinic's windows, making the cramped waiting area feel close. Mara stood near the doorway, scanning the small hall for signs of Seth, the injured hiker who had been found wandering in the forest. A nurse pointed her toward the far end, where a single room had been set aside for him. Mara nodded, then slipped inside.

She found Seth perched on a narrow bed with disheveled blankets pooled around his legs. A thin layer of sweat beaded his forehead and he clutched a plastic cup of water. He looked up at her, his gaze wary. She introduced herself in a low, calm voice, showing her SRD badge. He watched her as though he could not trust anyone but eventually he nodded once and motioned for her to sit on a plain wooden chair.

Mara lowered herself and set her field pack at her feet. "You're lucky the ranger patrol found you," she told him. "I'm here to learn anything you can remember about the man you crossed paths with and the creature you saw."

He took a shaky sip of water. "I...I didn't know what was happening until it was almost too late." His hands gripped the cup tighter.

"Take your time," Mara said. "Tell me how it started."

Seth explained that he had headed out on a multi-day hike to clear his head from college stress. He paused, breathing heavily, and his gaze drifted to the small window behind Mara. She studied him for a moment, aware that pushing him too soon might make him clam up. His arms bore scratches, scabbed and scaly around the edges while bruises dotted the skin above his wrists and elbows.

He finally exhaled and continued. "I got turned around on one of those side trails. After a few hours, I realized I was off the main path. That's when I ran into a man in a hooded jacket handing out odd postcards." He placed the empty cup on the side table then leaned forward. "He had a notebook too and kept drawing spiral shapes."

Mara's pulse quickened. "Do you remember what he looked like?"

"Middle-aged, messy hair, a little stubble. He seemed focused on me for several seconds, like he was studying my reaction to his postcards. He said something about unleashing the power of stories, but he didn't linger. He wrote spiral designs in his notebook then disappeared into the trees. I assumed a cryptid fan wanted attention."

Her teeth ground together. This matched Carter Vale's tactics. She had suspected postcards were a piece of his puzzle, feeding the viral chatter that gave the cryptid physical strength. She glanced at Seth's bandaged arm. "Then you saw the creature? How soon afterward?"

"It happened quickly," he said, his voice trembling. "I heard a deep groan echo and followed it, thinking it was an animal. It made me uneasy but I pressed on. My skin crawled at once. I saw movement in the brush and the creature was enormous. The moment I felt scared, it responded. It seemed to thrive on my panic."

Mara's chair creaked as she leaned forward and scanned his

expression. "Describe it." Seth's eyes clouded with distant fear. "It stood more than seven feet tall, maybe taller. Bony plates clung to its shoulders and back. They looked fused in some places. There was a spiral carved into its torso that gleamed when it moved. I swear the shape glowed." His breath caught and he swallowed twice before he went on. "It let out a low rumble. With every step I took backward, its presence grew stronger and the spiral glowed brighter as I panicked."

That detail matched the pattern Dr. Finch had outlined. The cryptid's power rose with the intensity of belief and fear. Mara kept her tone measured. "Did you see any sign of other hikers around you, possibly a couple named Jackson and Mia?" He shook his head. "No. I saw no campsite or other people. After I caught a glimpse of that monster, I ran. I stumbled over roots, injuring my ankle. It tore at the trees behind me or slammed into branches while I ran. All the while I felt it chasing me, or waiting to feed on my dread. I pushed through thick brush until my head spun. The next thing I remember is waking under a ranger's flashlight."

Mara studied the bandages on his arm and noticed deep gouges. "Did it cut you?" He stared at the wounds. "Not directly. I think I fell on something sharp while running. I heard it roar, but I never felt claws. Hard to say." He clenched his jaw. His eyes brimmed with lingering terror. "They told me I was dehydrated and feverish when they dragged me out."

She reached into her pocket, removed her phone, snapped a quick photo of the injuries, and lowered it. "We have a good idea who that man was. Carter Vale. He has been at the center of these sightings, distributing postcards and stoking curiosity online. We believe he is driving up fear on purpose."

He nodded, his mouth twisting in frustration. "He gave me those cards with spirals. I tossed them after I got spooked, but those images were already burned into my mind."

Mara tried to hide her grim satisfaction at that confirmation.

Vale's insertion of these symbols fed the entity by amplifying people's anxiety. She cleared her throat. "Seth, I know this is not easy, but your account helps. Dr. Finch, our data analyst, will piece together the pattern of how belief spreads. The postcards you saw are fueling all of this."

Seth let out a shaky breath and rubbed his palm across his forehead. "I wish I had known. I feel guilty, like I played into his scheme by acting on that fear."

Mara leaned back and scanned the bleak ward. "This is not your fault. Vale's manipulations are subtle and that cryptid grows whenever the population obsesses over it. You got caught in the crossfire."

His shoulders relaxed a fraction. He glanced at the half-drawn curtain covering the small window. "So you're going to stop him?"

"That's the plan," she answered, voice crisp. "We'll contain that cryptid and cut off Vale's ability to feed it. If you recall any more details, maybe something Vale said or the route he took, have the clinic pass that along."

Seth nodded. "I'll do what I can. I'm sorry I can't tell you anything about those missing campers. I never saw them."

She kept her face neutral, though disappointment nipped at her. "Understood." Mara rose from the chair and reached for her field pack. "Get some rest. Whatever you told me is enough for now."

He looked relieved that the questioning would stop. She gave him a small nod, then stepped into the corridor, closing his door behind her. Two orderlies shuffled past, giving her a glance that begged answers. She figured rumors about the so-called Bigfoot sightings had reached the staff, though they did not know the full truth about a belief-born entity. She tried to remember whether the local sheriff's office had an official stance yet. It was probably something vague like "wild animal on the loose."

Link's voice crackled through her earpiece a moment later. "Mara, how'd it go?"

She walked toward the side exit with brisk steps, phone in hand. "Vale was definitely there. Seth recognized him from the postcards, same spiral pattern as always. He also confirmed the creature has a glowing sigil carved into its torso." She paused and leaned against a wall near a vending machine. "He didn't see Jackson or Mia."

Link sighed over the line. "Finch is analyzing feed spikes from overnight. Carter Vale posted another cryptic update, but we haven't fully decoded it. Something about each glimpse fueling the legend."

She clenched her jaw. "I'm not surprised. Keep sifting. I'll be out in a minute." She ended the call, then walked past the vending machine, brushing off the stale smell of coffee from a corner stand.

Outside, the air felt damp and chilly. She spotted two sheriff's deputies near a parked cruiser, exchanging muffled words in concerned tones. She felt sorry for them. They were in over their heads, dealing with crowds, viral hype, and a threat that defied normal explanations. People thought it was a hoax or a marketing stunt, while the cryptid fed on every shared post and sensational rumor.

Mara found Finch hunched over a laptop at his desk. "I got the highlights from Link," he said. "Seth's story lines up with everything else we've tracked. That glow on the creature suggests a direct link to the fresh postcards."

"I want to see if the postcards had any unique text or a time stamp, but Seth only confirmed that they had the spiral. It was probably one more variant of Vale's pattern. Once we know how many people encountered them, we can guess how fast the cryptid is ramping up," Mara said.

"I'll run a search on local social feeds. There might be a few people bragging that they got free cryptid souvenirs. If so, they've likely posted pictures or teased them to attract more clicks."

"Check everything. I want to confirm the anchor location soon. Seth described how the cryptid's chest pattern shone strangely. It feels like a direct extension of Vale's plan." She drummed her fingers on the table. "If that anchor is deeper in the forest, these spirals might guide the cryptid back whenever it needs to recharge."

Finch sighed. "That's plausible. I'll keep you posted as soon as ARGUS finds a lead. Link's got the drones on standby, so we can expand our search radius near that old cedar grove at markers eighteen and nineteen. That place had odd readings on earlier scans."

"Copy that," she said. She stepped out of the trailer, her gaze flicking to a passing ambulance. Its siren was off, but the painted stripes glistened with moisture. She remembered the raw fear in Seth's face and wondered how many others were close to stumbling into the same nightmare. He was lucky that ranger patrol found him. She keyed the ignition and reminded herself to check in with the local offices about new missing-person reports. The cryptid showed no sign of slowing, especially if Vale kept seeding those postcards online and in person.

She glanced in the rearview mirror and noticed a local news van parked behind the clinic. A reporter leaned out a window, scanning the parking lot for a scoop. Mara exhaled. This region was descending into chaos, the environment Vale thrived on. She had no doubt the next wave of sightings would appear soon, fueling more frantic speculation. We need to cut the feed at its source. She set the SUV in reverse and pulled onto the main road.

Traffic was worse than usual thanks to visitors piling into the area hoping to catch a glimpse of the rumored Bigfoot or capture first-person footage. She inched forward in a slow line of vehicles, biting down mild frustration. The next step involved confronting Carter Vale's twisted sketches. If he was scrawling those sigils in notebooks, he might have set up a fresh anchor somewhere else, possibly near that rumored cedar ring Finch mentioned. Mara wanted to check it herself.

She pressed a quick button on her console to patch through to Dr. Sato. When there was no response, she left a brief voice note summarizing Seth's testimony. Without mentioning details that might spook local authorities, she explained the postcards, the horrifying description of the cryptid's bone plating, and the spiral's luminous effect. She asked for permission to escalate ground sweeps in the deeper sections of Gifford Pinchot, then ended the call.

When she finally cleared the traffic jam near the small intersection, she turned onto a back road. Towering pines lined each side, their branches heavy with droplets that slid off at uneven intervals. She kept her gaze high, searching for a possible vantage point. Vale often used hidden pullouts and side roads to distribute more flyers before vanishing.

A white truck passed her from the opposite direction and a cluster of tourists followed in an SUV. Everyone seemed on the hunt for the cryptid. She felt tension rise in her neck but she breathed through it. "Stay focused." She muttered. The plan was to track Vale's digital trail, corner him, and disrupt the anchor to break the cryptid's power. No one else ended up like Seth, traumatized in a clinic bed. She refused to let Vale keep turning the forest into his personal stage.

A few minutes later her phone buzzed with a text from Finch, who had discovered a new batch of social media chatter. She tapped it during a lull at a stop sign. Several accounts posted images of a spiral postcard pinned to a bulletin board near a café. One suspicious handle mentioned the phrase "The real show is sure to devour the nonbelievers soon." That line triggered alarm bells. Vale's skillful stirring of hype was not letting up.

Mara's next call was to Link. The moment he answered she said, "Keep an eye on that user handle. Cross-reference it with local IP addresses if you can. Vale might have multiple sock-puppet accounts stirring conversation. Or he might be letting followers handle it for him."

Link sounded frazzled. "Sure." I'll see what I can dig up. People keep retweeting a new snapshot of a carved tree trunk with the same spiral. I'll cross-check the location in real time with the drone feeds.

"Thanks." Mara said as she pressed the accelerator carefully. She returned her attention to the winding road, tires crunching small stones. The sky overhead turned a dull gray, hinting at more rain. She planned to stop by the SRD mobile command trailer once she reached the clearing near the forest border. The team would need an updated plan with Vale sowing fresh postcards.

She pictured the half-burned notebooks in Vale's van from earlier scuffles, though they had never fully pinned him down. The lines in those pages spelled out a blueprint for feeding terror to harness belief. She realized he was not a clueless bystander. He was the spark behind it all. Her foot pressed a bit harder on the gas.

"Seth was lucky." She whispered to herself. "Mia and Jackson weren't so fortunate." With that final thought beating at the back of her mind, she steered onto the forest approach. She intended to find Vale's notebooks or new anchor etchings. If the cryptid had that spiral carved into its chest, there must be a central site fueling the power. She refused to leave the forest until she had uncovered it.

A chill coursed through her body as she recalled the bruises on Seth's arms. She hoped her team could keep more hikers from enduring that fate. She recalled the look in his eyes when he mentioned the creature's glow, the stutter in his words that hinted at deeper scars. Finch's data said that fear acted like a power source. Vale understood that principle and tweaked it at every turn.

Mara keyed her earpiece again to confirm details with Link but paused. We'll regroup soon enough. Better to announce the plan once I have something concrete. She shut off the line. Her SUV rumbled onto a gravel shoulder as the pines pressed close. Despite the gloom, she kept her shoulders squared.

She considered her next move. She planned to talk to Finch again to cross-reference new sightings and isolate a probable anchor site. Carter Vale's postcards were critical evidence, and so were the frantic social media mentions. The spiral was more than a random design. It was a direct pipeline to the cryptid's center of power. Seth's story made one thing clear. The more people believed, the more unstoppable the entity could become.

As she left the clinic, her conversation with Seth sparked a surge of adrenaline. The postcards he described reminded her that Vale had orchestrated every rumor for maximum impact. She slowed as she approached the trailer's perimeter and prepared Finch and Link for the next step. Vale's twisted sketches had to be uncovered, and the cryptid's anchor had to be destroyed. She wrenched the SUV into park. Then she scanned the area for any sign of drones overhead. Moments later she knew Link was already surveying the region.

She sat for a moment near the trailer. This ends the moment we find that anchor site.

She recalled the chill in Seth's voice when he described the bone-plated torso and that shining spiral. She refused to let Vale push more people to the brink. She tucked her phone into a side pocket and stared at the tree line. Then she turned around and walked back toward the trailer.

Even as the cold mist clung to her jacket, she did not slow her pace. She planned to piece together every detail Seth had shared. Vale's postcards, the carved chest spiral, and those pinned around town all indicated a rising threat. She was prepared to face it head-on.

CHAPTER SEVEN

Cars jammed the edge of the forest as morning broke. Mara stepped out of the trailer and noticed dozens of phones raised, all recording the treeline.

She rubbed her stiff neck. Yesterday's search had dragged on and she smelled pine sap on her jacket. The shredded campsite left her frustrated. Sheriff Thomason's sparse team taped off the spot but no new footprints appeared during the dawn check. The missing campers were still unaccounted for and now a wave of cryptid chasers threatened to complicate everything. Seth's information confirmed much, and her desire to save more hikers from meeting a similar fate grew stronger.

She spotted Skyhook leaning against the VTOL hull. The pilot's stance was tense. "Finch wants to run more data," Skyhook said in a low voice. "He's picking up movement on ARGUS that lines up with all these new sightings."

Mara glanced at the crowd gathering near the ranger station's trailhead. A flimsy barricade, little more than a row of orange plastic tape, stood between the public and the deeper woods. Dozens of overly enthusiastic people wore homemade Bigfoot shirts. Some carried camera rigs, a few had microphones, and a few more fussed over phone gimbals. The sheriff stood by a patrol cruiser, a tired frown locked on his face as he talked to a deputy.

She walked up to him while passing a group that bickered about which trail to search first. One person insisted they had scanned a rumored footprint from the livestream, and the other boasted they had the best lens in the business. Mara shook her head. They acted as if they were producing a blockbuster.

"Here to see the circus?" the sheriff muttered when she reached him. A half-eaten doughnut sat on the cruiser's hood. His ballistic vest looked a size too small and his eyes carried the strain of repeated emergencies. "We're stretched thin," he said. "People keep pouring in. I have no leads on your missing kids, either. The campsite told us nothing new."

"Understood," Mara replied. She pointed to the forest boundary. "We need to secure certain areas. This crowd will get in the way."

He snorted. "Local commissioners want the roads open. They're hoping cryptid tourism will boost the region, even if it puts a few thrill-seekers in danger." He picked up his doughnut and stared at it, then sighed. "I lost count of how many vehicles arrived this morning. They all think they'll catch their million-view shot."

Mara's earpiece chimed. "Hey, boss, we're seeing an uptick in hashtags," Link said, sounding harried. "More cryptid vloggers announced they're on-site. A couple claim they saw a shape behind the brush near mile marker ten. Finch says the ARGUS system is mapping a fresh spike in internet chatter. Another wave of believers is fueling the data."

Mara grimaced. The swirling rumor mill made the cryptid stronger. She watched a trio of young men, eager and jittery. They argued over who would lead their livestream. One swung a selfie stick in broad arcs. They stopped to greet a breathless hiker who insisted he had heard heavy footsteps near a stream at dawn.

Mara forced her shoulders to relax and kept walking. A hush fell over some bystanders when her SRD patch caught their eye, but others snapped photos, likely posting them online. She imagined inaccurate headlines: "Federal Agents Confirm Bigfoot Attack!" That would add to the hype.

She found the ranger at a desk by the station door. He looked more drawn than last night with bags under his eyes. "I tried reinforcing the barricade, but that tape is a joke," he said. "We can't post rangers every hundred feet."

Mara asked, "Any unusual reports since daybreak?"

He nodded. "Someone found a weird spiral scratched into a tree about half a mile north. They left in a hurry when they heard snapping branches. I'm not sure if that was the wind or something else. I heard a rumor that Carter Vale's van was spotted at a truck rest area early this morning too."

Mara thanked him and returned to Skyhook's side. She sensed the pilot's frustration. Anyone could see the forest was becoming an amusement park for cryptid enthusiasts. "Stay close," Mara said quietly. "If these folks wander off-trail and run into something real, we will need a medic."

Skyhook tapped her flight cap. "Finch also wants a sample from the new swirl they found. It could be more of Vale's carving, the same pattern as near the campsite." She lowered her voice. "We have not pinned him down, but rumor says he has moved around the secondary logging roads. Local chatter mentions a battered van that matches his."

Mara scanned the line of vehicles parked in the grass. One was an old news van with a scribbled logo. Another was a squat SUV displaying a bright Bigfoot decal. She saw a red truck with a homemade sign reading "Bigfoot Or Bust." None belonged to Vale.

He is more careful than these folks and is probably enjoying the show from a distance.

She and Skyhook moved toward a cluster of larger rigs. Along the way they nearly collided with two monster hunters in camouflage. One recognized Mara from the day before and greeted her with an eager wave. "Any sign of that cryptid? Heard it tore up a camp," he said. "The net's going wild."

She kept her composure. "There are no confirmed findings yet. Stay on marked paths. This area has steep drop-offs." She did not bother detailing the real dangers. Extra warnings might inflame their imaginations. He offered a thumbs-up and jogged off talking into his phone. She overheard him promising his viewers he would find the beast before nightfall.

The sheriff trudged over. "I received word that more folks are pushing past the barricade farther to the west. One deputy asked them to leave and they recorded the entire exchange. It is going viral. That is drawing even more gawkers."

Mara's jaw tightened. "Is there any chance we can get assistance from the next county or the state patrol?"

He scowled. "We have put in requests, but that will take days. I might get a few extra people, but not enough to cover every corner. Meanwhile my missing campers case is stalled and Vale is out there passing around his cryptic flyers."

She glanced at the sky, hoping for a second of clarity. A few crows circled overhead. She could still hear camera shutters snapping below. "Fine. We will do what we can. We will keep an eye on the deeper trails. I will see if Link can jam some of the coverage. We risk fueling conspiracy theories but we might limit real-time sightings."

The sheriff shook his head, unconvinced. "Keep me posted. I'm about to check out the far side of the lot. There's a batch of people in off-road vehicles who claim they're staging a thorough search near the ravine."

Mara leaned in. "Please be cautious. The cryptid we're tracking is no hoax. If you see anything that looks off, call me or my team. We have sedation gear if it tries to engage."

"Got it," he muttered, trudging away.

She made her way toward the command trailer that Link had parked just off the gravel. Finch sat inside, hunched at his laptop. His eyes were red-rimmed, but he waved her in. Link peered at clusters of open screens on a wide monitor.

Finch massaged his temple. "Every wave of social posts spikes the cryptid's probability curve. I've got the trending tags pinned. A handful of influencers keep going live every ten minutes, filming random bush movements. People are sharing it all."

"Is there a pattern to Vale's involvement?" she asked. "I assume he posted something that kicked off this morning's frenzy."

Finch tapped a short clip that looped on screen. "This was posted around 4 a.m. under a known Vale sock-puppet account. Grainy footage of a silhouette, plus the same spiral watermark we saw before. That was enough. By dawn, half the cryptid-chasing channels pounced. Carter knows exactly how to feed them."

Mara set a hand on the folded map next to Finch's console. "We're dealing with a zoo out there. Half these people want bragging rights, half want a viral clip. Let's see if we can direct them away from the zones where the footprints were spotted. Maybe we can concentrate them somewhere safer."

Link glanced up from his station. "I can push a few rumor seeds about the cryptid being spotted near the main road, far from the ravine or any deeper trails. That might steer casual folks away from high-risk zones."

Mara nodded. "Try it. The deeper woods are where the real trouble lies." She paused. "But we'll need to coordinate with the sheriff. I don't want to cause more friction if he finds out we're seeding false leads."

Finch glanced at the data overlay. "Might be worth it to keep the crowd safe. Meanwhile, let's see about analyzing that spiral carving. One more cluster was reported near the southwestern trail."

She and Skyhook prepped to head out. Before leaving, she

toggled her earpiece. "Sheriff," she said, "we're going to examine that southwestern site. Keep me updated if any big crowd trouble flares." He sounded relieved, as if happy to have them scouting beyond the mess of onlookers.

They stepped outside. Around them, the crowd had grown louder. A small group lined up with handheld radio receivers, scanning for movement or anomalies. Mara noted that many wore protective boots and thick jackets, which at least suggested they understood how rough the terrain could be. She squeezed past a skinny teenager interviewing bystanders about the "Bigfoot phenomenon."

Skyhook sighed once they gained a little space. "Never seen so many self-styled monster hunters. They look eager enough to run straight into a ravine."

"Let's hope that doesn't happen," Mara said, voice flat.

They began their hike through a side path that led toward the southwestern quadrant of the forest. Dense undergrowth rustled at their ankles. She raised her coil carbine, scanning for signs of fresh footprints or any trace of the cryptid's path.

"It's too quiet here," Skyhook muttered.

Mara's reply was short. "Better than a mob. At least we can work without bumping elbows." She peered behind a thick cedar trunk. Broken twigs scattered in an odd pattern. It might be an old campsite or an animal's rummaging spot. She motioned for Skyhook to stay close.

Her earpiece chirped and Finch's voice came through. "We pinned Vale's possible location near the truck stop an hour ago. Doesn't look like we have fresh intel on him now. The chatter from the southwestern path is low, so you might catch a break out there."

Mara clicked her tongue. "Understood." She whispered so her voice would not carry. "We'll call if we find anything."

Further along, they spotted a flimsy tarp and the remains of a makeshift fire ring. No spiral sigils were visible. They found footprints, though many seemed old or half-erased by weather. She took pictures with her visor gear and logged them for Finch's reference. After half an hour, the forest thickened and the distant noise of the crowd receded like a fading memory.

Skyhook lowered her voice. "Think we'll see a real sighting today?"

Mara shrugged. "If the cryptid is drawn to hype, it might hang closer to the bigger crowds. There's more energy to feed it." She considered the swirling data patterns that Finch had shown her. At some point, it's going to show up again. It would be better if it appears near us rather than among uninformed bystanders.

They pressed farther until they reached a narrow stream. Water gurgled over slick stones. Mara knelt, scanning for prints. Nothing. She watched a faint reflection of pines overhead. Then she stood and brushed leaves from her pants. "No sign of Vale. No fresh spirals. The southwestern cluster might be a false alarm."

Skyhook nodded. "Then we should head back to the command trailer. Finch wanted to refine the data once we checked this area."

The walk back was quicker though they stepped around brambles and small gullies. At one point, they heard raised voices in the distance. Mara tensed, expecting something urgent, but it sounded like a small argument rather than distress. She figured a pair of cryptid seekers had bickered over who saw what first.

When they returned to the main path, the crowd had surged even more. Two local news crews were setting up cameras near the ranger station. Mara glanced their way, then quickened her pace toward the trailer. She wanted to avoid being interviewed. In her experience, one stray quote could spark chaos online.

Link was outside, fiddling with a drone in the sunlight. He nodded as they approached. "I nudged some rumor chatter about the cryptid near the road, but that only diverted a fraction of folks. The rest remain convinced the forest is teeming with sightings. Also, we got a short wave of new feeders on social media. Something about a local influencer claiming they heard roars."

"Roars?" Skyhook raised an eyebrow. "They probably heard a sick moose."

Mara's lips twitched in a small smirk. "People hear what they want to hear. Let's keep monitoring. If we find any leads, we'll act quickly. Meanwhile, we will manage the fallout."

Finch stepped out, waving a printout. "The share count on cryptid videos has risen again. Carter Vale must be behind the scenes driving the increase. We have to watch for that. The cryptid's energy parameters keep climbing."

Mara nodded. "We'll keep a close watch on likely spots." She surveyed the rows of vehicles and the throng of amateurs with cameras. Telling them all to leave would cause more mayhem. "We'll keep them safe if we can."

Skyhook crossed her arms. "At least we can keep the body count at zero for now."

Mara looked at the horizon. The day was only half over, and the crowd showed no sign of thinning. Tension hummed through the crowd of careless thrill-seekers. She hovered between worrying about the cryptid's next move and dreading the chaos these onlookers might stumble into. She wondered how long they could maintain their position.

She took a final look at the packed parking area, then motioned to the others. "Let's regroup. We'll do another pass around the perimeter at midday and see if any fresh footprints show up. Be ready to jump if the cryptid makes an appearance. That includes preventing Vale from slipping away if we learn his location."

As they split up, Mara spotted a tavern where enthusiasts and civilians chattered loudly about the sightings. They all headed inside, bracing for the next wave of attention.

CHAPTER EIGHT

Mara stepped through the tavern's narrow door, greeted by the electric hum of overlapping voices. She scanned the dim interior and noticed patrons crammed around small tables, each group immersed in cryptid lore. Screens on every table replayed the so-called Bigfoot livestream that started the frenzy, while a few paused on a shot of Carter Vale's face. The air smelled of stale hops and body heat.

She paused near the bar so her eyes could adjust. After two days in the forest, this crowded room felt jarring. Most of the chatter revolved around rumor chasing. Patrons described night sightings and waved phone clips like trophies. One man claimed the creature looked covered in thick bone plates while his friend insisted it was wet fur. Mara suppressed a groan. She reminded herself these were the civilians she was trying to protect.

She wove between rickety barstools, listening. A middle-aged woman in a neon windbreaker bragged she planned to film at a nearby ravine. Another insisted Gifford Pinchot locals were exaggerating everything for tourism dollars. Mara picked out references to the missing college students Jackson and Mia sprinkled throughout the chatter. Some insisted the pair had staged the entire thing for clicks while others speculated they were wounded or worse. The guesses became more outlandish with every retelling.

She approached a corner booth when the voices escalated. Four hikers argued about whether the cryptid had glowing eyes. They turned to her demanding an official stance. Mara answered in a calm tone. "We've had scattered reports. Nothing confirmed." She tipped her head slightly. "Stop wandering out there at night. My team is investigating."

One man scoffed. "Investigating? You mean stopping everyone from making a living out of local legends." He puffed his chest, clearly offended. "Your folks are scaring people out of the woods."

Mara's jaw tensed. "My job is to keep anyone from getting hurt. I'd be the last person to stand in the way of normal tourism, but this is a serious threat."

He shrugged. "Serious threat that's boosting business around here. We got folks driving in from three states over, hoping to catch a glimpse." He tapped his phone. "The bar's never been this packed on a weekday."

Mara glanced around. The place was indeed busier than typical for a late afternoon. She understood the tension. Locals saw the monster stories as profitable. Nobody seemed to grasp how that excitement fed the phenomenon. Instead, they celebrated the hype.

She moved to a table where a group hunched over a battered paperback with Carter Vale's photo on the back. The talk there was even more concerning. One man, possibly an influencer with a tuft of pink hair, claimed Vale was staging a new broadcast. The influencer said Vale slipped him a scribbled note that morning. He looked up when Mara approached.

"Hey, you government or something?" he asked, noticing the subdued SRD patch on her jacket. "Because if you're looking for Vale, I might know where he's going to be tonight."

Her shoulders stiffened. "I'd appreciate hearing that."

He raised his glass in a self-important gesture. "He told me to watch for the spiral to blow up tonight and encouraged me to bring my camera. It's going to boost my channel." There was a gleam of eagerness in his eyes. "He said he would give me access to behind-the-scenes footage. That is huge for me."

She forced a neutral expression. "And you believe him?"

"He wrote bestsellers in the old days, right? He must know how to capture an audience." The influencer laughed. "This Bigfoot mania is real, and I'm riding that wave."

Carter Vale had once reached literary stardom when his first book rocketed to bestseller status and brought him a period of success. However, fame proved a fickle mistress. The initial acclaim was fleeting, his next books failed to recapture that success, and he faded from the public eye. It seemed he was creating content now, and not the good kind.

Mara's stomach twisted. She could predict how Vale's plan would unfold. More people would chase the cryptid. That would spread more fervor online and fuel the creature's power. She felt an urge to seize the man's phone and shut this down, but that would only add to the spectacle. She had to play this carefully.

She asked for the note itself, but he shrugged. "I used it as a prop in a quick story post and then tossed it. I have the message recorded, though." He patted a battered phone on the table. "We can make a quick handshake deal if you want the footage. My social media is always open."

Mara said nothing. She tapped her comm earpiece, then spoke quietly. "Link, do you hear this? Some influencer claims Vale is pushing a big event tonight."

Link's voice came through faint but clear. "Yeah, I have it on record." He said. "I am cross-checking it against new chatter. There is a spike of midnight invitations on local feeds."

Mara turned away and let the influencer babble to the others about potential brand opportunities. She noticed the bartender wiping glasses and listening in. She approached him next. He was older, in a threadbare flannel shirt, and he nodded as she came up. "Guess you're the one they call Mara?"

She nodded. "I will not hassle your customers. I want to know if you have heard anything resembling a credible sighting."

He set the glass down. "No credible sightings at all. Mostly drunks claim they hear howls or see shapes in the trees." He scratched his chin. "One or two people said they saw spirals carved into a cedar trunk near the main trail. They said the spirals glowed after sundown, but who knows."

She frowned. "Did they give a time?"

He said, "Only that it was late. They had been coming back from a day hike when they saw something weird, and then they hurried out." His expression hardened. "I told them to move along. That story makes half these fools want to run straight there."

Mara thanked him and made a mental note.

Glowing spirals? Finch is going to love that.

She had no doubt the markings were real. Reports of that effect had surfaced earlier, though nobody had captured them on video yet. She stepped back into the main room and scanned each table for anything else of value.

She overheard a mention of Jackson and Mia. A couple hunched over their fries whispered that the missing campers had left a cryptic farewell message on social media. Another swore they spotted Jackson's jacket near an overgrown trail but never reported it because they worried about a trespassing fine. She felt anger simmer. People protected their recreational whims more than each other's safety.

She eased close to them. "Were you the ones who claimed you saw Jackson's jacket?"

Both jerked upright. The man tightened his grip on his drink. "Maybe. But it was a quick glimpse and we had to get going." He shrugged. "Wasn't sure."

Mara took a steadying breath. She imagined the heartbreak those kids' families must be enduring while thrill-seekers treated clues like gossip. "Try to remember where you saw it."

The man fumbled with his phone and pulled up a map. He tapped a trail intersection near the forest's northern boundary. Mara memorized the spot and quietly thanked them. "If you recall anything else, contact local authorities." She said, slipping away.

She switched to her comm. "Link, are you getting that coordinate?"

"Got it," he replied. "I'll dig for more social mentions in that area. Might find something about the missing campers or Vale."

Mara circled back to the bar's far end. She saw a small group in worn hiking gear, each talking about a run-in with the sheriff's patrol. They looked annoyed at the idea of any roadblocks or restricted areas. One man said, "Sheriff Thomason tried to post officers around certain trailheads, but that only made folks more curious." The others laughed, stoking each other's bravado.

That fit the pattern. The more authorities tried to clamp down, the more these explorers wanted to defy warnings. Marshaling them to safety was starting to feel impossible. She caught a snippet of conversation involving a man who claimed to see Carter Vale earlier in the day. He described a hooded figure passing out flyers from the back of a weathered hatchback but that detail did not match Vale's van. Possibly a decoy or rumor.

Another swirl of chatter erupted near the dartboard. Someone reeled in excitement triggered by a new post. Mara craned her neck and spotted a phone screen streaming shaky footage from an unknown location in the forest. The angle showed tall pines and a shape in the distance. The tavern crowd pressed in. Mara tried to see if it was legitimate. It looked far too grainy, likely a hoax. Yet the tension rose among watchers. They wanted to believe it was real evidence.

She gently elbowed past them without apology. Then she

moved into an open stretch of floor near the restrooms. The voices merged into an animated buzz behind her. She needed air. That swirl of cell phone screens and speculation reminded her of swarms of insects around a lamp. Vale had harnessed that swarm. He used each new post or rumor to push the cryptid into sharper focus. The thought rattled her.

She keyed her earpiece again, leaning against a cracked wooden divider. "Link, I'm stepping outside. Meet me on the main channel once I'm clear. Got too much background noise in here."

Outside, the wind carried a damp chill that felt cleaner than the tavern's cloying heat. Mara walked a few steps from the entrance and scanned the gravel parking lot. A battered pickup rolled by with its headlights off. She watched it fade around the corner. Then she heard Link's voice in her ear.

"All right, I'm cross-referencing everything you've gathered. People are definitely planning midnight meetups deeper in the forest. The chatter about glowing spirals is spiking too. Finch texted me that there's an unexpected jump on local boards contributing to that. He's running new numbers on ARGUS."

"Wonderful," Mara muttered. She pictured Finch hunched over his console as lines of swirling data spiked upward. The cryptid's strength would be boosted by each wave of attention. It is feeding on every post. She stared at the tavern's old wooden sign. They are cheering for it.

"Skyhook wants to know if you want pickup," Link continued. "She's fueled up and can land near the old logging road if you want a camp sweep tonight."

Mara exhaled. "Not in the dark. Too many amateurs wandering around. A stealth approach would be next to impossible with all these people racing in. We would risk hurting them or getting sightings posted."

"Understood. I'll let her know."

She heard the door behind her swing open. The influencer

with pink hair stepped out for a smoke, glancing at Mara as if expecting another official condemnation. She gave him a curt nod. He shrugged and moved to the far end of the parking lot.

That left Mara alone near a flickering neon sign spelling the tavern's name. She frowned at her reflection in the glass. She knew she was on a collision course with Vale's next stunt. She wasn't sure how many warnings she could issue before the crowd ignored her.

She returned inside, paid for a bottle of water, and headed back to the corner. A final check around the booths revealed no fresh leads. Plenty of folks repeated the same stories: nighttime howls, possible footprints in the mud, posted invites for group hunts. She wanted to stand on a table and shout at them to walk away, but she knew it would only fan the flames. With a nod to the bartender, she left the tavern.

Back outside, the air felt cooler. She sipped her water and focused on the next steps. "Link," she said quietly, "I'm done here. Let Finch know we have a rumored event tonight and that it's linked to more spiral sightings. The entire place is buzzing about it."

He sounded tired as he replied, "Got it. We'll coordinate. Watch your back."

She ended the call and trudged across the gravel, passing the battered pickup again. Its driver still lurked by the far side of the lot, phone in hand. She could almost feel the tension flood the evening sky, a hothouse of rumors fueling the thing they were all chasing.

They're fueling it faster than we can contain it.

She secured her jacket collar. Then she strode onto the main road, determined to circle back to the SRD trailer. The next few hours would be critical. Vale's spiral belonged in a data chart, but it was creeping onto every phone screen in the region. The forest had become an open invitation, and Mara feared that once midnight arrived, half those tavern patrons would be streaming the hunt live.

She headed for her parked vehicle, scanning the horizon for any sign of drones or local patrol cars. As she turned the key, she thought of the missing campers. She pictured their abandoned campsite, shredded tent, and the spiral carvings in the trees. Then she remembered the rumor about Jackson's jacket near the northern boundary. The phone in her pocket vibrated with an incoming message from Finch. She didn't bother reading it yet. She already knew it would confirm her worst fears about midnight events or rising belief metrics.

She rested both hands on the steering wheel. Another long night. That was the best she could predict. The final echoes of laughter from the tavern drifted through her open window. She drove off, headlights cutting across the empty highway, mind fixed on the next step: regroup with Finch, decipher the new numbers, and somehow halt Vale's spiral from sinking even deeper into the forest's dark corners.

CHAPTER NINE

As night enveloped Gifford Pinchot, Mara pushed deeper into the woods, the beam of her flashlight cutting a nervous swathe through the oppressive gloom. Each step on the damp, leaf-strewn earth felt like a gamble. The forest offered its chilling clues in rotation: massive footprints pressed too deep into the mud, fresh spiral carvings gouged into bark, or vicious claw marks raking down ancient cedar trunks. These stark and unsettling markers all pointed to the cryptid's recent passage but never to the creature itself. It was a phantom always a step ahead, leaving Mara with the gnawing sense of being led. Link's voice echoed her unease, his drone feeds showing the creature's erratic movements. "It's almost like it's playing with you, Mara," he muttered. The data suggested less of a hunt and more of a pointless pursuit designed to keep her circling fruitlessly.

The forest seemed to conspire in the deception, its shadows twisting familiar shapes into monstrous illusions, its silence amplifying every snapped twig into a pronouncement of unseen menace. Then, amidst the detritus of a hurried passage, trampled ferns and angry etchings, a glint of something out of place: a polished camera pod half buried. She secured the device, a flicker of hope that its footage might betray another player in this grim theater, one of the reckless influencers drawn to Vale's hype or even a misstep by Vale himself. The discovery did little to dispel the oppressive feeling of being outmaneuvered in an arena the cryptid knew intimately.

It was Skyhook who broke the tension of the solitary hunt when her silhouette appeared in the deeper gloom behind a stand of firs. Link, concerned by the increasingly erratic data and Mara's deepening foray into the creature's perceived territory, had suggested the pilot join her on the ground. Together they pushed onward until the treeline gave way to the damp chill of a narrow ravine. They found a fallen log with bark slick with moss and sat in the silence for two minutes, their breathing the only sound against the vast quiet. What did this creature truly want? Was it simply territorial, a beast agitated by their presence, or was there a more insidious intelligence guiding its evasions, a dark purpose woven into the fabric of Vale's manufactured nightmare? The forest offered no answers, only the heavy scent of pine and the unsettling feeling of being watched.

Mara sat next to the ravine, eased forward with one hand braced against lichen-coated rock, and peered into the dark slope below. Link's voice crackled in her earpiece, telling her that local dispatch had picked up a frantic call from a father at these coordinates. His trembling voice had mentioned a hulking figure towering over his family's tent. That same man had dismissed official warnings as hype a few hours earlier. Now he was begging for rescue.

Skyhook moved up behind Mara. "All I see is a mess of snapped branches," she murmured, shining her flashlight in a tight arc. Her gloved grip tightened around the heavier med kit slung over her shoulder. "Folks never learn."

Mara sighed without looking back. "They saw enough

tonight." She checked the EM coil carbine strapped to her chest. The muzzle pointed low, stowed but ready. "Link, you have eyes on any movement from your side?"

"A few scattered sightings posted online," Link replied through the encrypted line. "No consistent direction. People on CryptidWatch are lighting up the boards about roars and tree knocks. Data is a mess again."

Mara adjusted her visor to low-light mode. The ravine's rugged walls took shape as faint outlines, and a few battered ferns lay crushed underfoot. She reminded herself not to get stuck analyzing every clue. The father's family was out here, shaken. "Skyhook," Mara said, "I'll take point downhill. If you spot anything overhead, call it out."

They descended carefully. Each step rattled the loose stones that lined the path. Mara disliked the unpredictability of these hunts. The moment crowds started posting new angles and possible sightings, the cryptid gained a fresh spark of ferocity, and the father and kids had unwittingly fed that cycle by showing up with minimal caution.

Her earpiece buzzed again. "We have a new upload," Link said quickly. "Two teenagers posted footage of a large shape cracking a trunk in half. That might be your location. The timestamps line up."

Mara cursed under her breath and paused behind a rotting stump that reeked of moss and old wood. She aimed her flashlight forward in short bursts. "When you say two teenagers, do you mean the father's kids or another set of thrill-seekers?"

Link fell silent, then said, "Users are named Danny and Aiko. Teen vlogger types. Probably not the father's kids. Their channel is already blowing up with half the chat screaming about an 'unholy creature.' That won't help."

Mara's teeth clenched. "Copy that. Keep scanning." She flicked her head toward Skyhook. "We'll try to block that line of sight if we see them. Stumbling around filming is a perfect way to get mauled."

They pressed farther along the ravine's edge until they heard a faint sob. Mara lifted a hand to signal Skyhook, who drew her sidearm and kept low. Then Mara stepped around a broken log and spotted three silhouettes: a middle-aged man who knelt protectively in front of two children wrapped in flimsy blankets. Their campsite lay a few yards away, the tent collapsed and gear strewn around.

Mara approached in measured steps and kept her carbine angled. "Sir," she called, voice firm, "you called for help."

He jerked at her voice, not sure whether to be relieved or terrified. "You're the agent they sent?"

"I'm part of a special unit," Mara said. She knelt so she didn't tower over the kids. "Are you three hurt?"

The father shook his head, though his eyes darted around. "I… my kids are okay. They're scared." One child, a boy around nine, clung to his dad's arm. The girl, around thirteen, hovered nearby, cheeks streaked with tears. "That thing came out of nowhere," the man continued. "It was huge, with what looked like bone plating across its back."

Mara saw a beaten path behind them where brush was flattened. The father's tent lay skewed and the polyester was slashed. She nodded once, then activated her comm. "Link, we have them. Three civilians. None are injured, though the gear is trash."

"Got it." Link replied. "No sign of the cryptid on my feed. The new teenage vloggers are half a mile south of your position, filming in a clearing with a big boulder. They're yelling about proof of Bigfoot."

Mara exhaled through her nose. "Terrific. Keep me posted." She turned to the man. "We'll escort you out. After that, you'll need to clear the area. It's not safe, and you know that now."

He nodded, face pale. "I'm sorry. I read the warnings, but I assumed it was an internet hoax." He paused. "I—I messed up."

Mara stood and signaled Skyhook to assist. "Kids, gather anything you need that's still intact. We'll escort you to a safer spot near the ranger station. My partner has a med kit if anyone's feeling shaken."

Skyhook led them up the slope. Mara checked the perimeter, stepping over snapped twigs and a chunk of plastic from what might have been a lantern. Splatters of mud revealed large tracks heading deeper into the forest. Her heart rate ticked up as she noticed how deep those depressions ran. That indicated power beyond normal wildlife.

She tapped her earpiece again. "Finch, are you picking up anything from the ARGUS system? We see fresh footprints, large and spaced wide. Looks like the creature came through fast."

Finch responded in a low voice. "ARGUS is spiking with social media mentions, but I can't confirm the exact location of the cryptid. The father's call triggered more speculation, plus the teen videos. Your best bet is to track it physically. I'll guide you if we see a pattern in the data."

Mara trekked a few yards from the campsite. The ground dipped toward a line of cedar trees, each trunk thick enough to hide something monstrous. She turned her flashlight and glimpsed a broken chunk of wood that looked shaved at the edges. As her light played across the fragments, she spotted a tuft of coarse, dark fur snagged on a thorny shrub. She set the carbine aside for a second, slipped on evidence gloves, and carefully plucked the tuft free. It felt warm, as if the cryptid's energy still clung to it. That unsettled her more than she would admit aloud.

Skyhook's voice slid through the comm. "I have the family about twenty paces up the slope. We'll reach the top soon. Need help?"

"Stay with them." Mara said. "I'll be right behind you. I found something for Finch to analyze later."

A faint noise echoed from further downslope. A crack and then a rumble. Mara sank into a crouch and switched off her flashlight. She flipped her visor to thermal, letting the device do the work. The faint silhouette of a tall form flickered near the base of a cedar, broad shoulders shifting. Mara steadied her breathing. That had to be the cryptid. It seemed to pace slowly, as if sniffing the air.

Her pulse beat hard in her ears.

Do I push forward, or do I keep my distance?

She weighed the risk. The father and kids were halfway out, so they were safer now. This might be a rare chance to see how the creature reacted without a crowd in the way. It was a gamble, but knowledge was precious in these hunts.

She took three silent steps. The shape turned. Mara froze, feeling its gaze as a raw wave of menace. In that brief second, she realized the cryptid had recognized her presence. A chilling snarl reverberated up the slope, and the creature raked a hefty arm across a fallen trunk. The wood cracked with a sharp pop, sending splinters across the ground. She heard it let out a grunt that sounded like a challenge.

Mara pressed the side of her earpiece. "Link, stand by for possible encounter. If it charges, I'll hold it off for a moment, then retreat."

Link's quick reply: "Roger that. I'm mapping a route around your position for the father and kids. Finch says sedation darts might help if you get a clear shot."

She flicked the carbine's safety to off, ignoring the flutter in her throat. Online hype had soared in the last couple of days, fueling every rumor. That made it more vicious. She aimed the coil carbine at the trunk the cryptid had just destroyed, letting the reticle settle near a likely approach point. Nothing was there. Then the faint shape crouched behind the log, peering over with glowing eyes. She inhaled slowly, forcing herself to be calm.

"Come on." She muttered under her breath. She thought she'd like to see if sedation worked in the open but recognized she needed a clear shot. She squared her shoulders, took aim, and squeezed off one dart. It hissed, lodging in the log behind the cryptid. Her aim was off because it moved at the last second. She cursed.

The creature raised its head and released a roar that rattled Mara's bones. A jolt of adrenaline jarred her and she gripped the carbine tighter. She racked another dart, stepping sideways for a better angle, but the shape sprang into motion. Its massive frame surged deeper into the forest, branches ripping aside in its wake. Mara snarled in frustration.

She dashed forward, scanning for signs of blood or a direct hit. The sedative had missed. All she found was another ragged tuft of fur near the log. She pocketed it in a quick evidence bag, then stared into the gloom where the monster had vanished. Her mind churned. She realized it was more skittish than she had expected. It was not ready for a direct fight. But a cornered cryptid was an even bigger hazard.

Her earpiece popped with static. "Mara, everything okay?" That was Skyhook, sounding tense.

She took a breath. "I'm fine. The creature retreated, so I doubt it's going to circle back right now. I missed with sedation. It's gone."

"Understood." Skyhook said. "Family is safe topside. The father was all tears once we got him on even ground. I'll walk them to the ranger station's perimeter."

"Good." Mara replied. She stepped around the log and noted a patch of bark carved with a faint spiral shape. The edges looked fresh, a possible sign of Carter Vale's continuing meddling. She snapped a quick photo with her visor and shook her head. He's still out there, making sure the hype never dies.

She climbed the slope and slipped on loose gravel. Her thoughts flicked to the father's trembling children. One misstep would have sent them face-first into a cryptid that might have killed them. Instead they had a brush with terror they would carry indefinitely.

Better to see the truth than cling to rumors.

When she reached flatter ground, she spotted Skyhook standing with the father and children beside a broad cedar. The man looked more composed now, though anxiety radiated from him in waves. "Thank you," he croaked as Mara approached. "I feel like the worst parent alive. If I had known, I never would have brought them."

Mara gave a curt nod. "No one thinks rationally when rumors spread. Fear or fascination takes over. Focus on getting them home safe now."

He swallowed hard and turned to the kids. They clung to him, wide-eyed but calmer with the immediate threat gone. "Agent," the man said, "I won't fool around with this again. We're done with Bigfoot hunts or whatever you call that thing."

Mara wasn't about to lecture him further, so she pointed toward the path leading west. "Stick with Skyhook for an escort to the ranger's main checkpoint. We'll arrange a safe ride. After that, do not come back here until we tell you it's contained."

He nodded, eyes lowered.

Skyhook guided them up the trail, weapon holstered while Mara carried the med kit. Mara lingered behind, scanning the darkness. Images of that towering shape haunted her mind: plated shoulders, an unreal growl. She squeezed the tuft of fur in her pocket. That sample would be Finch's next puzzle, though they all knew the root cause lay beyond biology.

She tapped her comm. "Link, can you confirm if more spectators are drifting in? Or do we have a window to regroup?"

"Chatter about the teenage vloggers to the south. They're set on finding 'ultimate footage.' Don't put it past them to wander into your zone."

Mara sighed and scanned her surroundings one last time. "We'll break off soon, then circle back to check on those teens. No sense letting them become the next casualties."

She followed Skyhook, footsteps quiet on the damp ground. A

series of short shrieks echoed in the distance, and her muscles tensed. The cryptid's call faded and tension settled in her body. *We're not nearly done. This thing grows bolder every time its name trends online.*

She had a job: gather facts, keep people alive, and drive the cryptid into a final corner where SRD's methods would neutralize it. She had done it before, though never with this many onlookers.

We'll handle it anyway.

She soon reached the father and children, who huddled near a fallen trunk while Skyhook stood watch. Mara closed the distance and saw exhaustion etched on the kids' faces. "We'll walk you the rest of the way," she said gently, motioning them toward the forest's exit.

A short while later, she and Skyhook led them onto a nearby path, where the lights of the ranger station glowed a safe distance ahead. Mara glanced over her shoulder. The cryptid was out there, fueled by every rumor.

"Well," she said softly to Skyhook, "it exists, and it hates us."

Skyhook nearly smiled. "At least we know it's real. That means we can beat it."

Mara nodded, eyes flicking to the blackness of the trees. She pictured the swirling sigils carved around the forest. *That cryptid won't vanish without a fight. Still, her decision was made. She'd push forward, no matter how wild the threat became.*

She lifted her comm to radio Link. "Keep me updated on social feed surges. We'll need to set a plan for tomorrow. Right now, I'm dropping these folks off, then returning to the trailer for a game plan with Finch."

"Copy," Link said. "And Mara? Nice job making sure those kids got out."

She pressed her lips together for a moment. "They got lucky tonight. Next time, we handle the cryptid before luck is even a factor."

She walked on, guiding the father and children closer to the ranger's boundary lights. The family would be safe soon, but the forest behind her still echoed with a faint, distant howl. It beckoned like an unresolved challenge, one she planned to confront without delay.

/ CHAPTER TEN

Morning arrived with a cold bite that settled in Mara Bishop's bones. She stepped out of the SRD Mobile Command Trailer and scanned the low clouds beyond the forest's edge and she wondered how fast Carter Vale could disappear on a lonely stretch of highway.

Her comm crackled with Link's voice. "We've got that lead on Vale. Some tipster saw a man handing out cryptid flyers at a truck stop." Mara rested a hand on her EM-Coil Carbine. "Understood. Give me coordinates and keep an eye on any posts about that location." She shifted her stance and adjusted the tension on her vest straps. Skyhook crossed the muddy ground to stand beside her, posture steady despite the early chill. Mara signaled that they would lift off in the VTOL as soon as Link finalized the route.

They touched down near a cluster of trailers and semis parked on gravel that looked more like a bog. A flickering neon sign would have greeted them if the bulbs were not half dead. Mara walked toward the convenience store entrance and raised an eyebrow at the torn plastic taped over the door frame. She paused before going inside and keyed her comm again. "Link, be ready if I need more background on the local crowd." Then she stepped through the doorway.

A middle-aged cashier wearing a stained T-shirt looked up lazily from behind the counter. He did not seem pleased to see a uniformed stranger strolling into his quiet domain. Mara offered him a curt nod. A whiskered trucker hunched over a cup of coffee near a window, ignoring her. The store smelled of burnt beans and old fryer grease, with a few boxes of instant meals stacked by the entrance.

Mara approached the cashier, who watched her closely. "Looking for a man in a threadbare jacket who left some cryptid pamphlets here. Know anything?" The cashier snorted. "I get all kinds passing through. If you mean that older fella with the camera, he was here earlier. Seemed jumpy."

Mara pressed for details. "You remember what he said." She noted the man's tired sigh as he set his phone aside. He scratched his chin a few times with the back of his hand.

He said something about a legendary beast in the woods. Told me to pass out a couple flyers. I shrugged him off, but he pinned one on the board outside. The cashier flicked a glance at the door. "He left soon after in a camper van. Could be heading north."

Mara pulled out her phone, jotted a quick note, and then stepped away. She walked around the store's side and followed the sagging wooden ramp that led to a small bulletin board under a sagging overhead light. She spotted a damp flyer pinned dead center. Spirals filled the corners of the paper. Crude text read, "Witness the forest's true king." Ten days remain.

Mara felt annoyance coil in her stomach. He was definitely stirring the pot. She snapped a digital photo for Finch.

Skyhook emerged from behind the store, boots clacking against the wet gravel. "I've got a trucker who says this guy was filming the parking lot like he was shooting a documentary. The van was a heap, older than me."

Mara studied the flyer again. The spiral matched the images Finch had flagged as a key anchor design. Lower on the page, the text teased an upcoming reveal. She folded the paper and tucked it into an evidence pouch, ignoring a few curious looks from a passing customer.

They headed back toward the cashier to confirm which direction the camper had gone. The man behind the counter gave them a halfhearted shrug. "He pulled out onto the northbound highway and might have turned off on a logging road. Don't see that many folks heading deeper into nowhere, but sometimes it happens."

Mara thanked him and signaled Skyhook to follow. Outside, she checked her phone and saw Link's real-time feed. "No updated posts from ValeSightings, but Finch is analyzing that countdown. He wants any notes or pages we find." Mara glanced at the line of trucks rumbling in and out of the lot. "We'll try to see if the drones can track him from above."

They made a short loop around the perimeter, careful to avoid the swampy patches near the semis. A patch of charred paper scraps lay tangled in the weeds near an abandoned fuel pump. Mara knelt and picked up blackened pieces of notebook paper. Faint words in scribbled handwriting read "culminating location." Another passage mentioned watchers fueling the cryptid's strength. She bagged the fragments, her mind racing with the tension that had dogged her since the Gifford Pinchot business materialized.

He's dropping breadcrumbs on purpose. She looked over her shoulder at Skyhook, who hovered a few steps behind. "This guy wants an audience. He's building up to something."

Skyhook exhaled through pursed lips. "He's turning the forest into a stage. Should we do a quick search of the area by air?"

Mara nodded and touched the comm earpiece. "Link, can you patch a drone feed across the truck stop perimeter? We found partial notes referencing a culminating event. I want overhead coverage."

"On it." Link replied. "Give me two minutes to launch from the trailer."

Mara and Skyhook returned to the VTOL, which sat primed on a flat patch of ground near a flickering streetlight. They took off, ascending high enough for Link's drone to circle. Through the video feed on Mara's wrist display, the surrounding roads looked bleak, lined by pines and dotted with occasional rusted vehicles. No sign of a moving camper. She clenched her jaw. "He's probably long gone."

They set down again and hopped out. Mara decided to canvas any remaining corners of the lot. She found a damp cardboard box surrounded by empty energy drink cans. No sign of footprints or anything else that might lead them straight to Vale. The place felt hollow, as if he had swept through and left nothing but shredded clues.

Before leaving the truck stop, Mara questioned the old cashier one last time. He insisted that the visitor looked preoccupied with his camera gear. "Didn't buy much, either," the cashier added. "Just a coffee." He said the visitor had clutched it tightly and drove off as if the devil were chasing him.

Mara thanked him and departed. She and Skyhook lifted off once more, heading north. The forest behind them swallowed the horizon in a spread of conifers that looked endless under a dull sky. Mara kept her eyes on the ground below, studying every bend in the blacktop for a camper's silhouette. Static hissed in her earpiece.

Link's voice cut in. "We got fresh chatter on the net. Vale-Sightings posted a cryptic countdown message. Some references to an unveiling in a few days, though the location's not pinned."

Mara's jaw tightened. "Any mention of those half-burned notes?"

"Not specifically." Link said. "But the timing lines up with the next big social feed spike. Finch thinks Vale is feeding the hype on purpose." Mara's next breath sounded rough in her own ears. She wondered whether every cryptid hunter out there would surge into Gifford Pinchot at the worst moment.

Skyhook nudged a dial on her console to level their flight. "I'm not picking up unique heat signatures. We might have missed him by a good hour or two." She met Mara's gaze and added, "A camper van that old probably isn't blazing down the interstate. He's poking along some back road."

Mara flipped through the images on her wrist display. The spiral flyer glared back at her like an insult. She pictured Jackson and Mia, the missing campers who never got a second chance after their prank turned real. That memory drove her focus. Need to nail this bastard before more people vanish.

They traveled another twenty miles in slow arcs, scanning for anything resembling Vale's vehicle. The drone feeds turned up nothing. In frustration, Mara finally signaled they should head for a clearing Finch had marked on the map as a potential regroup site. The trees below parted to reveal a patch of flat ground near a small stream, so Skyhook guided the VTOL down.

When they landed, Mara stepped out into the damp air and pulled out the half-burned notebook pages. She leaned against the hull of the aircraft, reading the scattered sentences. Carter Vale's handwriting peppered the margins with references to watchers, a final proof of belief. Above those lines, she found an ominous mention of fueling legends by any means. She felt a spike of anger. "He thinks he can shape the story, and we're just extras swinging in the dark." She muttered, lowering the page.

Skyhook removed her pilot's harness. "We should see if Finch can reconstruct that text. Might be a hint about his endgame."

Mara passed her the page. "Send it over. Also have Link cross-reference the phrases about watchers fueling the cryptid's growth. Maybe we can guess where he'd host his so-called event." She paused, glancing at the dense pines around them. The forest was damp as usual, the air thick with the scent of rotting needles and soggy earth.

She contacted Link. "We're at the clearing you plotted. I'll transmit photos of Vale's pages. Patch them to Finch and see if we can piece together the next date or location." A rush of static filled her earpiece before Link's voice came through. "Got it. Upload away."

As Skyhook angled her tablet's camera over the fragments, Mara circled back to the cargo hold and retrieved a portable drone kit. She set it on a rocky outcrop by the stream to widen their search. Think like a trickster. Where would he hide if he wanted to watch chaos unfold? She scanned the tree line, not expecting an answer. The swirl of tension in her gut would not leave. She found herself hoping to glimpse Vale's worn camper lurching between the firs.

Skyhook studied her with a guarded look. "No sense in pushing further if we can't track him. You know he's toying with us."

Mara lowered the drone kit. "He wants an audience when he stirs up more panic. Pulling back might give him extra time."

Their conversation broke off as Link's voice echoed in Mara's ear. "Finch says the scribbles mention a spiral anchor. He's matching the text against older references from Vale's previous sightings. The pages are incomplete, but it sounds like Vale's building a show with the cryptid as the main act."

Mara exhaled slowly and her mind spun. She closed the drone kit. "In that case, we need tighter control on local chatter. The more folks hear about this, the stronger the cryptid becomes. If Vale is orchestrating a culminating event, we are already behind schedule."

They regrouped and drank from their canteens before climbing back into the VTOL. Mara's vision was locked on the horizon. "We will return to the command trailer, analyze everything with Finch in real time, and coordinate with Sheriff

Thomason if we must. I hate dealing with that man's attitude, but we cannot let local law enforcement stay in the dark."

Skyhook gave a terse nod and turned the ignition. The VTOL vibrated beneath them, and they lifted skyward once again. Mara felt the day's fatigue creeping in. *This is turning into his twisted script, and we are reciting lines.* She rubbed the back of her neck, refusing to let frustration cloud her judgment.

Back at a deserted meadow that served as a safer landing zone, they set the VTOL down. Mara hopped out, stretched her legs, and signaled Link to bring the mobile trailer closer. The trailer rumbled behind a row of tall pines, Finch at the console inside. She approached its open door. Finch peered over the top of his laptop, eyes ringed with tired circles. "We have partial text. It references watchers and a final demonstration of 'the forest's real apex.' We may have singled out a probable day: next Friday."

Mara pressed both palms against the metal entrance. "Then we have a countdown. Please tell me we have a guess where he will do it."

Finch rubbed his temples. "The data is incomplete. It might be the old growth near the Cedar Grove zone, though I cannot confirm. Vale is leaving fewer digital footprints than before. He is probably operating under different handles or offline."

Mara stepped into the trailer and studied the scattered lines of code on Finch's screen. She recognized references to social ratings, share counts, and the dreaded belief metrics that had soared after the last cryptid sighting. Her mouth thinned into a grim line. "He is fueling hype. By the time we corner him, the cryptid might be at full strength."

Skyhook leaned in. "Let's figure out the best vantage points for a stakeout. If he wants a spectacle, he'll pick a place where curiosity seekers can gather."

Mara lowered herself into a folding chair. "And we'll be waiting. We're dealing with a twisted ringmaster who wants the crowd hungry for more." She studied the burnt notebook scraps, recalling the swirl of text and that mocking phrase about watchers. Part of her wanted to tear them apart. Instead, she set them aside and gazed at the forest map pinned to one wall. We'll head him off. We have to.

She turned to Finch. "Run the new data. Find any patterns in local vantage points or spiral patterns carved into older logs. Also keep an alert for any more sightings of that camper." Finch nodded. He returned to typing, jaw clenched in concentration. The hum of the trailer's generator kicked in, followed by a beep on the ARGUS console.

Mara took a moment to collect herself. That flyer had promised a show, and Vale's talk of watchers ensured that more unsuspecting people might get pulled in. No matter how she looked at it, the tension kept growing. She leaned forward in her seat, determined to keep her mind clear.

She glanced at Skyhook, who offered a faint nod as if they shared the same unspoken vow. They had lost this round, but the hunt wasn't over.

CHAPTER ELEVEN

The creek glimmered under fading daylight. Mara crouched at the edge of the clearing, checking her EM-coil carbine one more time before nightfall. Finch stood nearby, typing on his open laptop. He mumbled something about belief metrics spiking over the last hour, then glanced at the sonic lure placed in the grass. Mara saw worry in his eyes. He always looked stressed, but tonight his shoulders were especially tense. Link hustled around with a bundle of cables, trailing a drone case behind him. At the treeline, Skyhook unloaded battery packs from the back of their transport truck. Her posture was confident and businesslike.

Mara rose from her crouch. "We good on power?" Skyhook nodded once. "Enough juice to run those spotlights until dawn." She set a heavy battery on the ground. "Assuming nothing savage tears them apart first." Mara exhaled. "We'll see how it goes."

They had chosen this location because Finch's analysis flagged it. Something about reflective pools and unusual night-time sightings pinned the cryptid's pattern here. Mara had asked him for more detail earlier, but he only shrugged and said that belief could intensify in spots that drew camera attention. Shimmering water gave the public a dramatic backdrop. That was enough for Vale to exploit.

Link trotted over, wiping sweat off his forehead with the back of his hand. "Spotted two drones overhead, ours. Probably more watchers working on their own underside. Social feeds say at least ten cars parked on that dirt road. Expect an audience by nightfall." Mara sighed. "Perfect." She looked around the clearing and noticed the reflective sheen of water pooling along the creek bed. Setting a trap where watchers might gather was a gamble, but they needed a chance to test their new approach. "We'll put the high-lumen spotlights in a ring around the perimeter. If this works, the bright shock might disorient the cryptid enough for sedation."

Finch lifted his gaze from his LCD screen. "So long as star-struck thrill-seekers don't wander too close," he said. Mara appreciated his concern, but she brushed it aside. "That's why we have the rope cordon." She pointed to a line of stakes and rope that Link had started to set up. It would barely slow down a determined crowd, but at least it warned them to keep back. She hoped the local sheriff's patchy coverage would keep the turnout small.

By the time the sun dipped beyond the treetops, the perimeter glowed with powerful artificial light. Skyhook flicked each spot-light on in sequence, creating a band of brilliance across the ground. Gleaming puddles caught every beam and turned it into a harsh glare. Mara thought it looked impressive to any onlooker who found it online. The sonic lure sat in the center, a small black disc hidden under a cluster of flat rocks. Finch said it emitted a frequency sequence rumored to attract unusual wildlife, though nobody had tested it on a belief-born cryptid before.

She heard murmurs and footsteps along the far edge of the clearing. A group of onlookers, phones raised, advanced past the rope barrier. Someone carried a small tripod that glinted under the lights. Some wore jackets with cryptid-themed patches, fixated on capturing the next viral clip. Their excitement hung in the air.

Link shook his head. "This is turning into a circus."

Mara tightened her grip on the carbine and kept her tone steady. "Stay focused. If the creature shows, we control the scene."

Finch stepped closer and spoke under his breath. "Looks like that tip on the cryptid forums said we'd be here. Probably Vale again leaking our location."

She stiffened at the mention of Vale. Carter Vale was out there somewhere coaxing the crowd to feed the monster. If he had posted GPS coordinates, the cryptid could become unstoppable when more onlookers arrived. She forced aside her anxiety and scanned the treeline. "Everyone watch your quadrant. Once we have a visual, Link cuts the drone feed to the public net."

He nodded. "I'll jam any signal not SRD-authorized as soon as we engage."

A twig snapped beyond the furthest spotlight, and Mara froze. She peered between the trunks until movement caught her eye. She adjusted her EM-coil carbine to standby mode and prepared the sedation darts. The hush that followed felt weighty. Then heavy steps raked the undergrowth.

The watchers stirred, enthralled by the thought of the creature's arrival. A man in a baseball cap stepped forward, phone raised toward the darkness.

Once brilliant beams swung that way, massive footprints appeared in the soil. The crowd pressed forward, ignoring the roped boundary. Mara heard a gasp as the cryptid's broad shape lurched between the pines. Its shoulders wore familiar bone-like plating that unnerved her. The creature towered above her memory, a sign of rising energy from the media attention. Moonlight and spotlights merged around it, casting the beast in a harsh glow.

She raised her carbine to her shoulder. "Skyhook, eyes on me. Finch, watch for the sedation effectiveness readout."

"Got it." Finch said.

The cryptid snarled and barreled forward. It trampled across the perimeter line and crashed into one of the tall lights. Metal rattled as the stand collapsed and sparks burst from the battery pack. Watchers pulled back in panic, but one bystander did not move fast enough. He toppled sideways when the cryptid's limb struck his chest. Men and women shrieked, and phones whirled to capture the chaos.

Mara locked onto the cryptid's torso, but her line of fire would have hit the wounded bystander. She ground her teeth and held her shot. The creature roared, shaking its head at the glare of the remaining lights. Then it pounded the ground as if disoriented by the sonic pulses. Debris rained on the crowd. A few watchers scrambled behind a fallen log, filming every second.

Skyhook sprinted toward the injured man. She slid to her knees behind him and reached for the small med kit at her hip. Mara took a step forward, looking for an opening to fire. The cryptid whipped back, bones jutting from its spine as if bracing an attack. She considered a direct shot to its chest but two overzealous bystanders scuttled into her line of sight, cameras raised high.

Link shouted, "I'm cutting their feed." He tapped frantically on his device and found six live cell signals streaming, which fueled the creature.

Mara's pulse hammered. She refused to let the creature injure more people on her watch. She switched the carbine to single-shot mode and edged around a cluster of watchers. A trembling figure darted across her sights, phone in hand and ignoring the danger. It was hopeless to line up a clean shot. The cryptid roared again and slammed its forelimbs into another spotlight, sending machinery clanging to the ground in a shower of sparks.

Skyhook motioned at her and said, "We have to move this guy or he's done. He's bleeding badly."

Mara scanned the hillside for a distraction. She pulled a flare from her belt and jammed the ignition. "I'm tossing it upslope," she yelled. "It might redirect the creature."

She hurled the lit flare. It arced through the air and landed on a mossy rise east of the clearing. A bright glow caught the cryptid's attention and it growled as it stomped forward. That gave Skyhook seconds to lift the injured man with help from two watchers. Mara stepped between them and the cryptid with her carbine ready. She flipped the safety off, every muscle taut. More onlookers spilled from the trees, lured by the noise. A cluster pressed forward, snapping photos. She wanted to order them back. Instead she let out a low curse and aimed at the ground near the creature's feet. She squeezed the trigger. The sedation dart sank into the soil, wasted.

The creature swung its scaled head toward the commotion. Its jagged shoulders rose and fell in a harsh rhythm as cameras flashed. Mara realized the sedation approach was useless with so many civilians in the way. No angle could guarantee a safe shot. Meanwhile the cryptid grew bolder as the crowd's frenzy drew more attention online.

Finch's strained voice came through Mara's earpiece. "We can't contain it with so many people filming. Social feeds are surging. The sedation formula might not be enough now."

She looked at the cluster of half-ruined spotlights, the jostling crowd and the creature's livid stance. Everything was falling apart. "We're pulling back," she called to the team. "We can't hold the perimeter. Everybody withdraw."

Skyhook gripped the wounded man. The watchers who had been helping turned as the cryptid reared up. Mara signaled Link. "Go now!" she yelled. They hustled toward the vehicles. Finch disconnected his gear as quickly as he could, slamming his laptop shut. Link snatched up the sonic lure remote, cursing under his breath. The last working spotlight toppled when the cryptid charged it and splintered the battery pack in a crackle of plastic pieces.

Mara saw swirling dust kicked up by the cryptid's pounding footsteps. She fired a second dart, but it barely grazed the monster's flank. The creature shrieked, pulled back a few feet, and then turned its attention to the watchers shoving for better footage. They scattered while their phones recorded. A flurry of digital pings shot across the net, each ping enhancing the cryptid's presence.

Her ears rang from the hum of broken lights and the crowd's shrieks. She pivoted and blocked a bystander who rushed forward. "Get behind the truck!" she snapped. The man hesitated, glanced at his phone, then hurried away. She sprinted after Finch and Link, who were already halfway to the dirt access road. Skyhook trailed with the injured man. Half a dozen watchers lingered, trying to film from behind a tree. Mara leveled her weapon at them. "If you want to keep your limbs, leave now." They dispersed.

As the team reached the vehicles, Mara glanced back. The cryptid swiped the shattered remains of a spotlight off the ground and flung it aside. Its eyes locked on the glowing flare still burning uphill and it charged up the slope, grunting as the neon fire sputtered. That might hold its attention long enough for them to disengage. At least no one stood in its path.

Link climbed into the transport truck, his hands shaking. "That was too close. The plan got torched once that tip leaked."

Finch dropped into the passenger seat, pale. "We lost two spotlights, half the battery packs, and at least one civilian was injured."

Mara slid into the driver's seat and pressed the ignition. Skyhook helped the wounded man onto a seat in the back, braced him, then slammed the door. "Drive," she said. "This guy's in shock."

Mara pinned her gaze on the road. The engine roared and they pulled away, leaving the ruined remains of their light trap behind. A few watchers scattered to the side, streaming on their phones. She wondered how many had posted live feeds. That coverage would spread in minutes, boosting the cryptid's strength all over again.

She took a steadying breath. "Finch, once we're out of range, prepare the sedation data for Sato. We may need a stronger dose next time." She paused, glancing in the mirror. "And check that man for internal bleeding if you can."

Skyhook raised a brow. "When we find a place to pull over, we'll do what we can until we arrange evac." She still looked furious about the watchers who had nearly gotten themselves killed. "How many were filming at once? It felt like half the county was there."

Mara spotted the battered remains of their perimeter in the side mirror. She groaned. "I counted around twenty streaming or snapping pictures. That's exactly what Vale wanted."

Finch rubbed the corners of his eyes. "He probably orchestrated that tip. It forced us into a fiasco, fueling the cryptid right when we tried to contain it."

Mara drove deeper into the forest roads that wound away from the clearing. She tried to shake off the frustration that clung to her. These operations were complicated and now Vale was actively undermining them. The passenger moaned in pain. Mara pressed the accelerator to get them to a stable location. Trees blurred past. Link fiddled with equipment while scanning for signals or blocking further feeds.

They reached a wider patch of dirt near an old signpost. The spot was far enough from the fiasco that the cryptid wouldn't chase them, at least not right away. Mara parked and slid out to help Skyhook treat the injured bystander. Blood stained his coat but he was breathing. Finch moved quickly, rummaging in the truck for gauze and antiseptic. Skyhook's training kicked in, her voice calm and authoritative as she instructed the man to hold still.

Finch finished taping a gauze patch under the man's shirt, then turned to Mara. "He'll hold together until we can get him to a clinic. We got lucky it wasn't worse."

She rechecked her weapon. The sedation cartridges were still half full. "Lucky my butt." She muttered. "We had a plan. Vale conjured exactly the right crowd to ruin it."

Skyhook slumped on the truck tailgate. "Got to adapt, right?"

Mara nodded. It was all they could do, though each passing day gave Vale more time to expand his cryptid experiment. She closed her eyes, steadying herself. The team had survived tonight, but she feared the next encounter might bring more chaos, and they had no guarantee how large the creature would be by then.

She leaned back into the driver's seat, feeling the adrenaline slowly ebb. Link hopped in beside her again, scrolling through endless feeds. "Online chatter is off the charts." He announced "Videos from that clearing are already hitting thousands of views each minute."

She turned the key and the engine coughed before settling into a steady rumble. "Everyone set?"

"Yes." Skyhook said, still leaning over their passenger in the back. Finch clutched his laptop with a drained expression. Link typed determinedly, no sign of letting up on his attempts to jam outside signals. Mara forced her gaze forward and nudged the truck down the winding route that led away from the failed trap site. The battered spotlights, shattered stands, and scattered watchers were behind them now. She intended to see if the next approach could truly corner the cryptid, but that would require new tactics.

She let a few moments pass, letting the forest slip by in a blur of darkness. Then she grimly admitted to herself that tonight's fiasco proved how unstoppable the creature could become when fueled by mass curiosity. Vale had orchestrated everything to sabotage them. She pictured the beast shredding the spotlight stands, the crowd shrieking, cameras rolling. That memory stayed with her.

Mara pushed the thought aside and focused on the road. She steered the truck toward the county highway and listened as the tires hummed over gravel. She could still picture the massive footprints pressed into the wet creek bank. The cryptid had grown and the sedation attempts had failed.

They drove on and left the shattered trap behind, uncertain what Vale's next move would be but certain he would keep feeding the monster until they found a way to stop him.

CHAPTER TWELVE

Mara stepped inside the command trailer, and the stale air hit her like a warning. Finch hunched over his laptop at a folding table that cramped his arms, eyes rimmed with fatigue as lines of data scrolled across the screen. She stood behind him, arms crossed, scanning the neon swirl of charts on the ARGUS interface. Each swirl represented a cluster of social-media mentions latching onto the bone-plated cryptid rumor that Carter Vale had stirred up. Link's steady string of OSINT feeds kept peppering Finch's display with new pings. Mara could see the tension behind Finch's frown as he zoomed in on a glowing spiral pattern on the map. He tapped the screen without looking up.

"You see that concentration?" he said. "Hashtags spiked overnight in a neat cluster around the main trailheads. Then we've got random sightings from hikers who mention the creature's plated shoulders. Every time someone tags or shares a link, new data points bloom."

Mara exhaled, keeping her tone level. "Any sign of Vale mixed in there?"

Finch shrugged. "He is lying low at least in terms of direct posts, but his watermark is all over these new streams like an echo that never stops."

She studied the satellite overlay, where red icons formed a spiral across the forested valley. Dots indicated possible sightings, maybe illusions to the untrained eye. She refused to call them illusions. To the SRD, this monster was painfully real. She felt her jaw tighten remembering how the first cryptid sightings ended: two missing college kids, shredded tents, and digital mania.

Link's voice crackled through the comm line. "Mara, I've got local chatter from Gifford Pinchot watchers. They're repeating rumor after rumor about some big footprint behind the ranger station. Something about scratched carvings again."

She tapped the small earpiece. "Any photo confirmations?"

"One or two phone snapshots. They're so blurred it's worthless for ID, but the shape of that spiral is clear if you zoom in." Link said.

A wave of frustration moved through her. The spiral. She pictured it carved into tree trunks, watermarked over Vale's cryptic footage, and even posted on cheap flyers. "Thanks, Link. Get me a location pinpoint on that station and patch it to Finch's feed."

"On it." Link replied and a faint clack of keyboard keys sounded behind him.

Finch swiveled in his chair and gestured at another set of lines crowding the main window. A looping replay showed short clips from random forest trails. They were stitched together from different sources but each snippet displayed the same swirling shape in the corner of the frame. "Every time Vale's symbol spreads, we see a surge in messages describing the cryptid as bigger or more aggressive. If all these sightings stack up, the entity is feeding on the hype."

Mara rubbed her eyes. "I can't remember how long it's been since we saw it physically. The trails have turned into a circus."

Skyhook spoke from just outside the door. She wore a grim expression. "You might want to step out here a second." She thumbed toward the thinning layer of sunshine outside. "We've seen more tourists flooding the tree lines hunting for Bigfoot bragging rights. The sheriff is losing his mind trying to hold them back from the restricted areas."

Mara moved to the trailer entrance and stepped down into the moist grass. The scent of pine drifted in on a cold breeze. A few yards away, Link checked a row of small monitors on a portable table. He tilted his head at Mara. "One local posted about stumbling onto fresh carvings up the slope. Finch, check your feed for that user tag. Video is shaky, but I ran an enhancement."

Finch's voice carried from inside the trailer. "Got it. I see a few frames showing a spiral etched onto a fallen log near what looks like old footprints. The angles are poor so we cannot confirm."

Mara looked at Skyhook. "Any sign of the cryptid's relocating?"

"Not sure. Drone sweeps turned up tracks that vanish into thick undergrowth. We can't confirm if it's the same tracks from earlier or fresh ones it made after another brief manifestation."

Mara's throat felt raw, as if she had briefed the team on this crisis too many times. "That means we still have no direct fix on Carter Vale or the anchor point that keeps this thing stable." She muttered. She angled back toward Finch. "What about Jackson and Mia's search grid?"

Finch sounded tired. "Still nothing. The deeper we go, the more carved markings we find, but we have no luck. We keep tracking new leads, but the forest is massive."

Her stomach churned at the thought of how long Jackson and Mia had been missing. The cryptid had already proven it could harm anyone unfortunate enough to cross its path. She stepped back inside and the stale air pressed in again.

Finch tapped a set of images that popped up on the laptop. Some showed older tree-bark carvings. Others depicted brief glimpses of a carved stone. He highlighted a time stamp from nearly three weeks ago.

"Vale might have planted these spirals well before the first big sighting. ARGUS is cross-referencing local folklore records. One mentions an old cedar grove tied to cryptid myths long before social media. If Vale scouted that site, we could be dealing with a perfect anchor spot."

Mara felt a pang of grim respect for Vale's planning. He was cunning, always steering people's attention where he wanted it. "So if we confirm an original carving, destroying it could starve the creature of its power," she said quietly.

Finch nodded. "An older rumor references a massive stump carved with spiral shapes that date back decades. It fits the pattern. I want to narrow the last known coordinates, but it's an unmarked patch of forest. If the local archives are accurate, it's tucked on a remote slope where old-growth cedar still stands."

Skyhook entered and boots squeaked on the trailer's floor. "You said an old stump in a cedar grove? The ranger mentioned a peculiar clearing that no tourist map shows. He thought it might be connected to local legends about forest guardians."

Mara eyed Finch's display. The swirl of data formed an ominous shape that glowed across the top-left quadrant of the forest map. "We'll try that lead. Link, set a drone flight plan for that quadrant."

Link's voice came through the earpiece. "Sure. It might take a while to calibrate. I'm juggling half a dozen feeds, and the interference out here kills my signal every ten feet."

Mara stepped around Finch's chair and said, "Do your best." The overhead lamp in the trailer flicked once then steadied. She gave it a withering look. "Generators on the fritz again?"

Finch sighed. "Bound to happen with all the hardware we're

running. We've got to keep it going long enough to finish these analyses."

She said, "He orchestrates each cycle. He drops a new hint, lets the rumor churn, fuels new watchers, then disappears before we can zero in on him."

Finch scrolled through replays of Vale's old watermarked videos. "He's a master at letting others do the work for him. The more reposts, the stronger the anchor grows. People keep tagging each other, half joking about sightings, then feeding the phenomenon."

Her gaze dropped to a short clip of what looked like a shape in the distance. The bone plating glistened in a fuzzy frame. "Explain how disbelief factors into that."

"Belief outruns skepticism online," Finch replied. "Debunkers share the same footage, adding more activity. It doesn't matter if the response is negative or positive. ARGUS sees it as amplitude."

Skyhook snorted. "We're swimming in a feedback loop. If the cryptid is real enough to scare people, it draws that fear as fuel."

Mara's gaze wandered to the cramped corner of the trailer where a half-packed med case rested. She pictured Jackson or Mia stumbling through the forest terrified. She set her jaw then opened the trailer door and gestured for Link to step inside. He followed, eyes darting to the laptop.

Link transferred a new feed to Finch's screen and said, "This user posted an older blog about a hidden glen with a giant cedar stump. The post mentions swirl carvings that have been there for years."

Finch brightened. "Coordinates."

Link shook his head. "Only vague descriptions. If that stump is out there, it might lie two miles off the main logging road."

Mara turned to Finch. "ARGUS can piece this together with older satellite passes. The stump might have been visible from above before the canopy thickened."

Finch's fingers flew across the keyboard. The main screen flickered between topographic layers and older image sets. A ghostly outline of a clearing took shape, mostly hidden by evergreen crowns. "This might be it," Finch said as he pointed at a faint circle. "If that's the site, Vale has a perfect spot to carve in private. No random hikers would be around to question him. That could be the anchor we need to eliminate."

Mara tried to mask her relief. A solid clue at last. "All right," she said. "We target that location next. Prepare a recon team. Skyhook can fly the perimeter with a drone. I want eyes on it before we trek in."

Skyhook dipped her head. "Sure. Conditions are decent for a quick pass. If we see anything suspicious, we will radio in."

Finch rubbed his temples. "I'll keep monitoring. The second you get visual confirmation of the stump, I'll cross-reference any updated social chatter with whatever carved images might match."

Mara placed a hand on Finch's shoulder with a brief nod to thank him. She saw he was exhausted, but they had no choice. They needed to act. "We'll rotate in some rest soon but not until we pin this location. Keep me posted if Vale shows any sign of life."

Outside the muffled roar of approaching vans drew her attention. A few more cryptid hunters or online streamers arrived. She stepped out and noted two vehicles and a smattering of adventurous types unloading gear. They stood on the fringes, scanning the thick pines for any sign of Bigfoot. The forest offered no reassuring silence. It was full of rustling branches and distant chatter.

Sheriff Thomason's SUV appeared and he stepped out with a grim expression. He walked over. "My deputies can't handle the crowds piling up. If you plan a big push into the forest, you'd better tell me so I can block off at least a few roads."

Mara nodded. "We have a lead on a high-priority area. Your cooperation helps. Keep people away from that quadrant if you can. We'll handle the rest."

He gave a reluctant grunt. "Fine. But do it fast. The county is about to get hit with a wave of cryptid fanatics who see it as a spectacle."

She watched him stalk off. The weight that threatened to drag them all down settled on her. In the trailer, Finch called for her. She climbed the steps again and found him pointing at an overlay. A new mention had popped up near the rumored clearing they suspected might hold the stump.

"Latest set of tracks from drone footage," Finch said. "Not conclusive but the pattern suggests heavier footprints than normal hikers. Possibly the cryptid itself or Vale leading it around."

She studied the coordinates flickering in the screen's corner, each readout mocking her need for speed. "We'd better check that location ourselves. Wait for Skyhook's sweep, and then we move in for a closer look."

Finch rose from his seat and reached for a battered jacket. His eyes met hers. "We do this carefully. We both know the cryptid won't stay passive if it's anchored there."

She lifted her chin. "I know. Time to push deeper into the pines."

Link lingered by the door and shifted his weight. "One more thing. The local ranger radioed that a couple of hikers spotted fresh markings in the direction of that potential stump site. The time stamps line up. Vale might be on site right now."

Adrenaline crackled through Mara's veins. "Then we can't lose any more time. Lock in final coordinates and get an aerial pass going." She shouldered her gear and ignored the exhaustion in her limbs. "The second we have eyes on that old cedar grove, we're heading out."

Finch closed the laptop and carefully placed it in a rugged case. He looked at her with a grave expression. "Mara, we can't underestimate how powerful the cryptid might be near its core. Don't rush in underprepared."

She paused. She considered the caution in his tone, but the drive to act overwhelmed any hesitation. "We'll be ready for trouble."

Skyhook popped her head through the door and confirmed that the drones were nearly prepped. Mara caught herself anticipating the coming hours: a nerve-wracking flight over dense canopies, cameras scanning for the hidden stump, and an unplanned encounter with a monstrous shape no longer content to hide. She felt a flick of dread beneath her ribs and decided to push it aside.

Never let it think we are backing down.

Finch started bundling extra scanner equipment. Link tapped out instructions for the overhead cams. Mara forced a heartbeat of composure. The swirling data on Finch's screen had cracked open a path to the cryptid's heart. That was enough for now.

She gave the group a curt nod and stepped outside to watch the last pale streaks of daylight fade into a canopy of shifting silhouettes. Beyond those trees lay either a rotting cedar stump or a labyrinth of worthless leads. She whispered a promise under her breath.

We need to find Jackson and Mia. They cannot stay lost forever.

Mara flexed her stiff hands. "Let's get that aerial recon. Then we move." She spotted Sheriff Thomason a few yards away as he halfheartedly spoke with a boisterous group of cryptid tourists. They brandished net guns and homemade Bigfoot hats. She knew the forest would swallow those amateurs if they got too close to the real threat. She exchanged a look with Skyhook, who simply lifted an eyebrow in resigned annoyance.

Mara checked her gear: sidearm, muzzle attachments, and field kit. She had done it so many times that the routine felt automatic. In her earpiece Finch's voice chimed with an update. "Mara, we are uploading the flight path. Skyhook is taking off in five."

"Acknowledged," she said softly. She felt that familiar rush of dread and determination swirl together like volatile chemicals.

We are going in circles unless we act now.

Link hurried over and glanced at the sky. "Clear enough for a quick pass. We just need a stable signal. If it dips out, I will reboot."

Mara breathed in the cedar-scented air. The thought of Vale gloating somewhere among the trees made her chest knot. "Stay sharp," she said. "Let's find that clearing first, then we close in."

Skyhook waved from near the parked VTOL and gestured for them to watch the initial drone liftoff. A small device rose, blades whirring. Mara's eyes tracked it as it climbed above the trailer and banked toward the treetops. It vanished into a sea of green.

She stepped away from the small huddle of monitors and let Finch and Link manage the feed. The wind bit at her face. It carried the faint echo of distant voices. There were more curious souls in the woods, all chasing legends they barely understood. The cryptid was more than an online rumor, though. It had already proved that.

Skyhook's voice cut through the static. "Drone is on course. I see heavy canopy. It might take a bit to confirm that stump."

A feeling of urgency flared in Mara's gut. "Let's hope we find it soon. Finch, keep me posted on anything that pings." She tapped the earpiece and got a quick affirmation. With that, she slipped a hand into her jacket pocket, braced herself for the next phase, and nodded to the rest of the team.

She felt a prickle of tension across her shoulders. "All right." She said in a low voice. "Let's move out."

They would find that stump. They would trace those carvings, no matter how tangled the forest had become. This data shadow they followed would lead them deeper into the dark, and Mara vowed she would go as far as it took. She took the first step forward, leaving the cramped trailer behind as overhead rotors hummed, carrying her team's hopes into the fading sky.

CHAPTER THIRTEEN

The early light filtering through the pines cast a jagged pattern across the ground, and Mara felt a rush of urgency spike in her chest. She adjusted the earpiece in her left ear as Link's voice crackled with fresh intel.

She stood beside the SRD Mobile Command Trailer, scanning the recent photos that flickered across Finch's ARGUS console. One showed a grainy shot of Carter Vale's beat-up camper parked near a dirt road tangled with fallen branches. Online chatter claimed Vale had been spotted handing out cryptid-themed flyers to anyone who paused long enough to talk. Mara's breath hitched at the thought of more bystanders lured deeper into this twisted show.

She double-checked the feed from two overhead drones. Her gaze roamed across a topographical map pinned to the trailer's interior wall. Marked with swirling lines in red, it revealed the remote logging roads snaking around steep ravines. A particularly obscure spur had become a hot topic in local social feeds. She tapped that area. "Link, confirm you can push live updates to our tablets if you see new posts about Vale."

He replied through the earpiece, sounding a notch more tense than usual. "You got it. Brace yourself. Buzz on cryptid boards has spiked by another ten percent in the last hour. People keep spotting that van. Others claim they saw shapes moving beyond the tree line."

Mara's jaw tightened as she glanced at the drone's status screen. "Nobody else gets hurt if we can manage it. Skyhook, prep the VTOL. I want to be in the air before more idiots storm that location for selfies."

She stepped onto the packed earth outside the trailer and felt a faint chill, like a blade pressed lightly against her skin. The messages pouring in indicated Vale was stoking mania. Her best guess was that he wanted more social proof, more adrenaline, and more believers. It all fueled the cryptid's hold over this region.

Sheriff Thomason's voice came in over a separate channel. He apologized that his department was pinned by a flood of calls regarding "Bigfoot sightings." The sheriff barely had enough manpower to keep a solitary deputy on standby. Mara had expected as much. "Any help is better than nothing." She muttered then asked Thomason to keep an extra deputy on the radio in case they had to form a perimeter.

Skyhook hefted a small med kit and strapped it onto her belt. She gave Mara a subdued nod. A slight tension bracketed Skyhook's eyes but she exuded calm focus. Together, they walked to the waiting aircraft, a sleek VTOL with pivoting thrusters that allowed it to land among thick stands of pines.

As they lifted off, a whirlwind of pine needles and moss swirled beneath them. In the cockpit, Skyhook toggled the flight path based on Finch's coordinates. Mara settled into her seat, gripping her EM-coil carbine. She carried extra sedation darts though she doubted the cryptid would appear without Vale's stagecraft. It might not matter. If they caught Vale in the act, they could detain him before more chaos erupted.

They soared over ridges draped in forest green. Link's voice occasionally cut through the cabin speakers. "People are gathering about a mile east of that logging road. They're calling it the Bigfoot block party. Unbelievable." He paused. "I'm skimming local streams, too. So far, no direct sightings of Jackson and Mia, but a few mentions of a shredded tent near the main trail got renewed attention earlier."

Mara's pulse drummed faster. "Stay on it. Let me know if anything relevant pops up." She adjusted her harness as Skyhook guided the VTOL over a rough clearing. Conifers clustered around it, their branches forming a partial canopy. The craft hovered, then settled with a gentle thud.

"If we can reach Carter Vale before the cedar grove, we will seize the opportunity. If we stop his antics, we might not need to destroy the grove. Above all, protecting the hikers, Jackson, and Mia is our priority. Is that clear?" Mara said firmly. She rarely asserted authority since her team was decisive and supportive, but in situations like these the tone felt natural.

Everyone agreed instantly.

Inside the quiet cockpit, she allowed herself one second of reflection. Carter Vale's trail had felt elusive since day one. He had a cunning way of appearing in crowds long enough to distribute flyers, hype his curated footage, then vanish. The chance of cornering him this time felt stronger than before.

She hopped onto the uneven ground. Morning glow filtered through the branches. The air smelled of damp bark and the tang of decaying pine needles. She spotted footprints in the muddy gravel, some deep, others half-smeared. A set of tire tracks cut a clear line toward a narrow logging path, and she crouched beside them.

"These look recent," she told Skyhook, pointing to the ridges formed in the wet soil. "They could be from the van. The tread pattern matches the images we saw earlier."

Skyhook's gaze roamed the treeline. "We might be right on his heels. Should we send a scout drone ahead?"

Mara nodded. "Do it. Link can pilot from the trailer. I'll stay on foot. If Carter's there, we don't want to spook him into running." She returned to the craft, grabbed a portable drone from a side compartment, and powered it on with a few taps. Skyhook gave a short thumbs-up as Mara opened her comm link to Link for remote piloting.

They pushed through the first hundred yards of the logging path. Broken branches littered the route. Some bore fresh scrapes as if a wide vehicle had forced its way through. Hunched ferns grew in clumps beside the muddy ruts. The morning air was cold enough to make each breath visible. Mara advanced with her carbine slung across her chest, boots pressing into the sodden ground.

She paused when she noticed odd drawings scrawled across a cracked trunk that had fallen across one side of the path. The familiar spiral pattern repeated in charcoal or soot, each swirl echoing the viral watermark that had ignited the cryptid mania. A slight pang of anger sparked in her. This was Vale's calling card. He might have left it to taunt them or simply to pump more hype into the environment.

You like your little spirals, Vale. One way or another, we're erasing every last one.

Mara gestured for Skyhook to check the perimeter. She kept her own stance low, scanning between the pines. The forest had that hush just before midday, broken only by the drone's soft rotor buzz overhead. Each step they took felt measured, as if the ground might give away a new clue at any second. She spotted crushed energy-drink cans near a tangle of roots. That brand had popped up at previous Vale sightings, either dropped by him or people enthralled by his cryptid stunts.

Her earpiece crackled. "Mara, I've got one deputy who says he can move in if needed." Link reported. "He's tied up with traffic near the main ranger station. I told him to be on standby. Also,

I'm reading new postings from local forums. They're turning that close-by trailhead into a viewing party."

A hint of irritation laced her voice. "A viewing party? Fantastic. Next thing you know, someone will try to charge admission." She drew a steady breath. "Keep me updated. I want to intercept Vale if he's anywhere near here."

Skyhook crouched near the trampled undergrowth and beckoned Mara over. "He might have camped here. The grass on that side is flattened in a big rectangle. There's residue from a small fire pit." She brushed aside dead leaves, revealing half-charred scribbles. Spiral shapes again, though not as clearly formed. "Probably more of his propaganda."

Mara reached down and touched the ash, feeling it crumble across her fingertips. She snatched a small chunk of the charred remains and dropped it in a sample pouch on her belt. "We might glean something about the timing." She pressed the radio button fitted to her vest. "Finch, do you see anything on drone feed that lines up with a possible camp?"

Finch's voice arrived in a subdued tone. "No direct signs of smoke or freshly disturbed sites, but the top-down view is mostly canopy. I'll switch to angled thermal. We might catch a heat signature if Vale's engine is warm. Also…just saw a cryptid-themed group post about that old logging route. Could be they recognized the area from his online photos."

Mara felt the back of her neck tighten. "So he's leaving bread crumbs for the fans. That might mean he's somewhere near, waiting for more gullible folks to show up. We'll keep going up this path. Let me know the second you spot anything unusual." She and Skyhook pressed on, weaving around a set of spindly trees that bent inward like crooked guardians.

The road narrowed, strewn with clumps of moss that squelched underfoot. Rays of sunlight slanted through the canopy and stirred hazy motes. Mara's ears stayed tuned to the faint drone overhead. She checked her carbine's load and confirmed that the sedation darts were set. If Vale tried something reckless, she intended to drop him without lethal force. The cryptid might be a separate story but Carter Vale was human.

A few minutes later her earpiece crackled again. "Mara, I've picked up additional sightings from a vantage near your location. Some users posted pictures of the van before it disappeared down an overgrown turnoff." Link sounded more alert now.

She let her gaze roam the treeline. "How far from where we landed?"

"Based on GPS markers it is about half a mile north. No fresh photos in the last few minutes, though."

Mara kept walking as damp pine needles muted her footsteps. "Understood. Keep analyzing. I want to be sure we are not about to walk straight into a trap." She paused near a set of scratches on an upright cedar trunk. They formed spirals again but were much deeper, almost gouged into the bark. The pattern triggered an old frustration in her. Vale seemed to relish defacing nature with these twisted shapes, each one fueling the viral belief the SRD fought so hard to stifle.

She stepped back and motioned to Skyhook to proceed. They inched along and spotted a partial clearing ahead. It held a few decaying logs piled at odd angles and a scrap of tarpaulin snagged on a branch. Mara scanned it through the scope attached to her carbine. No hint of movement and no sign of Vale. Only tree stumps and matted ferns.

They crept closer, watching every snapped twig. A sour odor of wet ash lingered. Then she found another patch of scattered cans and a single plastic bag. Inside lay soggy flyers bearing Vale's bright spiral logo. They were blurred around the edges but still distinct enough to read. She peeled one open carefully and expected it to fall apart. It showed a stylized cryptid silhouette above a swirling pattern and a date. Different meeting times were scrawled in pen, perhaps coordinating secret gatherings.

Skyhook exhaled. "He's trying to direct a crowd here as you guessed. Templated mass invites. This has Vale's signature all over it."

Mara dropped the flyer back in the bag. "He might be trying to get a live audience for some stunt. We need to find him before that crowd arrives." She slung the bag over her shoulder, determined to examine it more closely once they regrouped.

Ahead, thick brush blocked the path. Mara pressed a gloved hand against a cluster of branches and shouldered her way through. The undergrowth snagged at her legs. A few splintered stumps left from old logging attempts provided footholds. Skyhook kept her sidearm ready, scanning left and right. Mara felt a simmer of nerves in her gut. Vale had a knack for ducking out at the last moment.

She imagined him wearing that hollow grin, a camera in one hand and a spiral flyer in the other as he monologued about how belief could birth nightmares from imagination. The fact that he had proven it so effectively left half the forest on edge. She clutched her carbine and moved step by step until they broke free of the thicket.

A small clearing emerged. Rusted metal fragments gleamed in the dirt. They looked like scraps from an ancient vehicle but not the van they hunted. No fresh tire tracks appeared, only older grooves. Mara scanned the area and keyed her mic. "Link, check if there is another branching route near our position. This location seems a dead end."

"Will do." Link answered. "The drone feed is partially obstructed but I will overlay satellite images with your current coordinates. Wait one."

Mara tapped her foot and eyed the ridgeline behind them. A hint of sunlight edged the tall pines but the ground remained deep in shadow. She turned back toward the path and noticed an abandoned tarp draped over a rock. More signs of Vale's short-term stops appeared. Everything indicated he wanted watchers to chase him as if this were his personal stage.

On the comm, Link returned. "I see a narrower offshoot about one hundred yards south of your position. It is hard to tell how driveable it is. The van could have gone that way. Do you want me to send the drone?"

"Yes." She said. "We will circle around and meet it. If we find more tracks, we follow them. If not, we pivot to the next likely spot. Sooner or later he will run out of forest to hide in." She nodded for Skyhook to retrace their steps, mindful not to crush foot impressions that might confirm Vale's route.

They kept an alert pace back along the path. Now that they had glimpsed the extent of Vale's scattered materials, she felt certain he was near. He tended to leave more spiral marks and half-burned notebooks whenever he stayed in one area for more than a few hours. The question was whether he was alone or expecting a spectacle with unsuspecting fans. If they got him, it would be the end.

She checked the bottom of her boots and noticed claylike mud caked along the soles. "If we are lucky he has left ruts this direction." She said to Skyhook. A small patch of flattened grass caught her attention. She knelt next to it and saw a slight indentation matching a standard camper van's wheelbase.

Before she could call Link, her earpiece buzzed with static. "Mara, we have a minor spike on ARGUS. Folks on social media say they are converging near that vantage point. They claim 'the cryptid' was heard roaring."

Mara stood. "We cannot let the hype get any further. Secure a second drone net around that vantage if possible. We still do not have Jackson and Mia located so keep digging for leads on them."

"On it." Link replied.

Skyhook gestured for her to continue. "If Vale is toying with a big reveal, he might time it when more people show up. We could catch him pulling the strings."

Mara's voice carried a grim edge. "That is the hope. We land him, we shut down these stunts, and fewer people get tangled in this cryptid mania." She kicked away a broken branch blocking her next step.

Up ahead, the forest parted and an overgrown byway appeared, faint but visible. She recognized the outline of scuffed gravel dotted with ferns. Tracks cut a ragged stripe through the growth. This had to be the road Link mentioned. Mara glanced around and noticed more spiral scrawl carved into a trunk. Her pulse quickened.

She keyed the comm again, her voice quiet. "Link, we've reached that turnoff. Fresh tracks, spiral markings, and all the usual Vale calling cards. We're going in."

He answered instantly. "Got it. I'm adjusting drone positioning. You should see coverage overhead in about two minutes. Let me know what you find."

Mara signaled Skyhook to maintain a tight formation. The path sloped downward, framed by towering pines pressing in from both sides. The damp air carried a faint undertone of rotting leaves and upturned earth. Tension coiled in her gut and sharpened her focus. If Vale was close, she planned to corner him. She could envision him lurking around the next bend, camera in hand.

They pressed deeper into the forest, stepping around embedded rocks and tangles of wild vines. Loose dirt clung to their boots, and the hush amplified every footstep. She scanned for movement, determined to spot any sign of the van before Vale realized they were near. Each swirl of breeze hinted at savage shapes in the underbrush, but she heard only the flap of a distant bird's wings.

Her next step crushed a stray flyer beneath her boot. She lifted it, noticing the swirling design half smeared by mud. He was close. She handed it to Skyhook and moved on.

You're running out of room, Vale. We're right on your heels.

The path twisted under thick branches. In the gloom, broken twigs and crushed ferns hinted at a vehicle forcing its way past. Mara flexed her grip on the carbine as adrenaline pulsed through her. She pictured Vale's grin. The thought of slapping restraints on him drove her forward.

She and Skyhook kept moving until they reached a slight clearing ringed by tall pines. Skyhook motioned for her to stop. A short distance away, muddy tire tracks curved sharply out of sight, vanishing into thicker brush. It looked recent, the wet earth still holding crisp impressions. This had to be the route the camper had taken.

Mara raised her hand in a silent signal. Her heart hammered with readiness. They were close. They just needed to push on until the path revealed where Vale had slipped away. She tapped her comm. "Link, we're following probable van tracks. Keep that second drone overhead. We're not letting him vanish this time."

She set her teeth and stepped forward, braced for whatever might greet her around that bend.

CHAPTER FOURTEEN

The biting wind carried the scent of pine and damp earth, a familiar perfume that did little to soothe the tight knot of frustration in Mara's gut. Link's voice, a tinny counterpoint in her earpiece, kept a running commentary on Carter Vale's latest online assaults: fresh posts showcasing spiral-adorned brochures, sightings near a distant gas station, each digital breadcrumb designed to whip the #RealBigfootRevelations crowd into a fresh frenzy. Finch's grim forecast echoed in her mind. Every share, every click was arterial fuel for the cryptid, its power swelling with the tide of manufactured belief. Vale was out there, a puppet master pulling invisible strings, and the forest felt like his increasingly volatile stage.

Her boots crunched on the gravel path as she approached the makeshift barricade, a couple of orange cones and a Sheriff's cruiser made to look inadequate against the vast encroaching wilderness. The deputies there, faces etched with exhaustion, relayed their own losing battle against the relentless tide of thrill-seekers. "They're ignoring every warning, Lieutenant." The senior one said, his words heavy with resignation. He passed her a scrap of paper, a hastily scribbled note detailing a tip: Vale himself, bold as brass, had been sighted hours before, handing out his damn spiral flyers at a remote clearing off the main highway. He'd even had the audacity to tell a group of hikers that "Bigfoot is real, and the show starts at sundown." Then he vanished down an access road that, according to the smeared map, likely intersected Mara's trajectory. The coordinates were a burning brand on her HUD. With a weary nod of consent, the deputies parted their flimsy barrier, a silent acknowledgment of their own depleted resources.

This was the lead she'd been chasing, a tangible thread in Vale's web of digital smoke and mirrors. Skyhook, who had joined Mara as the reports grew more specific and the terrain more hazardous, moved with quiet professionalism at her side, her presence a steady counterweight to Mara's coiled tension. They pushed forward, deeper into the forest, the deputies' warnings about the escalating crowds fading behind them. The air grew colder, the shadows stretching long and distorted as late afternoon bled toward dusk. With each step, Mara felt the familiar tightening in her chest, a grim anticipation. Vale was close. She could taste his smug satisfaction on the wind. The clearing and whatever awaited them lay ahead.

Then, through a final curtain of damp foliage, the trees parted. The clearing lay bathed in the day's fading, burnished light, quieter than either of them expected. Mara's cautious steps barely disturbed the mossy ground as she signaled Skyhook to tighten their formation. And there it was. Parked at a haphazard angle near a shallow, leaf-choked trench, a sagging camper van loomed into view. Chipped paint exposed patches of determined rust, grime coated the tinted windows, and a length of duct tape clung precariously to the rear bumper. Every detail matched the intel they had on Carter Vale's mobile den. Footprints, hurried and overlapping, crisscrossed the muddy earth around it, but of Vale himself there was no immediate sign. Mara paused on the edge of the clearing, scanning the tree line for any sign of Vale. A hollow feeling settled in her gut as she pictured him filming them at a distance.

She raised a hand in a quick signal. Skyhook bent low around the trunk of a fir tree and scanned for tripwires or hidden cameras. Mara crept toward the van, her carbine tucked tight to her chest. The driver's door sat partially open and creaked on its hinges when Mara nudged it. The interior reeked of stale coffee and cheap cologne, a combination that set her teeth on edge.

She had expected Vale. Instead she found only signs of his hurried exit. An unsteady tower of crumpled fast-food wrappers blocked the walkway to the driver's seat. Papers covered with spiral sketches lay scattered across the dash. Several black cords snaked around the console and connected to a battered old camera wedged between the passenger seat and a half-empty carton of instant noodles. She pressed her palm against the hood to test for warmth, but the metal felt cold under her glove.

"Clear back here," Skyhook whispered as she stepped around to the rear door. She tugged the handle and the panel creaked aside, revealing a cramped sleeping area strewn with more cables, rumpled blankets, and half-torn spiral flyers. A couple of empty energy drink cans tumbled out and rolled across the grass.

Mara slipped into the driver's compartment. She pushed wrappers off the seat and carefully lifted a spiral-marked note-book from the center console. The cover displayed Vale's looping scrawl, identical to the watermarks he plastered on every cryptid video. She opened it and saw a barrage of frantic notes referencing specific times of day, social media traffic surges, and cryptid-related hashtags. The entries read like a blueprint for orchestrating fear, each bullet predicting the moment an online crowd would be ripe for a staged encounter.

Her breath shortened. It was confirmation that Vale was no random hoaxer but a calculating manipulator who understood how to feed mass belief. She flipped through a few more pages, absorbing the repeated references to "living nightmares" and "turning stories into truth." Margin scribbles spelled out twisted theories on how online attention shaped physical reality. The lines felt obsessive, each one festering with the same arrogant tone she had learned to expect from the man behind these broadcasts.

Skyhook huffed behind her. "He left in a rush, right? I am not seeing any sign of him outside."

Mara nodded as she scanned the final pages. "He probably got spooked by something and moved on. He must have realized we were close."

"Want me to start bagging evidence?"

"Absolutely." Mara muttered. She carefully photographed each page with her handheld device. "Finch will want every piece of information."

Skyhook retrieved a large plastic pouch from her belt and held it open. Mara slid the notebook inside, making sure not to smudge the cover. Anger flared as she imagined Vale priding himself on orchestrating another cryptid surge. She thought, He is dancing on the line between genius and psychopath.

She frowned at the scattered debris on the passenger seat. An empty folder bore the words "Camp Footage" on its pocket, but the folder's contents were gone. Next to it, a forest map showed circled areas with handwritten times. Long arcs connected the circles, presumably suggested vantage points for sightings. She tapped the page. "Looks like he is planning multiple vantage shots. He probably wants the cryptid on everyone's livestream by the end of the week."

Skyhook set her gloved hands on her hips. "He times these sightings so the biggest chunk of people see it all at once online."

"That's exactly what he's doing." Mara confirmed. She felt tension pulse behind her eyes as she pieced everything together. Vale understood that frantic crowds were the best accelerant, and the more watchers he captured, the stronger the cryptid would grow.

She stepped outside and inhaled the sharp scent of pine. There was no sign of Vale or a scuff of a shoe or a flick of a camera lens in the shadows. The forest was quiet, but she refused to let her guard drop. Her boots sank slightly into the damp earth as she circled the van, scanning the branches overhead.

Skyhook joined her. "Link said he intercepted chatter on some cryptid forum about this exact clearing. That must be how Vale baits people. He leaks rumors, times his stunts, and then ghosts the area."

Mara crouched beside the rear tire and noticed fresh footprints pressed into the mud next to a crushed soda can. The treads looked similar to footprints she had spotted at the campsite days earlier. He was here not long ago and probably left at midday.

Skyhook brushed aside a clump of dried leaves, revealing a phone charger that had been yanked from the van's outlet. "He left in the middle of something."

Mara lowered her voice. "He might be setting up for a bigger stunt. We should call Finch and see if there's a new spike on ARGUS."

She tapped the comms earpiece. "Link, you reading me?"

A crackle sounded. Then Link's voice chimed in. "Loud and clear. Did you find Vale?"

"He's gone." Mara said. "But there's enough here to confirm he's staging more cryptid sightings. Check for new hashtags or suspicious live feeds. He left in a hurry."

"Will do." Link replied. "Finch is cross-referencing belief-spike data with local cell tower logs. Let us know if you need a drone sweep."

"Keep him on standby." Mara said.

She lowered her hand, then pushed off her knee to stand. She looked over at Skyhook, who was already sealing the recovered items in evidence bags. "We should sweep the immediate perimeter for any more clues. I'll check the tree line."

Skyhook gave a brisk nod. "I'll handle the other side of this clearing and see if there's a path he used to loop around us."

Mara walked to the far side of the van, stepping carefully among scattered wrappers. A swirl of spiral sketches lay half-buried near a rock. She knelt and lifted a page. It referred to an updated plan for capturing the cryptid from multiple angles, as though Vale wanted to spook it close to the camera while remote viewers gawked. At the bottom, notes mentioned rumor drops about Jackson and Mia, plus some cryptic mention of "final reveal."

Her jaw tightened. She hated the possibility that Vale might still be dangling those missing college kids as bait for more hype. She placed the paper in a separate pouch. The dryness in her throat threatened to turn into a snarl, but she forced herself to focus. Anger could wait until she had concrete leads on the next staging area.

A series of quiet footsteps announced Skyhook's return. "No fresh trails that lead anywhere obvious. He probably had a second vehicle or a local contact. Could be half a mile out by now." She said.

Mara exhaled. "I'll ping Finch to see if there's any mention of new rental cars or suspicious transactions. The last thing we need is him bouncing around the region with no trace."

They moved back toward the van. Mara peered inside one more time, rummaging through a jumbled stack of receipts near the gearshift. Most had partial addresses in other states. A couple showed small-dollar snack purchases at local convenience stores. None offered clear direction about Vale's next move. She steeled herself and swallowed a spike of frustration.

The day was sliding toward evening, judging by the shifting light through the canopy. Shadows lengthened, creeping over the clearing. Mara swung her gaze around the perimeter, uncertain if Vale lurked behind a trunk or if he was miles away by now laughing as he planned his next broadcast. She pictured him leaning over his camera, whispering instructions for anyone who might chase the cryptid or feed the hype.

She grabbed her comms again. "Link, see if there's a new wave of watchers for any random forest stream. He might have planted a tip that we're not catching."

"On it." He said. "Finch just flagged a suspicious jump in mentions for 'bone plates' and 'forest sightings' near the southwestern trails. I'd guess Vale dropped hints."

Mara's pulse quickened. She stepped away from the van, scanning the horizon. "Pull up any old data we have on southwestern sections of the forest. Let me know if there's a known vantage or carved anchor site there."

Skyhook re-emerged from behind the van and slid the final evidence bag into her pack. "We can break down here. I doubt there's more to find unless we start tearing the floorboards apart. Although that might be an idea if we have time."

"We'll have the local deputies tow it to a secure lot." Mara said. "We'll give Finch a chance to rip every bolt out if he wants to."

The two of them backed away, metal debris crunching beneath their boots. Before leaving, Mara circled the front of the vehicle. Something glinted near the windshield wiper. She leaned forward, plucking a tiny spiral pendant from beneath the wiper blade. It was shaped like Vale's signature swirl, etched crudely on a flat disc that looked like tarnished aluminum. She turned it over in her fingers, frowning at the puncture marks around the edges.

Skyhook peered at the pendant. "He left a souvenir?"

"More like a calling card." Mara said. "He never wastes a chance to brag." She shoved the pendant into her pocket, annoyed by the offhand cockiness it represented. He believes he's unstoppable.

Skyhook swung her pack across her shoulders. "Let's hope he's not planning to escalate. Last thing we need is a crowd of clueless hikers in the crossfire."

Mara moved toward the break in the trees leading back to the main route, keeping her rifle in a ready position. "We'll do what we can to contain him. Once we get these notes to Finch, maybe we'll see a pattern. Then we strangle his little plan before it gets bigger."

They trekked through damp brush, stepping over a rotting log, and emerged onto a narrow forest path. Mara signaled for caution, though no one appeared to be in the vicinity. She caught a faint whiff of the coffee stink that clung to her from the van, and for a second she pictured Vale smirking into a camera somewhere, fueling the next wave of digital mania.

Skyhook's footsteps stayed close behind, the quiet rattle of her gear an odd comfort in the silent forest. By the time they reached a small clearing on the other side, Mara paused to contact Link again. "We're heading back. Pack up what you can from the command trailer. Once Finch sees these notes, we might have our next lead."

"Copy that." Link said. "We had some success matching those spiral carvings to older sightings. We'll share when you return."

The call ended, and Mara motioned Skyhook forward. They pressed on. Branches rustled overhead while the canopy shifted with the breeze. The faint hum of distant vehicles drifted from beyond the treeline, reminding her that civilization lurked just a short drive away. She found it maddening that a single manipulator could coax thousands of online viewers into fueling a lethal threat. Vale clearly depended on that audience to keep the cryptid fed and unstoppable.

After five minutes of steady walking, they spotted the edge of the logging road where their transport waited. Mara let out a slow breath. She stepped onto the gravel and scanned the horizon. The world appeared calm, but she knew it was a temporary lull. Vale's notes screamed of bigger events to come.

She and Skyhook stowed their gear in the back of their vehicle. Then they placed the collected evidence in sealed containers.

Mara started the engine and felt a jolt of pent-up energy pushing her onward. The image of Vale's scrawled pages lingered in her mind: lines of script describing the power of belief as a fuel source for nightmares. She clenched the steering wheel.

"Hang in there." Skyhook said, settling into the passenger seat with a brittle sigh. "We'll piece everything together fast."

"Yeah. We don't have a choice." Mara replied. "We're not letting him turn the forest into a slaughterhouse for his viewership."

The wheels rumbled on the logging road as they pulled away. Streaks of golden light fell through gaps in the branches, reminding Mara that day was slipping into evening. The location might have been tranquil in another lifetime, but every shadow felt like a reminder that Vale was no ordinary suspect. He was an instigator of belief, planting seeds for a harvest of nightmares.

Skyhook nodded thoughtfully. "When we get back, I'll patch these findings to Link. Finch can cross-compare with ARGUS. If Vale is heading to southwestern trails, we might cut him off."

Mara guided the vehicle into a smooth bend, tires crunching over loose gravel. "He wants maximum exposure for the cryptid, so he'll pick a place that draws the biggest onlookers. We'll try to intercept that plan. Otherwise, we risk letting him feed the legend even more."

They rode in tense silence, the tension thick in the enclosed cabin. Grime from the forest clung to their boots, and the acrid odor of old coffee still lingered on Mara's gloves. She eased her grip and exhaled, determined to stay sharp.

No more close calls. We'll shut this down.

She felt a surge of grim resolve. The cryptid would not be allowed to terrorize more innocent campers, and Vale would not slip away unchallenged. She pressed the gas pedal harder to reach the SRD trailer and funnel every piece of data into Finch's tracking algorithms. Silence settled over the forest around them as if it awaited the next confrontation.

"Next time," she whispered, "we corner him before he sparks another crowd frenzy."

She kept her eyes on the winding road and prepared mentally for the next phase of their hunt. Every detail gleaned from that van would shape their next move. She hoped they would arrive one step ahead of Vale's twisted schedule. This time she intended to sabotage his show before the cryptid's power climbed any higher.

CHAPTER FIFTEEN

The next morning, the trailhead erupted in chaos. A lone hiker burst from the pines, his shirt torn and blood slick down his arm. He dropped to his knees and gasped. Every flashlight swung toward him. Mara's stomach flipped. Here was the nightmare in flesh: first Seth and now this man.

Sheriff Thomason barged through the knot of onlookers, shouting for room, but phones rose above shoulders. Even with a bleeding man at their feet, the crowd edged closer, sniffing for spectacle.

Finch's handheld monitor shrilled. A crimson spike vaulted off his screen, the sharpest surge yet. "Vale just uploaded another video." He muttered.

Mara tasted iron at the back of her throat. The forest fed on the frenzy and grew stronger with every upload. "We lose this crowd, we lose the valley." She said.

Skyhook tightened the strap on her field kit and slid a sonic lure into her palm. "Then we pull it away before the next hashtag hits." She answered.

Just as Mara and Skyhook left the trailer, a rescue volunteer hurried toward them, wide-eyed. "We just heard roars echoing from that ridge behind the clearing. A group of vloggers went straight for it." He looked furious. "They almost pushed me aside to get there first."

Mara's pulse pounded. "Let's move." She said, glancing at Skyhook. "If they stir that thing up, we'll have chaos. Bring your med kit in case they get mauled." Her lips pressed into a hard line. She grabbed her EM-Coil Carbine from a cart next to the gear box and slung it over her shoulder. The sheriff was busy fielding yet another confrontation with a limping hiker who refused to leave. Mara signaled to him as she passed, letting him know they were pursuing the new lead. He nodded, exasperated, and resumed his shouting match.

She and Skyhook trailed the volunteer through the tangle of ferns and brush. Branches snapped underfoot, and the faint smell of damp cedar filled the air. Tension coiled inside Mara every time she glimpsed footprints leading off-trail. A few prints looked fresh, pressed into the muddy ground. She listened for any sign of cameras in use or yelling. Instead, the forest gave them the rustle of leaves and the distant hum of crowd chatter.

They reached a rocky ledge overlooking a shallow ravine. No sign of the vloggers. Mara motioned for Skyhook to set a sonic lure near a large fallen trunk. They intended to coax the cryptid away from popular routes. Once the lure was armed, they retreated behind a cluster of mossy stones, waiting for any sign of movement below.

Minutes passed. Then something heavy moved far to their right, a dull thump that carried through the canopy. Mara tensed, ready to switch her carbine from safety. Another sound followed, perhaps a muffled shout. She couldn't determine if the voice belonged to the vloggers or something else.

Are we about to see them become prey on a live stream?

She radioed Link for a drone feed, but he replied that the

thick treetops had limited visibility. Finch was recalibrating thermal imaging to pierce the deeper ravine though that would take a few minutes. Mara's mouth was dry. She swept her gaze across the ridge. There was no movement, no sign of Vale's presence, and an ominous hush.

Then a shrill scream echoed from the shadows below. Mara's stomach twisted at the thought of a cryptid encounter. She flicked off the safety and signaled Skyhook to circle toward a narrow slope leading down. If someone had been attacked, they needed immediate help. The volunteer behind them muttered a prayer and offered to keep watch at the top.

Skyhook pressed a hand to Mara's shoulder. "We go slow. Could be a trap. That group might not realize what they're dealing with."

Mara nodded once and led the descent. Turbulent thoughts swarmed in her head. Vale was stoking the flame and letting these fools wander straight into the beast's path. She pictured Jackson and Mia lost in this labyrinth. We still haven't found them, and now the entire region is turning into a spectacle. She forced that thought aside and focused on each careful step downhill.

Their progress slowed when the slope turned steep. Rocks slid under their boots, clattering. She winced at the noise. It felt like an announcement of their location. She caught a glimpse of twisted bushes below, but no sign of whoever had screamed. She heard no more roars or other movement. The only sound was the rustle of leaves. She signaled Skyhook to set up a vantage near a warped cedar trunk. Then Mara pulled out her binoculars and scanned for tracks or figures.

A faint beep came through her earpiece. Link whispered that Finch was ready to patch in a new thermal feed. Mara lifted a slim black device from her belt and synced it. A hazy color overlay flickered on the scope. Through that lens, she caught heat signatures that might be human shapes on the far side of the ravine. They seemed to be running. She guessed they were the vloggers, spooked by something. At least they were alive.

She hunkered in place for another minute, but no monstrous form charged out of the shadows. The forest felt deeply unsettled, yet the cryptid had already vanished to wherever Vale guided it next. Eventually, Mara signaled Skyhook that they would move back. They disarmed the sonic lure and took a long, looping route to avoid crossing paths with the stampede of reckless explorers. Returning meant regrouping and planning crowd control again.

When they reached the trailhead again, more vehicles had arrived. A few were roped off by the sheriff's men, but dozens of individuals simply parked farther down the road and cut through brambles. Mara felt her patience strain. We're spread too thin, and Vale is probably laughing. She kept her tone measured when she spoke into the radio, instructing deputies on which areas needed urgent coverage. Skyhook returned to the mobile trailer to share updated coordinates with Finch and Link.

Mara paused beside a battered sign, then flinched. She remembered the rules, so she set her thoughts on the immediate tasks. A deputy jogged over, breathless, to say that he had found a chunk of shredded fabric a mile down the northern trail that matched the color of Jackson and Mia's tent. She told him to mark the site and call in a second drone pass.

Stepping into the trailer, she saw Finch hunched behind his laptop, lines of code and streaming data reflecting off his glasses. He gave her a tense nod. Link stood nearby, relaying the day's updates into a secure channel. A wave of new hashtags scrolled across the overhead display. Each one promised a new vantage point, fresh sightings, or sensational rumors. Mara could sense the forest's energy rolling toward a flashpoint, guided by Vale's manipulations.

She closed the trailer door behind her, scanning everyone's exhausted faces. "We need a plan to keep these people from fueling the cryptid's rise." She said, voice tight. "Start triangulating the worst hotspots and deploy any staff we can spare. Nightfall will give Vale even more cover." She felt the ache in her muscles, but she forced herself to focus. Backing down now was not an option. She would hold this line, no matter how frantic the trails became.

CHAPTER SIXTEEN

Mara set her tablet aside and stared at the lines of text scrolling across Finch's laptop. Through the command trailer's small window, she saw headlights scattered on the county road, heading deeper into the forest. A low hum from the portable generator buzzed around her, underscoring the tension in the confined space.

She leaned over Finch's shoulder. "So this broadcast started about an hour ago?" Her voice sounded clipped to her own ears. Finch nodded, eyes flicking between data streams on ARGUS and a muted replay of Carter Vale's feed.

"Yes. Link caught it as it went live." Finch tapped a blinking graph. "We're seeing a sharp spike in chat room mentions. They're talking about the swirl on that boulder."

Mara made a fist, pressing her knuckles against the console. "He's goading them, leading them on with cryptic hints about a 'legend made flesh.' Great. People are lapping it up." She fought the urge to yank the entire rig free and smash it against the wall. Instead she took a slow breath and forced calm into her tone.

"Where does he keep filming from?" she asked.

Finch cycled through waveforms. "It changed location five

times in the last hour. The feed is partially scrambled. Vale must be piggybacking through multiple routers or a direct satellite link. Link's trying to isolate it but there's much noise on the net."

Her earpiece crackled. "Can you two see this?" Link's voice rose from the team channel. "It's gotten worse. He's now calling the cryptid the 'forest's rightful apex' and telling people to 'come witness it under the old cedar groves.' I'm seeing the chat blow up with fresh hashtags."

Mara squeezed the mic button. "Understood. Keep pulling logs. Let me know if anything or anyone references Jackson or Mia." She paused, glancing at Finch. "Still no hits on them?"

Finch shook his head. "No new sightings. The volunteer search teams posted their coordinates but they're too spread out. Jackson and Mia remain unaccounted for." He tapped a chart with rows of trending topic lines. "This is overshadowing everything else."

Mara felt frustration knot in her gut. She stepped around Finch and skirted the narrow aisle of the trailer. Outside, the forest smelled damp from the drizzle. The hum of at least three new drones overhead was enough to raise her hackles.

He's turning this place into a circus. She exhaled, then reentered to check the main console readouts again.

Finch pointed to an expanding cluster of data arcs. "ARGUS is updating in real time. This southwestern quadrant is lighting up. I think Vale is either heading that way to record more stunts or he's been there the whole time."

Mara studied the topography map on the wide screen. The southwestern quadrant had dense cedar stands popular with day hikers. Cell coverage dropped significantly along the older trails. She noticed multiple amateur-sounding drone frequencies feeding questionable footage to local media outlets.

"Damn it. If he's planning a big reveal there, the crowd will be massive," she muttered. Her earpiece lit up again. Skyhook chimed in. "No official flight restrictions on these news drones.

They're everywhere. I'm hearing talk about folks livestreaming from random trailheads."

Mara's mouth tightened. She turned to Finch. "Remind me again why we can't get more federal muscle to shut this down?"

He shrugged. "We're bound by hush-fund orders. Dr. Sato hammered that home. The higher-ups want minimal exposure and no direct sabotage of mainstream media. 'Contain but do not cause broader panic.' I believe that was their phrasing."

She gritted her teeth. "Vale is out there, feeding hype to thousands. Meanwhile, the cryptid is getting stronger with every view. That's broader panic." She snatched her jacket from a hook and headed outside without waiting for Finch's reply.

The unwelcome yet familiar crunch of tires on gravel pulled Finch sharply from his scrutiny of Vale's latest broadcast. Through the trailer's window, he saw Sheriff Thomason exit his cruiser with the usual lines of weary frustration etched deep across his face.

Thomason approached, shoulders stiff beneath his uniform jacket, and confirmed their suspicions without preamble. Vale's newest provocations had triggered another influx of thrill-seekers flooding into the already crowded woods.

"My deputies are stretched thin, Bishop," Thomason said, each word clipped with simmering irritation born of battling both an unpredictable cryptid and county officials concerned more with tourism than safety.

"Vale's pointing them toward the old cedar groves, and they're following him blindly. We can't shut down every logging road in the southwest."

Mara held his gaze briefly. A silent recognition settled between them. Vale was no longer fueling rumors. He was deliberately guiding his followers straight into the heart of the manifestation.

Inside the cramped trailer, tension thickened like an electric charge. Link hunched over his screens and his fingers raced across keyboards as he relayed grim news. ARGUS showed belief metrics skyrocketing, all converging rapidly on the ancient cedar grove Finch had flagged from obscure folklore and Vale's earlier hints.

"He's practically handing out coordinates, Mara," Link said, his voice strained by urgency. "The forums are flooded with GPS pins pointing directly to the grove. Vale isn't bothering with subtlety anymore. He is setting the stage for something big."

The provocative image of the chalk spiral etched on the boulder, coupled with Vale's direct references to the cedar grove, left little room for doubt: this was precisely the setting he had chosen.

Finch, cross-referencing Vale's recent taunts with archival data, stabbed a finger toward a cluster of trees deep in the southwestern quadrant. "That has to be the spot. The carved stump, the local 'totem' from the legends, aligns exactly with everything Vale broadcasted. He's calling us out and bringing every curious believer armed with a smartphone along for his finale." The burden of Jackson and Mia's disappearance pressed heavily upon Mara, their unknown fate another troubling piece in Vale's sinister game. They had run out of time for cautious maneuvers or chasing elusive clues. Vale had openly challenged them, and Cedar Grove was now the battleground.

"Gear up," Mara commanded, her voice slicing through the low hum of electronics. "Skyhook, prep the VTOL. Finch, Link, assemble every shred of intel we have on that grove. We're going in. It's time to pull the plug on Vale's twisted show, once and for all."

The SRD trailer, normally filled with a hushed intensity, surged into deliberate action. Skyhook had begun pre-flight checks on the VTOL and its rotors sent a steady, low-frequency vibration through the forest floor. Finch and Link, faces cast in the tense glow of their screens, compiled final threat evaluations, generated ARGUS projections for Cedar Grove, and tracked sudden shifts in online belief triggered by Vale's latest broadcast. Mara systematically inspected her combat rig, including thermite charges, an EM-Coil Carbine, and sedation darts. Each familiar piece offered grim reassurance as tension mounted. Within moments, beneath the rapidly darkening sky, the VTOL lifted off, its engines slicing decisively through the night air toward the southwestern quadrant and into the core of Vale's orchestrated event. The approach carried an undercurrent of anxiety, heightened by Link's drone imagery showing civilians gathering around the target area even before the team arrived.

Mara crouched behind a thicket of dripping ferns, listening to the steady murmur of phone chatter in the distance. The damp air squeezed past her collar and she felt the tension ripple through her shoulders as she adjusted her grip on the EM-Coil Carbine.

She edged forward until she had a glimpse of the overgrown canyon below. Link's voice came through her earpiece with a quiet crackle, letting her know they had at least a dozen thrill-seekers gathered around. They had torches, handheld floodlights, and a line of smartphone rigs pointed at a makeshift clearing. Mara exhaled slowly. Fantastic, a midnight circus of amateurs.

She gave a single hand signal. Skyhook moved along her left, scanning the perimeter for any sign of the cryptid. Finch had stayed back at the mobile command trailer, monitoring ARGUS readouts while juggling local feeds that suggested more would arrive if someone got a good shot of anything monstrous. Unfortunately, people with cameras rarely complied without a fight.

She stepped even closer, noticing the crowd chanting something about calling Bigfoot out of hiding. Some wore matching shirts with printed spirals, clearly feeding off online hype. Mara saw no immediate sign of Carter Vale, yet the entire scene felt staged. Link's voice nudged her again through the comms. "Signals are going out live, Mara. I can jam them at your call, but we have at least six different rigs. They're using multiple carriers."

Mara gave an annoyed nod to the night. "Do it. Kill their signal so they can't feed the beast from here." She moved down the slope and took care not to slip on slick leaves. The chanting continued below, punctuated by shouts of excitement. She signaled Skyhook and advanced into the ring of onlookers. Her presence drew a round of shouts and several phones swiveled in her direction. She never liked being an unwilling centerpiece in these videos. That reflex to flatten her posture flared in her mind. She pressed on, cradling her Carbine at a low angle. "Everyone, you need to shut this down. This area isn't safe." One influencer shoved his way forward, phone raised high. "Who the hell are you? You can't shut us down!"

Before Mara could respond, a snarl boomed from beyond the torchlight. Branches snapped at the tree line. Torches wavered, and half the crowd pivoted to face the darkness. The cryptid's silhouette burst into view. Plates across its back stood out under the torch glare. It let out a throaty roar that silenced every phone-wielding fool instantly. Mara's pulse hammered as she tried to line up a clear tranquilizer shot. Not again. She'd lost her cousin to a nightmare like this. She wouldn't lose anyone else.

Some in the crowd shrieked and retreated while others scrambled to capture the action, eyes wild with adrenaline. One influencer shouted, "Get it on camera!" The cryptid lunged. Mara bit back a curse. She ducked behind a boulder and adjusted the rifle's angle but frantic bodies swarmed between her and the beast. People bunched together and a few stood on tiptoes to film over each other's shoulders.

Link jammed signals in bursts, hoping to cut the feed and reduce the viral spread. Mara heard the abrupt hush of phones losing service. She locked eyes with Skyhook, who sprinted to drag a wounded bystander out from under the cryptid's reach. Another onlooker stumbled, clutching a bleeding arm while the creature's snarl rumbled across the clearing again.

The brute's arm slammed a shrieking woman aside, sending

her sprawling over a patch of slick grass. Mara moved forward, fighting frustration as she tried to find an opening for a dart. Terrified amateurs scattered across the clearing, some tripping over abandoned gear. The creature pivoted, bony plating glinting, then seized a tripod and hurled it. The flying metal clipped a man's shoulder, dropping him instantly.

She cursed under her breath. That was a powder keg. She needed the crowd gone. She fired a sedative dart, watching it miss by inches as the cryptid twisted in the gloom. A phone's spotlight skated across her eyes, forcing her to blink. "Turn that light away," she shouted. The offender froze then spun the phone wildly as more roars rattled the clearing.

Skyhook reached Mara's side, panting. "Four injured so far!" Another crash sounded as the cryptid lunged toward a small group huddled near a cluster of torches. Mara twisted, aware that if she did not separate beast from crowd soon, they would be in deep trouble.

She moved closer to the cryptid's flank and leveled the carbine for a clean dart shot. A panicked influencer darted in front of her with a phone. Mara snarled at him to move, but he seemed desperate to capture another viral second of terror. She shoved him aside and squeezed the trigger. The dart hit the beast near its shoulder, but it barely paused.

A fresh wave of shouts rose as the cryptid roared in their direction. Then it swiveled and glared at the nearest torch with a guttural hiss. Mara spotted more phones pointed relentlessly at the creature, violet lights on the screens glimmering in the smoky air. She tore another phone from a stunned bystander, ignored his protest, and hurled it out of reach.

Sounds of thrashing branches signaled the cryptid's abrupt retreat. Mara saw its horned silhouette fade into thicker brush. She hissed an expletive, shouldered her rifle, and stepped past the moaning people scattered around. A few had the sense to gather their wounded friends rather than continue filming. She eyed the circle of torches that still burned along the clearing's edge.

One shaky voice piped up from behind a half-collapsed canopy of branches. "I swear I saw a hooded figure filming. He stayed back there." Mara scanned that direction but saw only darkness. Her gut twisted. That had to be Vale. He must have captured everything: the chaos, the cryptid's assault, and the crowd's fear. It was the perfect reel to further hype the story.

Link's voice came through again. "Bishop, I see partial movement near your nine o'clock. Somebody is slipping out behind a fallen log. Might be him." Mara spun to look, nearly tripping over a broken tripod. By the time she maneuvered past a cluster of dimly glowing phones, that shape was gone. Vale had played them again.

She knelt beside a trembling young man with a bruised shoulder. He stared up at her with watery eyes. "That thing almost ripped us apart." She nodded grimly and scanned the battered gear around them. The crowd was in disarray, scattering into pockets of confusion. "You're lucky to be alive," she said in a flat voice. "Get out of here and don't come back. This is not a game."

She helped a deputy who arrived late and pointed him to the injured for immediate aid. Several onlookers demanded their phones, while others cradled bruises or stood in shock. Skyhook pulled a hissing civilian to his feet and steered him toward the trailhead, ignoring his barrage of complaints. Mara worked alongside them, guiding the crowd away before the cryptid changed its mind about retreating.

More branches snapped in the distance. Adrenaline flared in Mara's gut, but no new shapes emerged.

They gathered the scattered equipment. Link's localized jamming had forced the feeds offline for now, but the damage was done. The cryptid had already fed on the energy of that crowd. Mara felt a prickle of anger, wishing she could corner Vale once and for all.

She gathered everyone who remained, urging them to climb the slope back toward the main trail. "Go. If you see anything else, do not post about it. Contact local emergency services." A few muttered insults at her, others trudged away in sloppy lines. They seemed more concerned about lost phone signals than the injuries around them.

Skyhook stepped beside her as the last group hobbled past, leaning on each other. "We should do a final sweep. The beast might loop around." Mara tightened her grip on the Carbine. "Agreed." Her head was pounding. They inched around the perimeter of trampled brush and sputtering torches, searching for any reappearance of the monster. No movement came from the gloom, as if it had melted into the forest. "Looks like it's satisfied for the moment." She said, though the words felt hollow.

A fresh cluster of pained groans drew them back toward the center of the battered clearing. Mara and Skyhook tended to the injured and applied basic field dressings before passing them off to the deputy. She realized the crowd who rarely listened had seen enough to scatter in all directions.

Skyhook walked beside Mara and handed her a cracked phone they had recovered from the grass. "It was still streaming when I found it, but the signal was jammed. Probably worthless to Vale now." Mara took it without much interest. "He's got other angles. Count on it."

They handed the wounded off to the deputy, who called for an ambulance from the county road. The rocky ground around them glistened with spilled water canisters, scattered phone rigs, and a few shoe prints leading deeper into the brush. Mara rubbed her brow. "He's always one step ahead, but we'll pin him down eventually."

She and Skyhook gathered the last bits of abandoned equipment and tossed them into a makeshift pile for confiscation. She noticed her hands trembled slightly after that close encounter. Calm down. Focus on the next step. The cryptid had left behind no fresh blood, but the limited sedation dart might wear off quickly. She worried it would return. Worse, Vale would probably spin the incident into more publicity. The more publicity, the stronger the creature became.

Skyhook patted her shoulder lightly, though the pilot's expression stayed grim. "We got them to safety, at least. That crowd was a powder keg. It could have ended much worse." Mara nodded and scanned the treeline. "We're not done. He'll push for another incident. We'll track it before sunrise." The words felt hard as stone, and she meant every bit of it.

By the time they cleared the site and returned to the edge of the canyon, the hooded figure was nowhere to be seen. The forest loomed in darkness, and all traces of spectators drifted away. Mara watched from a distance, not letting her rifle drop from her arms.

She turned to Link and Skyhook. "We managed to push it back, but Vale is fueling that thing. Once he uploads his footage, we'll see a bigger surge. We need to intercept that anchor before he sets this forest on fire."

The deputy closed his door and rolled his windows halfway down. He gave Mara a nod, though it was muted by the chaos he had witnessed. "I'll take these folks to the local clinic, then rally more for tomorrow. Good luck." Mara stepped aside as he backed out, the tires crunching broken branches.

In the gloom, she and her teammates gathered their gear, stowing battered phones inside the ATV's side compartments. No one wanted to talk much. The night's tension clung to them like sticky sap. Finally, Link broke the silence. "What's the plan now?"

Mara faced the forest's open maw. "We regroup, fix sedation loads, and track that cryptid's path. I want fresh thermal sweeps, more drones in the air. Vale is lurking around somewhere. We'll find him." Skyhook gave a nod. "All right. Let's move."

They set out for the mobile command trailer, guiding the

ATV with its mound of confiscated gear rattling in the back. Mara's teeth stayed clenched for most of the ride. Too many near misses, too many eager watchers who refused to see reason. She glanced over her shoulder at the blackness of the canyon. Then she inhaled, letting the chill night air fill her lungs.

He got his perfect footage, but this is not over.

CHAPTER SEVENTEEN

As Mara and the team headed into the forest to find the grove, they saw a lean, bleary-eyed ranger standing near a worn sign-post too faint to read without stepping close. He gave Mara a short wave and beckoned her over. His uniform looked rumpled, and he clutched a metal thermos as though it was the only thing holding him upright. She approached and raised her hand in greeting

"I'm of no help," he said. "Too many corners of this forest and not enough rangers. Locals say there's a ring of cedars in the center. Folks have gone missing there for decades." He reached into a zippered pouch and produced a tattered map. "That path is half-erased now, but you'll find old carvings if you follow the ridge." His eyes flicked to her carbine. "Hope that thing makes a difference."

She took the map and studied it. The ranger's penciled markings showed a meandering route that curved into a dark patch labeled "Ancient Cedar Grove." Mara spotted scribbles indicating vanishings and sightings, each date circled. She nodded. "You've done your homework. Thanks for this." He shrugged wearily and pointed east.

She fed a quick update to Link and described the map as best she could. Static hissed. Then Finch's careful voice emerged. "ARGUS is reading a slight spike right near that grove. Could be where the master carving is hidden. Keep an eye out for worn symbols or deeper spiral etchings. If you find it, we'll plan next steps for removal."

Mara snorted softly. "That's the plan. Tell everyone I'll sweep the perimeter first. We will not repeat our mistakes. We will not stop until we find the grove, even if Vale stands in our way. He seems determined to lead us away from it." She pivoted away from the ranger and stepped off the main trail. She wove through ferns that brushed her shins. Larger cedar trunks loomed in every direction. Their massive girth and textured bark created plenty of hiding spots. She paused to place a small motion sensor on a trunk. A green LED winked to life before she moved on.

The grove ahead looked thick with centuries-old branches overhead that blocked much of the sunshine. The air felt heavier as she advanced. She stayed alert for the snap of twigs that might signal a large presence. Rumors suggested Carter Vale might have ventured here during the night to carve new sigils or film fresh footage. She disliked how quickly his broadcasts sent the public rushing toward danger.

Shadows played over roots that twisted across the ground. She occasionally glanced overhead at the forest canopy, which held a grayish gloom. The place was stunning in a primitive way but thrummed with tension.

She stopped at a thick trunk showing faint spiral scarring near the base. A single swirl was gouged deep. The bark had peeled back to expose lighter wood beneath. The pattern resembled those she had seen at prior anchor points, though this one was smaller. She pinged Finch to mark the coordinates.

"Got it." Finch replied. "We're seeing your feed from the body-cam. That spiral is consistent with Vale's signature, but it isn't big enough to be the primary anchor. Keep searching. The big one should be carved more prominently."

Her earpiece chirped. Link spoke fast. "Heads up. I'm intercepting a local radio call from a group of hikers. They claim they heard roaring deeper in the grove. No visual, but they're freaked out. Also, a few social channels say there's a crowd starting to gather at the trailhead. They want live coverage."

Mara grimaced. "Typical. Let them know this is federal property. If they don't leave, they risk tangling with my operation and whatever that thing is." She knew Link had limited means to enforce that warning, but it was worth a try. She advanced again, each step sinking slightly into damp earth. A spiderweb brushed across her arm, making her jerk back with a muttered curse.

The trail descended into a hollow. She kept checking her six, half expecting Vale to pop out with his camera rolling. The swirl-laden totem stump was the real objective. They had destroyed smaller carvings before, but the biggest anchor was always hidden in a more remote spot, fueling the cryptid's presence. She recalled Finch's theory that repeated re-sharing of Vale's footage kept the creature's power from fading. That same theory meant the final anchor might be so potent that any direct confrontation with the cryptid near it would be a nightmare.

A branch snapped on her left. She dropped to one knee behind a fallen log, scanning with her carbine raised. A cluster of leaves shifted, then stilled. She listened for heavier footsteps. Nothing. The hush returned, punctuated by distant cawing overhead. She rose and advanced in short, careful strides.

Skyhook's voice filtered into her earpiece. "All quiet from above. Minimal movement on thermal. A few medium-sized shapes, probably deer. No giant heat signatures. We'll keep circling. The quiet somehow unnerves me more than chaos."

"Copy." Mara said softly, silently agreeing with Skyhook. She reached a wide clearing ringed by cedars towering like columns in a cathedral. Massive trunks soared overhead, and the ground here seemed to sag in a shallow bowl. Needles and debris carpeted the area, making it spongy underfoot. She paused, scanning for any sign of carvings bigger than the one she'd already found.

A crow shrieked above, drawing her gaze. Sunlight barely brushed the forest floor, but in one slant of brightness she spotted fresh grooves on a trunk. They formed a partial spiral about shoulder height. She approached and pressed gloved fingers against the gouge. The wood felt damp. She took a photo using the device clipped to her vest and sent it to Finch.

"Looks deeper than the first one." She whispered. A chill crawled along her neck. She eased back from the trunk and circled to see if the mark continued on the other side, but there was nothing. The break in the bark ended abruptly as if someone had run out of time to finish the symbol. She returned to the clearing. The entire zone felt like the threshold of something more ominous.

Another beep came from her earpiece. Finch said, "ARGUS is fluctuating right now. We have a spike in regional hashtags referencing ghost lights in the forest. It might be a rumor, or someone might have seen a reflection from a camera flash."

"Understood." Mara said. She stepped around the clearing, her eyes roving for movement. "I'm not seeing the major stump yet. The ranger said it would be at the center of the oldest growth. It looks like I have more ground to cover."

Nearby, a fallen cedar angled across a narrow gap. Moss coated its length, and moisture pooled in its crevices. She climbed over it and left faint boot impressions behind. A hush settled over the area, broken only by jays calling in the distance. Link chimed in again, his voice tense.

"We have locals ignoring warnings. They're piling onto side trails and trying to capture footage for social media. The sheriff's office is short-staffed and cannot do much crowd control. Be prepared for random hikers wandering into your path."

Mara hissed a low oath. The last thing she wanted was some group of rowdy onlookers messing with a carefully tuned operation. "All right. I'll keep my eyes open for them. How's the feed from my camera?"

"Clear." Link said. "You can push another half a kilometer before we hit any blind spots. According to that map you have, the real grove is due east."

She navigated through a corridor of cedar trunks so thick the sun vanished overhead. A faint smell of rotted wood mingled with a sharper tang of sap. She noticed a muddy trail winding to her right. The ranger's map had implied a footpath there decades ago, but it had been swallowed by undergrowth. Mara clicked on her vest light, though the day was bright enough. These trees made midday look like dusk.

She paused to set another motion sensor on a trunk. The device beeped softly and confirmed activation. She circled behind a wide cedar whose roots curled against a slope. The ground there dipped abruptly into a depression lined with ferns. She stooped to see if any carvings hid beneath the fronds. There was no sign of spirals. She eased up and checked her corners.

A short crackle announced Finch again. "ARGUS just correlated a fresh post with Vale's account. He teased that the heart of belief thrives amid the cedars. He posted geotag info that leads to you."

Mara exhaled slowly. "Fantastic. He's directing an audience right to this location."

Link spoke next, his voice tight. "We are seeing increased forum chatter. People want a big reveal. They think it is a hoax or a staged show. Some are bringing camping gear for an overnight watch party."

She ran a hand across her brow. "Well, let's hope they are not insane enough to cross caution tape if we have to set up a perimeter. Keep me posted." She moved on, edging around thick brush that snagged at her pant cuffs. The hush grew heavier in that patch of forest or her nerves tensed at the thought that Vale was inviting more eyes to this place.

At the edge of the next clearing she found a circle of smaller spruces. In the center lay a rotted stump. Nothing about it resembled a spiral carving so she pressed deeper. Her mind flicked to the missing campers Jackson and Mia. They had vanished around here or near enough. She clenched her jaw. She needed to finish this before more people vanished.

A scuffing sound rustled from behind. She twisted with her carbine leveled and her finger near the trigger guard. Through the gloom she spotted a figure in a black hoodie stumbling out from behind a trunk with a phone in his hand. He froze, eyes wide.

"Whoa." He blurted, raising his hands. "I thought... I was trying to find Bigfoot."

Mara lowered her weapon slightly. "Turn around. It's not safe. The local sheriff wants everyone out."

He gave a stiff nod and swallowed hard. "Okay, I'm leaving." He backed away, brushing branches aside until he disappeared into the trees. She shook her head, uncertain whether he would retreat or circle back. People rarely heeded a warning when they thought a viral spectacle was at stake.

Her comm beeped. Skyhook reported, "No sign of Vale's van from above, but we have a suspicious cluster of vehicles parked near the old trailhead. At least eight. Could be day-trippers or actual cryptid chasers."

Mara pressed forward. A deeper hush enveloped the next stand of cedars and she glimpsed a spiral carving near waist-level on a trunk. She swept her foot through a clump of leaves and that revealed a faint path. As the forest parted slightly, a dim shaft of sunlight streaked across an area choked with thick underbrush. She stepped closer and saw that the trunk to her left featured multiple swirl lines, each set at a different angle. She snapped a photo for Finch.

Soft footsteps rose behind her. She whirled around again, keeping her carbine tight to her chest. A father with two teenagers in tow stood there, his eyes filled with worry. He wore a flannel jacket and carried a modest hiking pack. "Sorry." He whispered. "We heard weird noises and got lost."

She jerked her head toward the way they had come. "You need to leave. This zone is off-limits. There is a dangerous presence here. Go now." The father nodded quickly. They sidestepped around her and hurried off in the direction she pointed.

Mara muttered an expletive under her breath. She advanced carefully, rounding a huge cedar whose roots formed a natural arch. A short slope dipped into a gloomier space. She paused and scanned the area with the muzzle of her carbine. The ground was pooled with dark water in places but she saw piles of stones that looked deliberate. One bore the spiral pattern etched on top, faint but unmistakable.

She opened her channel. "I'm seeing more condensed patterns. This might lead to the main anchor. I'll keep going a bit further."

Finch replied, "Got it. We're sending potential extraction routes to your HUD. If you confirm the anchor's location, we'll plan to send in the rest of the team."

Mara inched forward. The hush thickened. An occasional drip from overhead branches broke it. A swirl of ferns parted and revealed what looked like a partial clearing. Her chest tightened. She stepped out and found a wide ring of massive cedars. The air carried a resinous odor, and she caught sight of a tall stump near the center. It was six feet high, its top hammered with swirl carvings. Something told her this was the place Finch had warned about.

She paused a dozen yards away and scanned for movement. No beast in sight. She circled left to get a better angle. Lines of scarred wood ran in looping arcs across that stump, forming a pattern that made her stomach tense. That has to be the final anchor. Finch had said the largest anchor was often hidden in the oldest part of the forest, and this certainly fit.

She raised her comm. "I think I've found it. Big stump, spirals carved deep all around. Vale will show up eventually."

"All right," Finch said. "We'll coordinate. Hold position, but do not engage with any brute force. We need to plan this carefully."

Mara nodded to herself, eyes locked on the carved stump. She advanced a few paces and snapped photo after photo. Each swirling groove looked fresh. The spiral lines glistened with dampness, and in one deep groove she counted scratch marks that could indicate the cryptid had used its claws to deepen the carving. The possibility made her uneasy.

She stepped back into the cover of a nearby cedar trunk and pressed her shoulder against the bark. She realized they had to move quickly. People were streaming in from all sides, thanks to Vale's twisted invitation. If the cryptid emerged now, the chaos would be worse than any past confrontation.

She scanned the undergrowth for signs of movement. Nothing. She whispered into the comm, "I'm standing by. You can send in the rest of the team. We'll map out a strike plan."

At that moment, an amplified voice crackled across a distant speaker. She stiffened and peered through the trees, but she saw no one. The voice was faint, as if it came from a portable device broadcasting an echoing message. She picked out only a few words. Something about "truth in the forest" and "living legend." It had the smug ring of Vale's style.

She clenched her jaw. Vale had a sense for drama. She suppressed a wave of frustration and steadied her breathing. Soon, the others would arrive, and they would have to remove or destroy that trunk before Vale lured an entire audience to watch a monstrous demonstration. She stayed behind the cedar trunk, heart pounding.

"I'm in position," she said into her mic. "We'll do this by the book. Send in backup now."

She kept her carbine up, eyes locked on the stump. An over-cast glow lit the circle of cedars. The forest gave no immediate sign of life, yet the sense of dread only grew. She knew the real showdown was coming, and the anchor was here, waiting to feed a monster that thrived on every rumor.

That was where she needed to end her search for now.

CHAPTER EIGHTEEN

The air within the Ancient Cedar Grove was dense, saturated
with the smell of age-old rot, damp earth, and the sharpness of
freshly exposed wood. Mara advanced carefully, her movements
controlled and precise, each step nearly silent on the thick bed of
ancient needles. Ahead stood the reason for their urgent pursuit:
the totem stump. It loomed larger than any image had suggested,
a massive twisted relic of cedar, easily six feet tall and twice that
in width, its jagged top a grotesque altar to Vale's dark creativity.
Intricate spirals, fresh against the worn wood, wound across its
surface. Some were shallow and tentative, others carved deep
with fierce certainty. Thick amber sap seeped from these inci-
sions, catching the dying light and making the markings appear
alive. This was the center of the disturbance, the primary anchor
Finch's ARGUS had pinpointed, surging with every passing
moment due to intensifying online belief.

Skyhook moved silently at Mara's side, her easy confidence
muted by the solemnity of their surroundings. She had discreetly
landed the aircraft about half a kilometer east, leaving a nervous-
looking county deputy, a supposed local liaison, overwhelmed,
tasked with guarding their approach. Mara doubted the deputy's

effectiveness against Vale's expected maneuvers. Link's voice buzzed in her earpiece, giving a grim update from online channels: social media was ablaze with speculation, hashtags proliferating rapidly, intensifying the frenzy. "Onlookers are still bypassing roadblocks, Mara," Link reported. "Vale's likely broadcasting right now, urging them to come see the 'true king's throne.'"

Mara pushed aside the external turmoil and focused on the immediate task. The thermite charges felt solid in her pack, each canister promising a cleansing fire in stark contrast to the vitality pulsing from the stump. Finch spoke quietly through her other earpiece in a steady stream of caution and data, underscoring the risk. "The energy surrounding the totem is escalating quickly, Mara. ARGUS shows belief metrics nearing critical levels. Disturbing the anchor too significantly now could cause an unpredictable response."

"Understood, Finch." Mara retrieved the first thermite charge and knelt at the base of the stump. Her gloved fingers meticulously explored its rugged bark until she found the precise spot Finch had described. The wood felt ancient and cool, yet she detected a faint vibration beneath the surface echoing the wave of online panic. She discovered a shallow hollow near the ground, partially hidden by an overhang, and placed the charge inside. With a click it armed and a small green indicator blinked in the dimness. One in place.

The stump's size required a cautious, deliberate placement of each charge in what felt like a delicate task around the heart of the cryptid's power. Mara moved methodically and remained alert to any changes in the grove, any sign of the creature's arrival or of Vale's interference. Finch's earlier caution echoed in her mind: introducing foreign energy could provoke the entity immediately. Skyhook maintained vigilant watch, her weapon drawn, head turning constantly to scan the shadowed gaps between the massive cedars standing sentinel around the clearing.

"Deputy reports a small group heading up the west slope," Skyhook whispered, barely disturbing the oppressive stillness. "They claim Vale himself directed them here, promising 'real magic.' One of them seems to be streaming live."

"Link, can you disrupt their signal if they breach our immediate area?" Mara asked, focusing on positioning the second charge within a deep knothole.

"Already on it," Link confirmed. "But offline recordings will inevitably surface later. Vale is counting on it."

Of course he was.

Mara pictured him hidden nearby, filming smugly, the thought fueling a cold resolve in her chest. She secured the third charge within a deep fissure on the stump's northern side, the spirals twisting around it like malevolent veins. The indicator glowed steadily green. The remote detonator clipped to her belt felt heavy, a promise of decisive action.

Finch's voice sharpened. "Mara, ARGUS is spiking uncontrollably. Vale's feed must be live, directing major attention toward your location. The energy field around the stump is dangerously volatile. A sudden release now would be unpredictable."

"How close, Finch?" Mara's hand paused over the final charge.

"Imminent. The entity might appear at any moment, or the anchor itself could react violently because of the intense belief energy. The spirals' structural integrity is becoming dangerously unstable."

Mara exchanged a quick, tense glance with Skyhook. Twilight had thickened the shadows, intensifying the grove's sinister atmosphere. The distant eager voices of thrill seekers grew louder, signaling an approaching crisis. Mara took the last thermite charge, its red warning label stark against the gloom, and wedged it into a crack near the stump's jagged edge. Another click armed it. Four charges now surrounded the anchor.

She stepped back with the detonator in hand, its tiny green signal pulsing in sync with her quickened heartbeat. A systems check confirmed the charges' readiness. "Finch, Link, Skyhook," she said, slicing through mounting tension, "charges are set. Awaiting your ignition order, but this crowd won't stay back much longer." Their nearing voices rose, excitement and chaos intertwined. The carved spirals seemed to ripple subtly in the growing darkness, poised to release Vale's carefully crafted horror.

She moved toward a patch of ferns. Her boots sank into damp mulch, which released a faint, mossy scent.

Two minutes later, she spotted self-styled investigators perched on a fallen log. One had a shiny phone rig balanced on a tripod, while another rummaged through a backpack stuffed with extra lenses. Their hushed excitement made them oblivious to any warnings about the cryptid. A tall man among them waved toward her. "Hey, you with the feds?" he called. "That Bigfoot is real, right?" Mara kept her voice steady. "You need to leave this area. I'm not repeating myself." She saw their skeptical glances. One woman shook her head and pointed her camera at Mara as if she wanted a statement. Mara turned away. She tapped her communicator. "Link, can you jam as many local data streams as possible?"

Link's sigh crackled in her earpiece. "I'll do what I can, but these folks have hotspots, phone boosters, you name it. Carter's broadcast is pulling record numbers. If he's close, he might be tethering them to his own feed to ramp this up." Mara accepted that they would never block everything. Vale had always been careful with his signal distribution. He wanted the biggest possible audience.

A deputy's voice echoed toward her from somewhere near the grove's edge. Mara edged forward and stepped around a large cedar that bore an acorn-sized spiral carving. Frustration welled again at how orchestrated this was. Vale had teased the public with a slow trickle of images, fueling curiosity and turning a quiet forest into a stage.

She caught a glimpse of him through a gap in the trunks. He wore a hooded coat with a handheld camera pointed outward and a calm posture. A single lens glinted. One more broadcast from him would spark new hashtags and more believers. She lowered her stance to avoid alerting him. The cryptid could appear at any time after it sensed the watchers' energy, the fresh rumors, or the carved sigils. Mara crept behind a gnarled root and raised her binoculars.

Vale did not appear concerned about stealth. Mara had no idea when or how he had entered the premises. But the fact that he was here filming was not his biggest worry. He angled his camera upward to capture the lattice of spiral etchings near the tree's midpoint. A passing deputy raised a hand while trying to shoo Vale away, but the watchers behind him had their cameras rolling. Vale stepped around the deputy and beckoned the onlookers to follow. Mara swore under her breath and keyed her comm. "Finch, how strong is the cryptid's baseline now? I need a number." Finch replied in a subdued voice, "We're at a ninety percent threshold, which is extremely high. That means it's probably bigger than we last estimated, or more aggressive. It is hard to say which."

All right, enough.

She keyed the comm again. "Finch, see if you can remote-hijack Vale's stream. Break it or scramble it. Link, keep suppressing local signals as best you can. Skyhook, if you have a clear shot on Vale from overhead, let me know." She paused as she glanced at the stumbling civilians in the distance. "On second thought, wait for my mark. Too many bystanders."

She advanced quietly with her rifle held tight and scanned for Vale's hooded silhouette. She heard a deputy yelling, "You all need to move back." The watchers' voices overlapped into a dull roar of speculation. Mara crept past a cluster of ferns and found herself only twenty paces from Vale. He angled his camera at a tall trunk carved with multiple spirals. A few watchers with phone rigs hung back, filming him. She felt the energy surge from their collective belief.

Her finger slid closer to her carbine's trigger guard. She wasn't sure how fast the cryptid might come crashing in. The thermite bombs ringed the big stump at the heart of the grove, but Finch had stressed that the anchor needed a direct blast to destroy it. If the creature or the watchers got in the way, the entire plan would become a disaster. She tried to think of a safe way to lure Vale out of the grove, somewhere with fewer cameras. He seemed determined to stay in this ring of cedars.

Vale shifted, glancing around with the casual air of someone who wanted to be seen. The swirling pattern on a trunk behind him caught the morning light. He tapped the bark, then angled his camera again. Mara exhaled quietly, edging behind a large root. Two watchers pointed in her direction, possibly noticing her figure. Vale saw them wave, paused, and turned. Mara stayed low, pressing herself against the trunk.

Link hissed in her ear: "He's definitely streaming something. The feed is going viral. People are commenting like crazy. They think a physical showdown is coming." Mara gritted her teeth. She recognized that if she moved on Vale now, the watchers might rush forward for a better angle. That would be the exact moment the cryptid would love to appear, fueled by their collective hype. She needed backup or a quick distraction to get Vale alone.

Then a new voice rose from deeper in the grove: "Where's the proof, Vale?" A few watchers snickered. Vale pivoted, camera in hand, and motioned them closer. The spectacle was building. Mara whispered, "Skyhook, set down in that clearing we scouted. I'll try to herd Vale that way. Finch, keep an eye on the belief metrics. If the cryptid shows up, ping me immediately."

She heard the faint hiss of the VTOL descending. Branches

rustled from the gust of wind created by its thrusters. Hidden behind the trunk, Mara took a brief moment to check her weapon's sedation darts, though she doubted they would stop the cryptid this time. She also double-checked her extra magazines, aware that if Vale ran, she had to chase him quickly.

Creeping forward, she peeked around the trunk again and saw Vale inch deeper into the grove. She could tell by his body language that he planned something dramatic, likely wanting the crowd to swarm in. Another man stepped forward, camera out, yelling excitedly, "This is it, right? Show us if you're not messing with us." Vale just smiled, then raised his camera as if to capture the entire ring of watchers.

Mara took a risk and tiptoed closer. She considered calling out to the deputy to evacuate anyone too close to the center, but the deputy was already arguing with a cluster of obstinate onlookers. A beep in her ear signaled a message from Finch. His voice was subdued: "Mara, the cryptid's amplitude is at critical. This entire area is soaked with hype. If Vale streams anything else, it might appear." She recognized it as the final warning before chaos struck. Her boots crunched softly on a layer of needles. She inhaled, set her shoulders, and stared at Vale, who was now only a dozen steps away.

Feeling forced to act, she stepped from behind the trunk. He turned his head and saw her, his camera lens glinting. Their eyes locked across a short gap. The watchers stirred uneasily, their smartphones raised in every direction. Vale's mouth quirked in a half smile. Mara thought, "He wants me to make this public." She tightened her grip on the rifle and took a step forward.

Before she could speak, Link's voice hummed in her earpiece: "Bad news, Mara. Another large crowd arrived from the slope. They're filming each other too. There is no sign of the cryptid yet, but it cannot be far." She shifted her stance and gauged whether she had a window to grab Vale quietly. He seemed content to let the cameras run. She wondered how many thousands of viewers had already tuned in.

Vale angled away and slipped behind a large cedar carved with fresh spirals near the base. He led the crowd somewhere and knew she was on his tail. Mara exhaled sharply and moved after him. He was fast, disappearing behind the thick trunk. A swirl of murmurs swept through the watchers. Mara snapped a quick look behind her to ensure no onlookers trailed too close. At least the deputy had corralled a few.

She pushed on, weaving through elbows and phone screens. Vale's shape reappeared a few steps ahead, half shrouded by leaves. She paused behind a greenish stump and steadied her approach. The hush of the crowd made her tension spike. Vale seemed poised for his final reveal. Mara clenched her jaw, aware that the cryptid could crash in from any side and turn watchers into victims.

Link chimed in: "We cannot jam his broadcast effectively. He has hopped to multiple backup channels. People are urging him to push forward. This is exactly what he wants." Mara's pulse hammered. She remembered how in earlier incidents Vale had teased glimpses of the cryptid until it attacked, leaving terror in its wake.

One more step and she spotted Vale. He stood near an old signpost just inside the grove's main boundary. A frustrated deputy waved watchers back, but they fixated on Vale's camera. Skyhook's voice came in: "I'm down in that clearing if you need extraction. Say the word." Mara nodded to herself.

Vale's manner was unnervingly confident. He held the camera high for a slow pan, letting people see the etched spirals and the towering cedar. His hood cast a shadow across his expression. The watchers hovering nearby looked entranced by the spectacle, ignoring any notion of danger.

Mara felt her chest tighten. This scenario was a tinderbox. She planned to keep Vale in sight until the others arrived to help.

She lifted her rifle again, intending to warn him that he was out of time. Then Finch's urgent tone broke over the comm: "Mara, the cryptid's signature just jumped. Be ready."

Vale pivoted and stepped behind an enormous trunk that nearly dwarfed him. He flicked his hand to gesture his devotees to hang back. Mara steadied herself. She had to stop him from turning this into a bloodbath. She moved with deliberate care, passing thick brush and ignoring the stares of watchers who dared approach.

She could see Vale's back in partial silhouette as the overhead light caught his camera lens. He filmed the swirling patterns carved overhead before posting an announcement online. The thought made her stomach coil with anger. She hoped that Link would hamper the feed enough to keep new viewers away. Still, the crowd in the grove was too large. Even if the broadcast ended, dozens of phones captured the scene. Vale had set the stage perfectly. Mara resolved not to let him throw the final switch.

Her feet crunched on pine needles as she advanced, unwilling to lose him again. Her comm crackled. "Mara, new arrivals on the eastern slope." She closed her eyes. More watchers, more phones. She tightened her grip on her carbine and pressed on until Vale had nowhere to go. If she had to drag him out of the grove to stop the final show, so be it.

She peeked around the trunk, searching for his hooded figure. He had vanished behind a thick cedar. Faint chatter drifted from the watchers, uncertain whether to follow him or stay put. Her pulse pounded in her ears. Something about Vale's calm disregard felt ominous. She set her jaw, each step steady, her gaze fixed on the spot where she had last seen him.

She spotted him deeper in the grove, content to remain in the cameras' crosshairs. A wave of muttering rose from the watchers as their phones tilted upward to capture Vale filming spiral carvings. Mara drew a steady breath and promised herself he would not lure more people into danger. Finch's updates warned that the cryptid might appear as hype reached its peak.

Vale raised his lens to the canopy, probably recording the swirling patterns etched along a towering trunk. His posture radiated the quiet confidence of someone completing a personal masterpiece. Mara followed in silence, determined to stop him before he used the watchers as pawns. She stepped behind the next trunk and paused. Link's voice crackled. "Heads up, Mara. He's boosting the feed again."

She braced herself. Vale drifted out of sight, slipping behind another cedar. Ignoring the startled whispers of the watchers, she advanced once more. The next move might decide whether they could contain the cryptid or watch it rampage across the grove. Mara shifted her weight and pressed on, ready for whatever final trick Vale planned. She would not let him turn this into a global spectacle of fear.

CHAPTER NINETEEN

Twilight settled across the grove, draping gray shadows through the towering cedars. Mara watched her portable searchlights create a wide perimeter around the carved stump. The air, smelling of wet bark and old needles, felt heavy. Skyhook's voice via earpiece confirmed aerial support from the VTOL hovering above. Civilian onlookers drawn by rumor and Vale's hype pressed against the makeshift barricade, ignoring deputies' calls to stay back.

Mara had followed Vale, who was half-hidden and camera-ready, orchestrating the scene like a theater performance. Her frustration simmered. Confronting him now would only fuel the crowd's frenzy. A deputy rushed over, reporting more thrill-seekers breaching the perimeter to the south. Mara directed him to scare them off, warning of active charges in the area, which was a necessary exaggeration to ensure their safety.

The sonic lures shifted to a discordant, throbbing pulse. Link's voice came through comms: "Strong hits on the boundary. Cameras show a silhouette... Might be the creature, might be Vale playing games." The belief charts spiked further. Mara took position near the stump, her EM-Coil Carbine ready. She could feel the electric buzz in the air fed by the crowd's nervous energy.

A scatter of pine needles rustled, then parted. A shape the size of a moose slid through the haze. White bone plating caught a stray beam of light. A startled cry went up from someone beyond the barricade. Phones rose in unison. Mara's stomach tightened. She remembered how the creature had seemed smaller days ago, more uncertain. Now it looked bigger, chest wide and shoulders bristling with bone ridges.

"Skyhook, confirm." Mara said. "Confirmed visual." Skyhook replied from overhead. "We also see Carter Vale panning the camera side to side. He's definitely streaming." Mara gritted her teeth. "Understood." She murmured a few instructions into her mic, then advanced two steps toward the stump. Civilians at the barricade struggled to see the monster, so some drifted even closer. Another irritated command from the sheriff's deputies rang out, but it did nothing to stop those who wanted a better shot.

She needed the beast closer to the stump for the thermite to do its job. Link's voice piped in again. "I'm going to dial up the lure's power. Brace yourself."

The noise ramped to a harsh beat, and the creature let out a low growl that vibrated through Mara's boots. She heard branches snapping. On her left, Finch hissed in frustration at a new spike on his screen, describing how every snippet of video posted in real time was fanning more interest. She prayed their partial data scrubs were at least limiting the spread even if they had not shut it down.

A sudden hush fell over the clearing. The cryptid stepped forward, revealing the ridges of hard bone on its back and arms. Its eyes glowed in the artificial lights, and thick muscles bunched across its torso. Mara caught a glimpse of the spiral carved into its chest, a twisted brand that pulsed faintly. It is a walking symbol, she thought. The more they believe, the stronger it gets.

She eyed the stump and considered the hidden thermite. It would ignite soon.

Vale's camera lens angled to capture the monster's approach. His stance suggested confidence in his twisted plan. The onlookers cried out in awe and terror. One man stumbled forward, phone extended, desperate for a close-up shot. Mara snapped at him, "Get back." He froze, eyes wide, then scrambled behind a deputy. The cryptid snarled, but it stayed fixated on the stump as if the carved anchor beckoned.

Mara signaled Link with a quick gesture. The next wave of sonic pulses began, but the creature barely reacted. It raised its head, flared its nostrils, then clamped its gaze on a pair of bystanders who were too close. She cursed under her breath and motioned Finch to her side. She whispered, "We have to force it in. If it charges those idiots, we lose the advantage." Finch tapped more commands, adjusting the pattern of the lure to draw the beast left, away from the crowd.

Skyhook announced from the VTOL, "I can swing the spotlight to corral it if needed." "Do it," Mara said. A bright shaft of light cut through the dark, raking across the cryptid's flank. The beast rumbled low in its chest, shifting toward the stump as if seeking relief from the glare. It stomped closer and the ground seemed to shiver. The watchers near the barricade finally started backing up as they grasped how massive it was compared to a human silhouette.

Mara's hands tensed around the carbine. She was prepared to fire sedation darts if it veered toward the crowd, though Finch had cautioned that the creature was likely too strong now for a mild dosage to drop it. They had prepared for every possibility. She spotted Link perched behind a portable console near the edge of the clearing. He gave her a nod: everything was set to blow if necessary.

Vale took a few daring steps forward. He described the cryptid to his streaming viewers as though narrating a spectacle.

His voice carried in the hush. Mara heard him proclaim that viewers were about to witness a living, breathing legend. She debated telling him to shut up, but she chose not to feed his performance.

A series of clicks from the deeper woods suggested more watchers possibly with other cameras or overhead drones. Finch had jammed certain frequencies, but that still left enough band-width for phone streams. Mara's gut twisted. They had to act now or the crowd might never leave alive.

She raised her gloved hand, signaling a readiness call. Finch readied the remote in his bag, the one that would prime the ther-mite. She needed the cryptid square in the center of that stump ring. Just a few more feet would guarantee that the blasts struck true. The creature paused, scanning the lights. The rumble in its throat rattled the air.

A heavy impact shook the ground as the beast lowered its front limbs and prowled a step closer. Its eyes glinted in the searchlights, and Mara saw the carved stump reflected in that dark gaze. A fresh wave of voices rippled across the onlookers. Panic mingled with excitement. She wished the entire crowd would realize how lethal this was.

She inched sideways, aiming her carbine at the creature's broad flank. "Finch, you got full readiness on those charges?"

"In position." Finch muttered. "Thermite armed. Say the word."

Skyhook's spotlight tracked the monster's bony plates. Muscles rippled beneath that natural armor. Claws scored deep into the soft forest floor, leaving fresh grooves. Link's sonic lures shifted pitch. An eerie whine cut straight to Mara's nerves. Through the haze of overlapping lights, she watched the cryptid tense as if it were about to lunge.

Anxious figures at the barricade held their breath. The hush deepened. Then a single voice at the back chanted the cryptid's rumored name. Someone else took up the call as if they were summoning it. Mara tried to ignore that surreal moment. They are feeding it even now.

Vale's camera lens glinted. He whispered something that Mara couldn't catch, though she guessed it was a line meant for his loyal viewers. He shifted his angle to capture the cryptid's entire frame. Every second of it fueled more online chatter, which Finch claimed propelled the monster's power curve. Mara kept her aim steady.

The beast rumbled a deep, guttural noise, then advanced until it reached the edge of the searchlight ring. Its bone plating shimmered under the beams, giving onlookers a sickeningly clear view. Another wave of phones lifted, bright screens capturing each second. The moment felt razor-thin, every breath balanced between chaos and the plan they had laid out.

Mara steadied herself with a final inhale. She flicked the safety off her carbine with a click that seemed too loud in the hush. She saw Vale's camera tip upward, focusing on her for a single heartbeat. Then he swiveled back to the creature, apparently eager for the main event. She studied the cryptid's body angle. Its eyes locked on the spiral carving scrawled on the stump.

A primal howl broke from its jaws, echoing across the grove. A few watchers shrieked and scrambled away. Some still tried to film. Mara drew a line of sight that placed the monster and stump in the same frame. She threw a quick glance to Finch, who tightened his grip on the detonator.

Something cracked in the undergrowth. The beast's hackles rose, and it turned left in a stiff motion. The watchers gasped, uncertain if it would charge them or move closer to the anchor. Vale leaned forward, perched on the tips of his toes, and focused the camera. Mara's pulse thundered in her ears.

She took a slow step to encourage the cryptid, creeping to the right so it would follow the arc of the lure's hum. Her heart hammered. The next movement could seal everything.

The creature's eyes flashed. It lowered its head. Mara raised her carbine, exhaling as she prepared for it to cross into the kill zone. Vale's camera remained locked on the beast. The watchers braced, anxious for the show. The hush settled again, charged with raw tension. The cryptid's shoulders lifted. Its claws tore furrows in the dirt. Everything narrowed to that single moment when it finally lunged toward the spiral stump, drawn by that maddening siren call.

Mara's muscles coiled, ready to spring. She wanted it a few more yards closer. She braced herself, hearing Finch's unsteady breathing behind her. A faint beep from Link's console signaled another spike in online chatter. The cryptid roared, teeth bared, and stomped forward. Searchlights blossomed off its plated back. Phones lit up from dozens of vantage points. Vale inched forward too, as if he craved a perfect shot.

All of it converged on that ring of tarps, carefully hidden. Mara took a half step back, finger hovering by the trigger. She scanned the spectators, silently urging them to back away. The beast drew a ragged inhale, sounding like wind through broken reeds. Then it raised its head high, letting out a thunderous challenge that pounded through the grove.

Mara exhaled, one thought guiding all others. We do this fast, or we're done. She lifted a hand, signaled Finch to be ready, and fixed her gaze on the monstrous shape about to cross into the trap. The crowd stared in fascination. Carter Vale stooped for an even better visual, broadcasting to many viewers.

A raw growl tore through the air. The cryptid gathered itself and charged, closing the last gap between it and the spiral stump. Mara's heart hammered with each thud of its clawed feet. "It's in the ring," Link snapped in her earpiece.

She sighted along her carbine. Finch tensed behind her, remote in hand. Vale aimed his camera, capturing its approach. At that instant, the cryptid reached the carved stump's outer edge, shoulder ridges scraping a searchlight stand. Shock rippled through the watchers, and some began to flee.

Mara tightened her grip and swore under her breath. The beast's red eyes locked on the anchor. She saw muscles flex and adrenaline spike in her veins. She inhaled once.

Then everything seemed to hold still.

CHAPTER TWENTY

The cryptid emerged with a thunderous bellow, stomping across broken branches and flattening undergrowth. It towered above the watchers, bone plates gleaming under the floodlights. Mara's mouth went dry. It was larger than she had ever seen. Online chatter seemed to have fed its growth. She heard frantic gasps from civilians scattered around the grove, some jockeying for camera angles of their own.

Deputies shouted for people to back up, but curiosity won out. One influencer wearing a thick coat stumbled too close. The monster's massive limb lashed out, ripping a chunk of bark off a cedar trunk as it swung. Mara dashed forward holding her carbine in one hand. She caught the influencer by the collar and yanked him out of the path of a sweeping claw.

"Get clear," she snapped, helping him scramble behind a leaning searchlight. He stared at her with panic in his eyes, then bolted toward the outer ring of onlookers. Mara recentered herself and scanned the cryptid's dorsal plates for a clean shot. She flicked the carbine's safety off and thumbed the sedation dart selector.

Skyhook's voice crackled in her earpiece. "Got the spotlight on its left flank. Draw it toward the stump."

"Copy," Mara said. She glanced at the massive cedar stump behind the creature. The swirling spiral was visible even from where she stood. She could bet the anchor was surging with power.

She traced the cryptid's path as it stomped past a cluster of panicked thrill seekers. A second spotlight blazed overhead courtesy of the hovering VTOL. The beast snarled at that harsh beam, shoulders tensing. Mara fired two sedative darts into its side. Both landed but the cryptid barely slowed.

Finch came through her comm. "Those darts aren't going to cut it. The creature's scale has gone beyond our earlier dosage."

Mara kept moving, hugging the trunk of an old cedar. "Got it," she muttered. She heard Link over the radio calling for deputies to regroup. The plan hinged on forcing the cryptid to the stump where they could trigger the charges. The crowd was making it impossible to line up a direct path.

Ahead, Vale circled with his camera keeping a measured distance from the beast as it smashed another floodlamp. Metal clattered across the ground, sparking for a moment before the light died. Mara gritted her teeth and glanced around for improvised solutions. The cryptid roared, shaking the branches overhead. She felt debris rain down on her vest.

Deputies tried to corral bystanders away from the core of the grove, urging everyone to evacuate. Some people listened, drawn by the rising threat. Others lingered, desperate to witness a final confrontation. Mara wanted to shout curses at them all. Instead she signaled to one deputy with a curt nod and pointed toward an unguarded gap near the stump.

She sprinted across a patch of churned soil, bracing the carbine close. A shallow crater spoke to the beast's strength. Branches and splinters lay everywhere and the reek of raw sap filled the air. A bystander on her left coughed at the gritty haze swirling in the fog. She ignored him and refocused on the cryptid's flank.

The monster plowed through a ring of smaller cedars, splintering bark. Mara fired another pair of darts, aiming for exposed flesh near the creature's front shoulder. It roared at the sting and snapped its jaws. Through the steam of its breath, she saw that the sedation was too weak to slow it. Each online feed probably fueled it more.

Skyhook's voice returned. "Be ready with the lure. We'll try to push it from above."

Mara tugged a small disc from her belt, the sonic lure. She twisted the dial and watched the device's indicator glow. That abrasive whine could set the beast off, but it might drag it exactly where they needed it. Finch shouted something about a second wave of onlookers arriving near the perimeter, but she tuned him out. This moment demanded focus.

She tossed the lure underhand toward the stump. It landed near the spiral insignia carved into the wood. A piercing hum spilled into the night, and the cryptid jerked its head as if drawn by the noise. Mara exhaled and stepped back to lure it further inward with her presence. The monster angled toward her. Its black eyes shone with raw aggression.

Another thrill-seeker tried filming from a vantage behind the stump. The cryptid whipped its arm out and smashed the remains of a fallen cedar trunk. Splinters launched in all directions, and Mara ducked. One deputy shouted for a medic, though she spotted only superficial wounds on the few who had scattered to the side.

Carter Vale's quiet grin unnerved her. He looked enthralled, as though each bit of destruction was a triumphant scene in his script. She wanted to yell at him. She wanted to drag him away in cuffs, but the cryptid moved again and pulled her attention back to survival.

"Positions," Link said over comms. "It's approaching the stump. Thermite is standing by."

Mara inched along the perimeter to ensure no one else threatened to get in the crossfire. The monster's broad back faced Skyhook's spotlight now, which offered a partial blind spot for Vale's camera. Yet Vale adjusted his angle, determined not to miss a thing.

Branches and brush cracked under the cryptid's feet. That rhythmic hum from the lure pulsed against Mara's eardrums. She marveled at how the creature's body looked bigger than the last time they engaged. Online hype loves this. She forced the thought aside and gritted her teeth.

Everything erupted when the cryptid took a sudden sidestep, nearly trampling a deputy who had run in to help escort a bystander. Mara rushed to intercept and tucked her weapon to the side. She shoved the bystander forward and hooked her arm around the deputy's vest. The creature's giant claw swiped at them and sliced the air just inches from her face. She felt the shock of that near miss as a rush of warmth across her cheek.

She rolled to the ground and shoved the deputy away, ignoring gravel that rasped her forearms. Her carbine clattered. She could just make out Finch's voice in her earpiece, but she heard only her own breathing. That was too close, she thought, and struggled to stand. Overhead, the cryptid bellowed again and wove dangerously near the stump.

Skyhook angled the VTOL's spotlight in a harsh beam, pinning the monster against the cedar trunk. The lure hummed. Mara staggered forward, retrieving her carbine. She double-checked the sedation chamber even though she knew it was useless. The cryptid swung an arm at the stump. Wood splinters flew as its claws raked across the carved spiral.

She activated her comm. "Get everyone out. This is about to blow."

"Roger." Link said. "Ten seconds once you confirm the big guy's in range."

Vale's camera lens glittered with reflected light. He inched closer, trying to catch the cryptid's face in a perfect shot. Mara felt her frustration boil over. She took a slow breath. She had no time to drag him out of there. The creature pivoted, rattling its plated shoulders as it advanced on the lure's location. She saw the swirling mark on the stump and realized it was glowing from the combined energy of the watchers.

Her vision wobbled for a moment as adrenaline spiked. She steadied the carbine, though it no longer served to sedate. If necessary, she would draw its attention to protect any onlookers. She heard Finch in her earpiece. "The anchor's supercharged. Link has the charges armed."

The cryptid stepped directly in front of the carved stump, lifting its bone-plated arms in a posture that screamed rage. Celestial beams from the searchlights rimmed its silhouette, accenting every segment of plating. The monstrous shape snarled at the sonic lure, then smashed it. The hum faltered, replaced by mechanical shrieks. Mara braced to see whether those shrieks would draw it a few steps farther into range.

Several spectators huddled behind a partially downed cedar on the opposite side. A deputy herded them out, waving a flashlight in frantic arcs. Carter Vale slipped behind a split trunk, rolling film. Mara glimpsed him wiping sweat off his brow with one hand while he zoomed in with the other.

Her lungs felt tight as she realized how quickly belief soared when so many were filming. Argus data must be off the charts. She suppressed an urge to swear.

We're almost done.

She took a single step forward, gripping her carbine, scanning for any last stragglers. The cryptid roared. Its massive claws slammed into the cedar trunk behind the stump, showering them in a storm of bark chips.

Mara caught a glimpse of the anchor's spiral. It pulsed in time with the creature's rage, feeding on the eyes locked onto it from all sides. Link's voice cut through the chaos. "Mara, can you confirm we're ready to go?"

She adjusted her stance. "I confirm. Ignite the charges on my mark."

The cryptid twisted its head as if smelling the thermite. Mara inched sideways, not wanting to draw it away from the kill zone. Another deputy signaled the all-clear on the far side, so she raised a hand in acknowledgment. Then she watched the creature brace its arms on the stump as though transfixed by the carved lines. She imagined Vale's grin behind that camera.

Her breath caught in her throat when the cryptid bared its teeth. The ring of searchlights pinned it in place, but it was thrashing, grunting, and smashing at the stump's base. She heard the structure crack and saw the spiral's edges split. Her heart hammered at the possibility that the stump could break before the thermite fully destabilized it, but there was no time to hesitate.

At last, Link's voice came in her earpiece. "We're set. Just say the word."

Mara tightened her grip on the carbine. She glanced at Vale's silhouette and frowned. He was capturing every second, hype pouring onto the web and fueling the beast even in these final moments. She cursed under her breath, flicked her comm switch, and braced herself to give the command. Her mouth felt dry, but the chance to end it was too vital to waste.

Finch shouted in alarm, reminding her that they had only moments before the cryptid tore the stump apart. She signaled to Link with a clipped tone. "On my count. Three...two...one... Mark."

She glimpsed Carter Vale's face in that instant. He looked transfixed as though the entire scene fed his grand narrative. But one question bugged Mara: if Vale had spent a lot of time conjuring this cryptid, why was he grinning at its destruction? The cryptid roared again and smashed aside a half-broken searchlight. Mara stayed poised and held her breath while Link prepared to trigger the devices. One more second. Her mind buzzed with everything that had led them here.

Then she heard Link's final pronouncement in her ear. "Engaging."

Mara braced herself behind a cedar trunk, pressed one gloved hand against the rough bark, and steadied the carbine in the other. She stared at the monster's shape, ignoring the cameras and Vale's fervent filming. The reflection from the searchlights made her squint. She tasted copper on her lip where she had bitten down a second earlier.

A faint beep signaled the final count. She exhaled, knees bent, and hoped the thermite would do its job before the cryptid tore someone apart. Vale kept filming. Bystanders huddled at a safer distance, watching in morbid fascination. Mara's earpiece clicked.

Link's voice came through. "Igniting now."

She swallowed her nerves and hunched low in preparation for the explosion. Smoke and sparks would fill the grove and neutralize the anchor completely. A coil of tension rippled up her spine as she kept her gaze on the cryptid. This had to work. It was the only way to clip its power and erase the twisted spiral fueling it.

The monster twitched, glowering at the stump. Mara steadied her stance. She could almost feel the swirl of viral attention. Then the pressure in the air shifted. Her grip tightened on the carbine, her heart thudding. She saw Carter Vale's camera angle shift, capturing her at the edge of the grove. She forced down a snarl of frustration aimed at him.

Link counted down softly. Mara braced, certain that every second of chaos was about to get louder. She held her breath. The final click in her earpiece confirmed there was no turning back.

CHAPTER TWENTY-ONE

Cornered and shaken, the cryptid howled to draw attention. It lunged forward and struck the ground with thick forelimbs. Fragments of soil scattered. Onlookers shouted. Mara dashed to the far side of the stump and pressed flat against the trunk, the remote detonator in her hand. Her breath caught when the creature screeched again. The sound vibrated through her bones.

She peered around for Vale. There was no sign. She gave a quick nod to the deputy on the perimeter, who was keeping two streamers from entering the clearing. Then Link's frantic voice crackled through her earpiece. "Mara, that video feed is at peak numbers. It's now or never."

"Finch, status."

"Holding steady. The lines are connected." Finch replied. "Say the word."

"On my mark," she said.

She clenched the remote's arming switch. The cryptid stomped once more and shook the stump. She glimpsed movement overhead as the VTOL angled its light. Moments later, the beast swung a massive limb at a cluster of searchlights beyond the stump. Metal stands toppled with a crash and sparks fizzled near the base.

Mara pressed the button. She heard the thermite charges ignite. A flash of white-hot brilliance erupted beneath the tarp. Heat lashed the air and the stump's center glowed. Liquid light poured down its sides and the spiral carving vanished beneath the molten rush.

The cryptid screeched. It threw its head back as bone plating cracked with each tremor. Vibrations rippled through the clearing and watchers crouched behind logs. The air reeked of cedar and scorched earth. Mara covered her mouth with her sleeve as the stump collapsed under the intense reaction. Ash and sparks vaulted skyward, dancing in the glare.

She felt a blast of heat that forced her to stumble backward. The cryptid's body contorted as if the meltdown at the stump had severed its link to the living world. Its plated exterior peeled open to reveal swirling embers. Then it dissolved into columns of ash. Chunk by chunk, the remains collapsed. For a tense moment, the clearing filled with harsh noise as steaming fragments sizzled on the ground.

Mara caught sight of Carter Vale ducking behind an uprooted tree at the perimeter. She took a step toward him, but swirling ash stung her eyes and she lost sight of him. "Skyhook," she barked into her earpiece. "We have a runner on the west side. Check for Vale."

"Copy," Skyhook said. The VTOL's searchlight swept the area, illuminating scattered crowds.

Mara coughed and lowered her sleeve. She waved at Finch, who rushed forward with a handheld sensor to measure residue. A deputy jogged by with a fire extinguisher, though the thermite's final glow quickly waned. Soot coated the yard-wide crater where the stump had stood.

"It's gone," Finch said quietly, stepping to Mara's side. "I'm reading no further entity activity."

Mara nodded, eyes watering. "You did good. Everyone else, watch for Vale."

A wave of relief rippled through watchers at the perimeter. A few daredevils broke from cover and aimed their cameras at the crater despite the choking air. Deputies yelled for them to fall back. The charred remains of the stump produced a noxious haze overhead. The cryptid's final ashes settled into scattered lumps at the stump's base and left a smoldering impression of its spiral lines.

Mara locked her carbine. Her gloved hand trembled. That massive creature had vanished in a burst of flames but the man who conjured it was still out there. She turned to Finch. "We need a location on Vale's van. Now."

Finch wiped sweat from his brow. "Link is scanning license plates at the northern checkpoint. We'll see what we can find but he might have snuck around us."

"Keep me posted. I'm not letting him vanish." Mara pressed her lips together and searched the treeline for movement.

A few feet away, an exhausted deputy coughed into his shoulder. "We're clearing stragglers from the center, ma'am. We'll gather statements from anyone we can catch."

"Appreciate it." She stepped toward the scorched crater and surveyed the site. The cryptid's last ragged calls still echoed in her mind. Onlookers were already sharing highlights on social media and ignoring the smoldering debris around them. She tuned out their shouts.

Skyhook landed the VTOL in a clearing to the east. She stepped out in her flight suit and nodded at Mara. "No sign of Vale from above. He could have joined the crowd or circled through those side pathways. Flashing the spotlight turned up nothing."

Mara tilted her head at the swirl of disturbed air near the crater. "He's slippery. If we can't pin him down tonight we'll track him tomorrow. He won't get far."

Skyhook gestured at the crater. "At least that thing won't rise from the ashes. The stump anchor is toast."

Mara's gaze fell on the molten stump. "We ended it here so that's something. Thanks for the cover."

Skyhook gave a tight smile. "Better than facing it alone."

Finch walked closer, analyzing his handheld sensor. "Residual energy levels are dropping. The crowd is still talking about it online, but with the anchor gone the entity can't re-form."

"Which means mission accomplished for now." Mara's eyes swept the perimeter again. She noticed groups of watchers scurrying off, hoods up, phones out. At least half of them wore big grins as though they had witnessed a spectacle. She found that reaction infuriating.

She tapped her earpiece. "Link, do we have any final leads? Or should we start cleanup?"

Link sighed over the comm. "No luck picking up Vale's phone signature. I might have to run a deeper search once we regroup at the command trailer. The crowd is messing with the feed."

"Check the usual truck stops. He likes to hide out there." Mara muttered. She stepped aside as a deputy escorted a trembling man to an ambulance. Thin lines of soot streaked his cheeks. Others coughed behind them, some stumbling away from the crater's fumes.

Finch knelt to scoop a charred piece of cedar near the stump's base. He tucked it in a sample bag for further study. Mara gave him a small nod. "I'll coordinate with the sheriff about local coverage." She paused. "I'm surprised no one got themselves killed."

Skyhook sighed. "A few might be too rattled to appreciate that. Anyway, we should pack up. The meltdown took care of the cryptid, so recontainment isn't necessary."

Mara turned away from the crater. "Right. I'll handle the immediate handoff with the sheriff. Finch, help me finalize statements from the local volunteers. Then we regroup at the trailer."

She felt another spike of tension and half expected Vale to appear in the shadows. The memory of that monstrous presence lingered, but the forest smelled only of scorched sap and raw ash.

She strode toward the perimeter, picking her way past broken searchlights and scattered phone cases. The watchers parted to let her pass. One hopped forward with a question on his lips, but a deputy shoved him back. She glimpsed a grainy phone screen displaying a replay of the cryptid's final moments. Some website had already shared the meltdown footage. Great.

At the taped boundary, Sheriff Thomason waited with arms folded. His face was lined with exhaustion. "I suppose that's it."

She nodded. "Yes, the cryptid's gone. Vale escaped, but we'll chase him when we have a better lead."

He adjusted his hat, then looked across the clearing at the smoking remains of the stump. "It's a mess, but I'm glad you put an end to that creature."

She let out a quiet breath. "We had no other choice. We'll do a sweep for any other sigils in the morning. Thanks for your help with crowd control."

He shrugged. "I hope we didn't lose any idiots in that stampede. My deputies will hold the lines while you do your final checks."

Mara thanked him and motioned to Finch, who was reviewing sensor data. Together they approached the command trailer's temporary vantage. The official containment protocols demanded evidence collection, witness statements, and sweeping the vicinity for leftover anchor carvings. Some of that would have to wait until morning. Now the SRD had to confirm Vale's location or at least block his exit routes.

She paused at the edge of the trailer steps. "Finch, upload that raw sensor data. We'll see if the stump's meltdown neutralized all offshoots."

"On it." He hooked his device to a console.

Skyhook approached, carrying her pilot's helmet. "Link's

inside, trying to track Vale. I can do a quick pass in the VTOL if you want."

Mara glanced at the forest's dark outline. "Give it a try. He might still be in range."

Skyhook nodded and set off. Meanwhile, Finch's screen flickered with lines of data, each representing the baseline energy in the area. The lines plummeted after the thermite detonation. Mara watched for a moment then glanced at the clearing. Deputies guided the last watchers away from the stump. Embers still glowed under the ashen surface.

She stepped inside the trailer. Link was hunched over a workstation and scanned license plate logs. He shot her a look. "No match so far."

Mara placed a hand on the back of his chair. "Keep digging. He can't vanish into thin air."

Link pointed to a cluster of blips on the screen. "There are multiple vehicles with plates hidden by mud or deliberately obscured. It could be any of them."

"Run them anyway," she said. "We'll coordinate with highway patrol if he tries to slip out of state."

Link nodded. "You got it."

Outside, the VTOL engines lifted off once again, their beams shining across the treetops. She lowered her gaze to her hand on the carbine's grip.

Calm and no mistakes now.

After she checked sensor readings with Finch, she stepped down from the trailer to face the crater one last time. Smoke whirled in the moonlight. Deputies organized a barrier around the charred ground to keep onlookers out overnight. She kicked aside a broken camera stand and searched for clues Vale might have dropped.

Nothing. The meltdown site was a burned wreck but it was free of the cryptid. They had cut off its anchor at the root. She felt relief tempered by the knowledge that Vale's method could surface elsewhere if he got a chance to plant another sigil. She wanted to chase him but the immediate job was done.

She lowered her voice as Finch came up beside her. "You don't see any other hot spots on that readout?"

He shook his head. "No. This was the main anchor. The swirl patterns are gone. The internet might talk about it for days but the physical bond is severed."

Mara glanced around. "I'll rally the team for a final sweep, then we'll sign off with the sheriff."

She shouldered her gear and walked toward the deeper part of the forest, double-checking the perimeter. The hush of the watchers had died down, replaced by occasional murmurs or the crackle of shortwave radios. She took a few steps and scanned the trunks. No fresh spirals. No footprints matching Vale's usual boots.

A faint echo of relief vibrated along her nerves. She signaled to the deputies that the area was secured. Then she circled back to the trailer where Finch was logging a final note.

He gave her a quick nod. "We'll do a full gear pack in half an hour. I'll start analyzing residual data. Link's still searching for Vale's signature on the highways."

She stepped inside, flipped off her earpiece for a moment, and let the static hush in her head. She laid the EM-coil carbine on a side bench and unbuckled her vest.

The memory of that scorching meltdown lingered, seared in her mind. She had seen belief take monstrous form before, but this time the crowds and cameras poured so much energy into the cryptid that it threatened to become unstoppable. Only the thermite forced it to unravel. A wave of gratitude washed over her as she remembered Finch's calculations, Link's jamming attempts, and Skyhook's overhead cover. They had saved many lives.

She exhaled and switched her earpiece back on. "All right,

everyone. We'll wrap. Good work. We'll keep searching for Vale but the cryptid is neutralized. That's a win."

Mara pulled on her jacket, still shaken by the ordeal. At least this forest wouldn't see that creature again. She stepped outside and looked toward the smoldering stump site, satisfied that it posed no further threat.

Her hand tightened around the carbine's sling. Carter Vale might have slipped away, but she knew this fight wasn't over. She crossed the clearing and called for the team to finalize perimeter sweeps and coordinate with local authorities. Tomorrow she would examine every clue that led to Vale. For now they had closed this chapter of his grim spectacle.

She glanced around once more, nodded at a deputy closing the final gap in the barrier, and walked toward the glow of the SRD trailer. The thick haze of smoke and adrenaline still hung in the air, but she felt calm now that the cryptid was gone. She pressed her lips together and stepped through the trailer door, prepared to handle the aftermath.

CHAPTER TWENTY-TWO

The inferno that devoured his creation was, Carter Vale had to
admit, visually spectacular. From his meticulously chosen
vantage point, a shadowed declivity choked with sword ferns and
fallen cedar limbs at the very edge of the totem grove, he had an
unparalleled view of the pandemonium. His modified broadcast
camera, a high-definition marvel he had painstakingly assembled
from scavenged and specifically ordered parts, drank in every
flickering flame, every panicked face, and every billow of acrid
smoke clawing at the twilight sky. The air thrummed with a
symphony of chaos, with the crackling roar of the thermite
charges consuming the ancient stump, the distant approaching
wail of sirens, and the closer more satisfying chorus of human
fear, gasps, shouts, and the occasional high-pitched shriek.

His creature, the magnificent bone-plated terror he had
painstakingly coaxed into existence from the fertile ether of
collective belief, was dying. Or rather, unmaking. It thrashed in
the searing heat, its formidable form contorting and its roars
shifting from primal rage to bewildered agony as the sigil-carved
anchor that bound it to this plane was violently and systematically obliterated. Vale's face, mostly hidden by the deep cowl of

his mud-stained jacket, remained unreadable. He adjusted the camera's zoom to capture the balletic way the creature's plated shoulders peeled away and dissolved into embers that danced and died in the swirling updraft.

A part of him, the part that still clung to the vestiges of artistic pride, felt a pang. It had been such a perfect manifestation, more robust and more terrifyingly real than his previous smaller-scale experiments. The other part, the dominant calculating core of Carter Vale, suppressed that fleeting sentiment. This was not an end but a transition, a dramatic climax that would echo through the digital ether for weeks, months, or even years.

As the last recognizable fragment of the creature slumped into the incandescent ruin of the totem stump, a faint tremor passed through Vale's lips. It was not a smile of joy or a frown of despair. It was…appreciation. He could see the SRD agent Bishop even now, a silhouette of furious, frustrated action near the epicenter, her team fanning out to impose order on a scene that was chaotic. They were such predictable pawns, always reacting, always one step behind the narrative he so carefully wove. He watched them tend to the injured, their movements efficient but ultimately futile in the grand scheme. They thought they were containing a threat. They had no idea they were merely players in his far larger, far more ambitious production.

The world that had once forgotten him, that had relegated Carter Vale the author to the remainder bins and the dusty shelves of second-hand bookstores, would now remember Carter Vale the myth-maker. This spectacle, this visceral brush with the impossible, would be seared into their collective memory, and he, the unseen hand guiding the strings, would be the architect of that fear.

"The story." He whispered, his voice a dry, papery rustle lost in the crackle of the dying flames and the rising hysteria of the crowd, "isn't over. It's merely turning a page, my eager audience. A much, much darker page." His eyes, gleaming with feverish light in the reflected glow of the burning stump, scanned the panicked faces of the onlookers still huddled at the grove's edge. Their terror was palpable, a rich, intoxicating perfume. Yes, this act had concluded. But the show, his magnificent, terrifying show, would go on.

The sirens were closer now, their discordant wail slicing through the smoky air, an irritating punctuation mark to his otherwise perfect finale. Overhead, the thrumming beat of the SRD's VTOL grew louder, its powerful searchlight beginning to cut impatient swathes through the dissipating smoke and the dense canopy. Time to make his exit. The performance was complete, and the artist must now vanish before the stagehands grew too inquisitive.

Vale lowered his camera, the recording light blinking off with a soft click that seemed unnaturally loud in the sudden lull of the flames. He retracted the zoom lens with a practiced, gentle twist, his movements economical and precise despite the urgency of the moment. With the camera nestled securely in its padded shoulder bag, he melted back from his observation point, deeper into the embracing shadows of the ancient cedars. His escape route, chosen days ago, was a faint game trail that snaked away from the grove, bypassing the main access paths now likely swarming with deputies and persistent, foolhardy thrill-seekers.

He moved with the silent grace of a forest creature, his worn, mud-caked boots making barely a whisper on the damp carpet of pine needles and decaying leaves. He kept to the treeline, a fleeting shadow among deeper shadows. Clusters of onlookers, their faces pale and etched with terror and morbid fascination, were stumbling away from the smoldering grove, their phone screens held aloft like desperate beacons in the encroaching darkness. He passed a group huddled near a fallen log, their voices a low babble of "Did you see the size of it?" and "It just… fell apart!" Amateurs, he thought with a curl of his lip, so easily awed, so easily manipulated. Their belief was a crude, blunt instrument, but potent nonetheless.

A sheriff's deputy, younger than the rest, his face smudged with soot and tight with fear and adrenaline, swung a heavy-duty flashlight in a nervous arc. The beam sliced through the under-growth, illuminating a tangle of ferns just feet from where Vale had paused behind the massive, gnarled trunk of a lightning-struck hemlock. Vale froze and pressed himself flat against the rough, damp bark. The scent of ozone from the recent strike, still faint, filled his nostrils. A single bead of sweat, cold and sharp, traced a path down his neck, then disappeared beneath the collar of his hooded jacket. He didn't breathe. He didn't blink. He became another knot, another shadow in the forest's deep tapestry. The light lingered, swept back and forth, then with a grunt of frustration from the deputy moved on, its beam spearing the darkness further down the slope. Vale remained motionless for ten heartbeats, then resumed his silent retreat, a ghost in the periphery of their manufactured crisis.

Before he approached the grove for the final act, he took a small detour. Near the original campsite, where Jackson and Mia's little prank had so fortuitously provided the initial spark for this grand conflagration of belief, he planted a carefully curated piece of misdirection. He tucked a shred of neon-green tent fabric identical to the scraps Mara Bishop and her team had collected earlier beneath a moss-covered boulder that Finch's drones would have mapped. He even scuffed the earth around it, creating the illusion of a brief struggle. A little something for Bishop and her bloodhounds to sniff at, a false trail to lead them deeper into the labyrinth while he and his more valuable assets were long gone. It was a small detail, unnecessary perhaps, but Carter Vale prided himself on his attention to narrative structure. Every good story needed its red herrings.

He sidestepped a discarded strip of yellow police tape, its stark "CAUTION" a laughable understatement given the evening's events. A news van, its satellite dish swiveling skyward like a metallic carrion bird, was parked haphazardly on the muddy verge of what passed for an access path. He slipped behind it and joined a straggling group of self-proclaimed "cryptid hunters" making their hasty exit, their voices loud with tales of bravery and near-misses. Their chatter provided the perfect acoustic camouflage.

Further down the invisible logging trail, a path he had marked on his detailed topographical maps weeks ago, he veered sharply left, pushing through a thicket of salal and huckleberry bushes. Beneath a broad, low-hanging canopy of interwoven cedar branches that concealed it from view, he located the oilskin-wrapped satchel he had stashed earlier that day. His fingers steady and sure unfastened the leather buckles. Inside the satchel, nestled among spare high-capacity batteries, a compact water filter, and a vacuum-sealed pack of emergency rations, were his backup solid-state hard drives, pristine uncompressed copies of every second of footage, every surge in belief metrics, every terrified gasp from his adoring unwitting audience, and his most precious collection of spiral-bound notebooks.

He pulled out a notebook with a weathered dark faux-leather cover, already softened with use and embossed with a deeply pressed spiral sigil. A tight, wolfish grin touched his lips as he cradled it. This was where the true power lay. Not in the fleeting manifestations but in the meticulously documented methodology, the seeds of a dozen new legends, a hundred new nightmares, all waiting to be cultivated.

The camper van was exactly where he had left it, nestled deep within a small forgotten clearing, shielded from the main logging road by a dense screen of young hemlocks and a draped camouflage tarp that blended seamlessly with the forest floor. Dented, its once-white paint now a patchwork of primer, rust, and caked-on mud, its tinted windows were opaque with grime, reflecting the gloomy twilight like dead eyes. It was an ugly utilitarian beast, but it was his castle, his laboratory, his escape pod.

He slid into the driver's seat to the familiar scents of stale coffee, cheap cloying sweet air freshener (a futile attempt to mask gasoline fumes), and the metallic tang of ozone from his jury-rigged electronics a perverse welcome home. Papers scrawled with sigil variations, chaotic constellations of interconnected hashtags, and hastily sketched maps of ley lines and belief hotspots still littered the cracked dashboard. This was his true scriptorium. He paused before turning the key and peered through the grimy windshield. Through the dense lattice of trees, he could just discern the distant frantic pulse of emergency lights painting the smoke-filled sky above the now-silent grove. Fools, he thought with genuine but fleeting amusement in his eyes. They scurried about tending to superficial wounds and congratulating themselves on a hollow victory while he, the true artist and architect of their terror, was already miles away preparing his next act.

A sudden deafening roar of engines ripped through the quiet forest. Above the canopy, the SRD's VTOL, a monstrous predatory insect, materialized, its powerful searchlight knifing through the darkness and sweeping the logging road with brutal efficiency. Vale's hand froze on the ignition key. He killed the barely visible parking lights instantly and his breath hitched. The beam, a blinding white spear, painted the trees to his left and then swung with terrifying speed illuminating the hemlocks that shielded his van. He held his breath and tensed every muscle as a flicker of unwelcome fear sparked within him. The light seemed to linger for an eternity, pinning him in its glare and threatening to expose his sanctuary. Then, as quickly as it had appeared, the beam veered away and arced further down the logging road following the most obvious path of retreat. They hadn't seen him. Or perhaps, in their arrogance, they hadn't considered the possibility of such a mundane, well-camouflaged hiding place.

He waited until the percussive beat of the rotors had faded into the vast indifferent silence of the wilderness then, with a quiet click that sounded deafening in the enclosed space, he turned the key. The old engine, coaxed with a familiar grumble and a plume of acrid exhaust, coughed to life. Without headlights and relying on his intimate knowledge of this forgotten track and the faint ambient light filtering through the thinning canopy, Carter Vale guided the lumbering camper van deeper into the forest, a ghost slipping away from the scene of his triumphant, terrifying masterpiece.

The van bumped and swayed along a forgotten forest service road, its suspension groaning in protest with every rut and pothole. Miles now separated him from the smoldering chaos of the totem grove. The dashboard lights cast his face in eerie, shifting shadows of green and orange, making his features seem sharper, more predatory. He reached up and brushed the small hand-carved wooden spiral talisman that dangled from the rearview mirror with fingers stained by soot and the faint sticky residue of pine sap. It was a crude, almost primitive thing, whittled from a piece of lightning-struck cedar he had found deep in the Olympic Peninsula years ago and stained dark with a concoction of iron oxide and his own blood, a small symbolic offering. But its power, or rather the power it represented, the potential it unlocked, was immeasurable.

His mind, no longer consumed by the immediate logistics of escape and observation, drifted. Not to the recent inferno, nor to the grotesque beauty of his creature's unmaking, but further back, to a pivotal moment that shifted the course of his existence. The memory surfaced, sharp and crystalline despite the intervening years: a younger Carter Vale, not yet fully consumed by bitterness but already restless, hungry for something more than fleeting, fickle applause of the literary world. He saw himself hunched in the dimly lit, dust-choked archives of a small, forgotten county historical society in rural Maine, researching local folklore for a novel, another desperate attempt to recapture the elusive spark of his early success. The air in that cramped room had been thick with the scent of decaying paper, brittle leather bindings, and the faint, unsettling aroma of forgotten secrets.

He remembered the weight of the old, ledger-style journal in his hands, its calfskin cover cracked and brittle, its pages yellowed and foxed with age. It was the personal diary of a nineteenth-century clergyman, a man who had apparently dabbled in more than scripture, his entries a curious mix of theological musings and meticulously recorded local superstitions, tales of things that lurked in the deep, impenetrable woods of the northern frontier. And there, sketched repeatedly in the margins of a particularly dense, faded passage describing strange, unsettling occurrences near a ring of ancient standing stones, was the spiral. Not the precise, geometric spiral of a nautilus shell but a more organic, hypnotic swirl like a galaxy in miniature or a fingerprint of some vast, unseen intelligence. Primitive yes but undeniably potent, radiating a subtle, subliminal energy even from the faded ink. Accompanying these sketches were cryptic, barely legible annotations in a different, more hurried hand. Credendo Vides, belief gives it form. Historia carnem desiderat, the story craves flesh.

A shiver cold and electric traced its way down his spine then, a sensation he remembered with perfect clarity even now. It was not just the words but the conviction behind them, the unnerving certainty of that long-dead annotator. He had been skeptical of course. Intellectually he dismissed it as the ramblings of a deluded mind. He believed then that the world was a mundane, predictable place governed by the immutable laws of physics and the dreary machinations of commerce, not by forgotten symbols of ancient folklore and the nebulous power of collective willpower.

But the seed, once planted, took root, festering in lingering recesses of his mind. He began to test it discreetly at first as a perverse intellectual exercise. He tested it with small, subtle manipulations of online forums, anonymous seeding of carefully crafted stories around obscure local legends, meticulous tracking of resulting ripples of belief and faint, imperceptible amplifications of fear and fascination. He recalled with grim satisfaction a minor incident years ago, a localized panic in a remote coastal village in Newfoundland triggered by whispers of a half-seen amphibious thing that haunted coves shrouded in fog. The details were deliberately hazy even in his own meticulously curated memory, a necessary precaution against unforeseen forensic intrusion. But he remembered the thrill, the intoxicating dawning realization that the sigil, the carefully constructed narrative, and the burgeoning instantaneous power of the internet when artfully combined worked. The raw, pliable clay of human fear and fascination could indeed be sculpted into tangible, terrifying forms. The clergyman's annotator had been right. Belief sufficiently focused, sufficiently amplified, could indeed make stories walk.

A symbol... yet it unlocked everything. He murmured now and traced the worn, familiar contours of the carved spiral talisman as it swayed gently before him. The sigils, he knew, were not his invention. He was a conduit, a visionary who had rediscovered their latent power or had been subtly guided to them by whispers from darker, ancient corners of forgotten lore. The old journal from the Maine historical society had contained a barely visible bookseller's stamp on its flyleaf, an obscure, unreadable insignia that, after months of patient, obsessive research, he had tentatively traced to a defunct nineteenth-century esoteric society, a clandestine group rumored to have explored the mechanisms of belief and manifestation. He had branded the Gifford Pinchot legend with that ancient mark, embedding it in the digital DNA of every shared video clip and carving it into the very fabric of the forest, the trees, the stones, the earth itself to anchor the creature and give his terrifying story roots in the unyielding soil of the physical world.

His thoughts snapped to the two campers, Jackson and Mia. Their clumsy adolescent attempt at a Bigfoot hoax, broadcast live to a handful of amused online thrill-seekers, had been the initial spark, the unexpected comically mundane catalyst that fortuitously accelerated his meticulously planned timeline for the Gifford Pinchot manifestation. He had monitored their livestream while his own sophisticated recording equipment stood ready nearby and anticipated the inevitable convergence of their trivial narrative with his far grander, more terrifying one.

When their feigned surprise curdled into genuine unscripted terror as his carefully seeded narrative began to bleed into theirs, as the whispers of the forest deepened and the shadows coalesced into something monstrous and real, he was there, a silent, unseen chronicler filming from the concealing darkness. Their dropped phone, its lens pointed at the shaking, out-of-focus undergrowth and streaming their shrieking escape to a growing audience, became a viral sensation born of their fear and his art.

Retrieving them later, dazed, disoriented, and on the verge of hypothermia from the muddy fern-choked gully they had blundered into in their panic, proved insultingly easy. He had decided to move them from the immediate vicinity of their abandoned campsite just hours before those persistent federal pests, led by the officious and resilient Agent Bishop, started sniffing around with their buzzing drones and meticulously gridded search patterns. An inconvenience certainly, those two mewling college students, but an inconvenience that creative narrative restructuring could mold into a significant opportunity. Their fear, their continued mysterious disappearance, and their inevitable story would all serve a greater, enduring purpose. It might be a sequel to the Gifford Pinchot legend or something even more…ambitious. He allowed himself a quiet chuckle. The narrative possibilities, he mused, were endless. They were far more valuable alive and terrified under his careful artistic curation than as mere anonymous casualties. Their story, he decided, was not yet fully written.

The old camper van, its engine sputtering a familiar, rhythmic protest against the strain of the climb, finally rumbled onto a stretch of relatively smooth, paved two-lane blacktop. Rain, which had eased to a persistent, misting drizzle, now began to fall with renewed intensity, smearing the accumulated grime on the windshield into opaque, greasy streaks. Vale switched on the wipers, their worn blades juddering a noisy, protesting rhythm across the glass, a discordant counterpoint to the insistent hiss of tires on the wet, slick asphalt. He was heading north, putting as much distance as possible between himself and the lingering inconvenient official attention now focused on the smoldering ruins of the Gifford Pinchot grove.

A massive, brightly illuminated billboard loomed out of the misty darkness, its garish colors a jarring intrusion into the monochrome landscape of rain and night. It advertised the latest formulaic thriller by a blandly handsome, smiling mannequin of an author, "Michael R. Thorne: The Crimson Cipher, the Unputdownable Number One Global Bestseller. Soon to be a major motion picture." Sharp, corrosive envy tightened Carter Vale's chest, clenching around his heart like an icy fist. He remembered with a clarity that could still wound a time when his name had graced the hardback jackets, when he had briefly entertained the illusion of literary significance, of a legacy etched in words.

He vaguely recalled the name Michael R. Thorne. He probably wrote the kind of lowest-common-denominator, airport-bookstore tripe that Vale had in his idealistic youth vehemently and publicly despised, the kind of shallow, predictable drivel that sold millions.

His own literary heyday, if it could be called that, seemed a distant, forgotten lifetime ago. He had a brief flicker of success in the vast, indifferent publishing world. Three novels, meticulously crafted, each one a heartfelt attempt to say something meaning-ful. One, a sprawling historical epic that had consumed nearly a decade of his life, had even brushed the lower rungs of a national bestseller list for three weeks. He remembered the rush of that minor triumph and the anticipation of each new royalty state-ment and each inquiry from a film scout.

Then came the slow, humiliating slide into obscurity. He recalled with vividness a particularly galling book signing for his third and final published novel. It took place in a cavernous, impersonal chain bookstore in a sprawling suburban mall. A teetering pyramid of his unsold, unloved copies stood near the entrance, and only five people showed up during the allotted two hours. One of them, an elderly woman with vacant blue eyes and the faint scent of lavender water, patted his hand and asked with devastating innocence "Would you ever consider writing some-thing… you know… real?"

The question, guileless and unintentionally cruel, stung more than any scathing review from literary critics.

And the reviews…oh, the reviews. Those carrion birds of literary ambition were always circling, always eager to pick apart the still-warm corpse of a writer's dreams. "Derivative," one had sneered, dismissing his carefully researched historical detail as "mere window dressing for a hollow narrative." "Lacks authen-ticity," another had proclaimed, questioning the psychological depth of his characters. One particularly venomous piece published in a widely respected national literary supplement had eviscerated his foray into non-fiction. It was a meticulously researched, if overly sensationalized, account of a local, unsolved missing person case from the 1950s. The critic had accused it of being riddled with "unsubstantiated hoaxes and wild, irrespon-sible conjecture." That critic, a smug tenured academic whose own literary output consisted of a single unread monograph on obscure seventeenth-century poets, had mockingly suggested that Vale's stories would only achieve true significance "if they somehow managed to leap off the page and physically accost the reader."

His grip tightened on the van's worn steering wheel. His knuckles showed white under the faint green glow of the dashboard instruments. The irony, oh, the bitter irony, was a corrosive acid in his gut. The public, those fickle, sensation-hungry masses, had yawned and turned away from his crafted prose and earnest attempts at thoughtful storytelling. Yet now they obsessed over his manufactured monsters and staged spectacles of primal terror. Thousands, tens of thousands, no, hundreds of thousands, had hung on every grainy terrifying frame of the Gifford Pinchot creature. Their frantic misspelled comments flooded chat rooms and their shares and retweets made his fabricated legend go viral in a matter of hours.

"They wanted real? I'll give them reality," he thought, a grim feral smile playing on his lips. He was an artist of a new, more visceral, more potent kind. His medium was no longer the anemic inadequacy of ink and paper. It was the raw, pulsating, malleable power of collective belief and primal fear. He was an architect of tangible experience, a modern-day god of belief breathing life into the dark forgotten corners of the collective human imagination. The fleeting, insignificant fame of a critically acclaimed, commercially unsuccessful novelist was nothing compared to the raw, intoxicating, world-shaping power he now wielded. The literary establishment that had spurned him and the reading public that had ignored him now trembled before the tangible echoes of his terrifying creations. The irony was that they were all complicit. They wanted to believe. They craved the thrill, the terror, the validation of their deepest, darkest fears. He was merely providing a service. An exclusive, memorable service. The world that had once forgotten him would now remember Carter Vale not as a failed author, but as a legend himself, the man who made monsters real. They would remember him for eternity.

Hours later, as the first pale, anemic fingers of dawn began to probe the bruised eastern horizon, the rain finally eased, replaced by a persistent, chilling drizzle that hung heavy in the air. Vale, his eyes gritty with fatigue but his mind sharp and alert, pulled the weary, mud-spattered camper van into the mostly deserted, oil-stained parking lot of a sprawling, anonymous twenty-four-hour truck stop complex somewhere in eastern Oregon. The neon sign of the attached all-night diner, a greasy spoon called "The Wanderer's Rest," buzzed fitfully with lurid pink and bilious green bulbs casting a sickly glow over the wet, pockmarked asphalt. He needed black, scalding coffee. More important, he needed to erase his recent digital footprints.

He fired up a battered, heavily modified tablet computer inside the van's cramped living quarters, its screen covered in a spiderweb of fine cracks. He connected it by a shielded cable to a compact satellite uplink antenna he had disguised as a luggage rack on the roof. His fingers flew across the touchscreen with surgical precision as he navigated layers of encrypted servers, proxy chains, and anonymous routers. The "ValeSightings" livestream archives from the Gifford Pinchot event, the raw unedited high-definition footage of the creature's appearance and fiery demise, and the terabytes of captured chat logs filled with terrified, believing commentary were all wiped, fragmented, and scattered across the digital void like ashes on the wind. He chuckled, a dry rasp devoid of humor. Let Agent Bishop and tech specialist Finch chase those digital ghosts. By the time their bureaucratic forensic analysis produced any actionable intelligence, he would be long gone, already seeding the ground for his next ambitious project.

Before severing the satellite connection, he allowed himself a final browse through the chaotic currents of online forums and social media. The Gifford Pinchot "Bigfoot" incident, as the predictable mainstream media had already dubbed it, was still trending globally. Viral content exploded: frenzied speculation, endlessly looped blurry screenshots, and breathless eyewitness accounts that morphed with each retelling, embellishing the legend, deepening the mystery, and solidifying the belief. He scrolled and admired the chaotic beauty of his handiwork. A separate, smaller thread, almost lost in the noise of the Gifford Pinchot aftermath but steadily gaining traction and belief, caught his eye. Reports from the East Coast. A different kind of fear. An older, perhaps more potent legend. "Winged creature with glowing red eyes spotted over the Wharton State Forest." "Strange, bloodcurdling shrieks heard echoing through the desolate heart of the New Jersey Pine Barrens."

A predatory smile touched Carter Vale's lips. The Jersey Devil. An American classic. So much rich, preexisting folklore to exploit. Such a wonderfully evocative, inherently terrifying descriptive palette: leathery wings, a horse-like head, glowing red eyes, and the cloven hooves of a demon. Yes. This had potential, immense potential. He tapped a folder on his tablet labeled "Project: Barrens." A grainy, indistinct image filled the cracked screen: a dark, menacing silhouette, vaguely horned, with vast folded wings against a stark, moonlit backdrop of dense, forbidding pine trees. It was an old photograph of dubious provenance, one he had unearthed from an obscure out-of-print collection of paranormal hoaxes. With a little digital enhancement, a little narrative embellishment, and the subtle insidious application of his signature spiral watermark, it would serve as the perfect visual seed. His finger hovered over the icon in his editing software, ready to brand this new legend.

"One legend feeds another," he murmured. His eyes gleamed with a renewed sense of purpose. "The narrative, my dear, gullible audience, must constantly evolve, must always escalate." This was not merely about conjuring individual monsters or isolated spectacles of terror. It was about the grand, overarching tapestry of belief itself, about his unique godlike ability to harness its raw elemental power, to become the unseen, unacknowledged puppet master pulling the delicate, invisible strings of global consciousness. Gifford Pinchot had been a stunning, unqualified success, a triumphant proof of concept on a grand, operatic scale. But he now realized with a fresh invigorating surge of ambition that it was only the beginning. It was the overture to a more complex, more terrifying symphony.

He powered down the tablet. Darkness in the van's cabin was absolute, broken only by the faint residual glow of the dying embers of his ambition on the cracked screen. The sprawling truck stop complex outside was quiet now, sinking into the predawn torpor that precedes the daily onslaught of diesel fumes and weary travelers. Only the distant mournful rumble of early morning semis on the unseen interstate, like the breathing of some vast sleeping beast, disturbed the heavy, rain-soaked stillness. He started the engine. The old motor coughed and sputtered in protest before finally catching and settling into its familiar uneven but reliable rhythm.

He pulled the lumbering camper van slowly out of the deserted, oil-stained parking lot and back onto the slick rain-swept highway. He switched on the radio and tuned it to a crackling indistinct all-night news station. A breathless announcer was just recapping the "ongoing and increasingly bizarre Bigfoot mania" that had gripped Washington State, quoting shaken incoherent eyewitnesses and speculating wildly about the "mysterious officially unexplained explosion" that had reportedly occurred deep within the heavily cordoned-off Gifford Pinchot National Forest. Vale smirked, his lips curling in contempt. He turned the volume down until the announcer's voice was a faint tinny murmur and an irrelevant footnote to his own grand narrative.

The night was dark and mist swirled around the unassuming van as it sped eastward. He began to hum a tuneless, slightly discordant melody, a fragment of a half-forgotten folk song from his childhood and a counterpoint to the rhythmic slap of the worn wiper blades against the grimy windshield. His mind had drifted into the New Jersey Pine Barrens where he imagined carving potent sigils into the gnarled bark of pitch pines and planting whispers of bloodcurdling terror in online forums and local superstitions.

He glanced at the small crudely carved spiral talisman dangling from the rearview mirror, its dark stained wood absorbing and subtly amplifying the faint ambient light from the dashboard. A line from one of his earliest, most obscure, and commercially disastrous novels, a dense allegorical gothic tale exploring the shadowed liminal spaces between folklore, faith, and madness, surfaced unbidden in his mind, a fragment of his own forgotten narrative.

"Monsters." He whispered to the empty, indifferent passenger seat, his voice a low sibilant hiss blending seamlessly with the wind buffeting the van and the ceaseless rhythmic drumming of rain on the fiberglass roof. "Never truly die. No, not as long as their stories are told. Not as long as there is someone…someone like me…to tell them."

The red grime-streaked taillights of the old camper van receded into the misty rain, fading into the darkness of the American night. The legend of the Gifford Pinchot creature would echo briefly in the relentless news cycle. But its unseen author, Carter Vale, was already scripting his next more terrifying and enduring chapter.

The stage was set and the audience waited. He knew with unshakeable certainty that darkness craved new stories.

CHAPTER TWENTY-THREE

Smoke cast a thick cloud across the grove, burning Mara's lungs as she circled the destroyed stump. Charred splinters crumbled under her boots, and she brushed a trembling hand over her forehead. Her gaze darted toward a shout from across the clearing. She saw Vale's damaged camper van lurch away from a cloud of ash. The vehicle bounced down the slope, and its tires spat dirt as it vanished behind a stand of towering conifers. A blistered branch swung in Mara's path, forcing her to duck. She tasted the acrid tang of thermite residue on the back of her tongue.

He fled before the cryptid had blasted. This was not his purpose. He is planning something else.

Skyhook's voice crackled over Mara's earpiece. "I'm too far out. We need a minute to get airborne." Mara pressed a hand to her vest. "Do what you can. Link, see if any camera network is picking up that van."

A burst of static signaled Link's attempt to comply. She heard him mutter curses as he sorted through local feeds. Mara's eyes roamed the scorched debris. The cryptid was gone, reduced to a heap of ashen fragments scattered near the splintered cedar stump. She felt relief, but it came with a pang of frustration. Vale was making his getaway.

Nearby, a dazed onlooker moaned. Mara forced herself to focus on immediate priorities. She crouched beside the influencer who had slammed into a fallen trunk when the cryptid lashed out earlier. The young man clutched his shoulder, eyes wide as if he was reliving the moment the creature dissolved. Blood soaked the sleeve of his denim jacket.

"Sit tight." Mara said. "Skyhook will patch you up."

He sputtered something about seeing Vale rush through the haze. "He pointed a camera at the ashes from far away, then sprinted for that van. Is this some twisted stunt?"

Mara tugged a bandage roll from her vest. "That stunt nearly got people killed." She pressed the bandage to the influencer's wound, holding firm until Skyhook arrived with her medical kit.

Skyhook stepped around a tangle of scorched branches and dropped to one knee beside them. She wore her flight harness, helmet still latched under her arm. "I see we have an arm injury. Let me handle it, Mara."

Mara gave a curt nod and leaned back on her heels. She scanned the perimeter. The cryptid's meltdown had drawn watchers from the trees, phones raised high. Some recorded the drifting ash, and others pointed their lenses toward Vale's exit. Now the crowd milled around in confusion. A few shouted questions at Mara, but she waved them off and put a hand to her earpiece.

"Finch, you found anything in the remains?"

His voice carried the same edge of exhaustion she felt. "Still scanning. Tissue is charred beyond recognition, but I might salvage a sample. If we tie it to the anchor's destruction, we can finalize the post-op analysis. Nothing unusual so far."

Mara twisted around to see Finch kneeling at the pile of cinders. He wore sterile gloves and fiddled with a half-melted container meant for scrapings. She appreciated his thoroughness, but her nerves were too raw to care about fine details now. "Copy. Keep me posted."

A short distance away, a county deputy sprinted across the clearing, boots crunching through ash. She nearly tripped over a fallen branch before catching herself. "Sheriff Thomason wants to know if you have eyes on Vale's van."

Mara shrugged. "He tore off. No unit in position to chase him?"

"Everyone is tied up with injuries and crowd control. It's chaos."

Mara set her jaw. "Listen, tell the sheriff that blocking the main exit is still crucial. Even if we missed Vale on the old logging road, we can try to catch him farther down."

The deputy hustled off. Mara closed her eyes for a moment, inhaling the lingering stench of melted sap and burnt wood. Irritation built beneath the crisp uniform calm she tried to maintain. Vale had orchestrated every second of this. He wanted that dramatic conclusion. He had recorded the cryptid's final moments and was likely uploading or editing footage right now. Her teeth clenched at the thought.

A hiss of static from Link disrupted her simmering anger. "Mara, local street cams show no sign of the van. Either he moved off-grid or he's tampering with the feed. I've got nothing."

She muttered a curse. "Then we regroup here and manage the aftermath. Keep trying. He can't vanish without a trace."

He gave a grim acknowledgment before dropping off the channel. Mara let her stare wander over the battered remains of drones that had crashed during the chaos. The clearing was riddled with scorched earth and twisted shapes from the cryptid's final rampage. Finch's voice rose as he warned curious onlookers not to step near the ash. Some folks demanded an explanation but he refused to say more than a vague reference to a chemical hazard.

A loud groan emerged from behind one of the toppled evergreens. Mara moved to investigate and found two hikers shivering in the cold drizzle, leaning on each other for support. They had bloody scratches on their arms. Their expressions danced between awe and terror.

She directed them toward the sheriff's makeshift triage zone near the edge of the grove. "Go see those deputies for first aid. You're lucky the worst is over."

One hiker coughed, wincing at a sharp pain in his shoulder. "That…that…was it real? I swear it looked like bone spikes on that thing. Then it crumbled."

Mara wished she had an easy answer. "Get patched up. Let the medical folks handle the rest." She guided them until a deputy hurried over, offering water and bandages.

Glancing back at the broken stump, Mara tried to stir her focus. The cryptid was neutralized, and that was the main objective. Destroying the anchor had collapsed its power, leaving only smoldering chunks. Yet Vale had slipped away, and if he was brazen enough to record everything, he would stir new waves of hype online. People would swarm the area again, ignoring the danger.

She stalked toward Skyhook, who was finishing the influencer's dressing. "We need to secure the perimeter soon. How is he?"

Skyhook exhaled. "He'll live. Nothing too deep."

A new voice chimed in behind them. Sheriff Thomason trudged up, face taut with tension. He removed his hat and wiped sweat from his brow. "Saw Vale's ride vanish. My deputy tried radioing a patrol car down the road, but they're tangling with a pileup. We have to let him go."

Mara felt her pulse thud at her temples. "Of all times for a traffic jam."

"Got folks driving up here the minute they see the slightest rumor." Thomason rubbed the back of his neck. "We're lucky it didn't turn into a stampede."

She nodded. "I can't spare a chase crew anyway. I need the entire team for crowd control and first aid. My pilot's out of position, and Link's got no leads."

He nodded. Frustration thickened the silence. Then Thomason jerked his head toward the swirling ash. "That...thing. I guess it's done? We don't have to worry about more attacks?"

Mara studied the blackened circle of ground. "Not from this cryptid. The anchor is destroyed, so it's gone. But Vale got what he wanted. Keep your men alert in case he tries something else around here. One thing I can assure you: if there is no Vale, then there is no cryptid."

Thomason grunted and strode off, barking orders at the nearest deputy. Mara stood there for a moment and waited for her heartbeat to steady. The crowd was thinning, though a handful still lingered near the fallen cedar trunk, phones raised high. She wanted to confiscate every device pointed at the scene, but that ship had sailed. The story was out there. Another wave of online chatter would follow soon enough.

Finch approached with a sealed evidence bag holding a small sample of ash. His face revealed exhaustion mixed with relief. "I've got what I need, though this might not reveal much. Still, I'd like to run quick scans with Argus to confirm the meltdown. If the reading is stable, we can confirm it's over."

Mara nodded. "Go for it. Then we regroup with Link and pack up."

His eyes flicked toward the ditch where the cryptid fell. "We pulled off the main mission. Feels hollow with Vale gone, but it's a victory."

She crossed her arms. "It is. Next time, he won't be so lucky." A bitter taste crept into her mouth as she thought of Vale's smug expression. She was certain he had filmed every dramatic second. That footage would be gold for him. She could almost see the viral headlines. This was a twisted stepping stone to his next stunt.

A harsh cry drew her attention. Another influencer stumbled out of the bush, camera phone still rolling. She had a shallow cut along her cheek. "Where's the monster? I heard it was right here."

Mara waved her off. "It's gone. Get yourself to the triage corner if you're hurt."

The woman nodded, trembling. She edged closer, ignoring Mara's attempt to move her away and angled her phone as if trying to record an exclusive interview. "Folks online say some mysterious federal team just toasted Bigfoot. Is that you guys? Is the government covering everything up?"

Mara stiffened, stepping back to avoid the lens. "We're assisting the county with public safety. That's all."

The influencer pressed forward, eyes glittering. "People are gonna want proof. They'll call me a liar unless I share footage of the big meltdown."

A savage retort threatened to slip from Mara's tongue, but she clamped down. Instead, she gestured for a nearby deputy to intervene. "Ma'am, please cooperate. We have injured folks who need immediate care."

After the deputy guided the influencer away, Mara breathed out. Her nerves throbbed as she felt the toll of the frantic conflict. He had planned it all to make a spectacle. She hated giving him that power.

Skyhook tapped her shoulder and pointed to a battered drone that lay half-buried in ash. Mara stooped to retrieve its camera module. "We can salvage some data from this," Skyhook said. "Might see if Vale or his prints show up on the final feed."

"Attach it to Finch's gear. Let's see if we get a shot of what direction he ran off."

Skyhook nodded. She headed for the command trailer. Mara surveyed the forest floor and resisted using the banned word that described Vale's van. Ragged branches, scorched ferns, and scattered footprints painted a portrait of chaos. She stepped carefully between them to avoid slipping on damp ash mixed with soft soil. Her back tensed each time she recalled Vale's triumphant dash to his getaway.

Link's voice returned. "No dice, Mara. He's in the wind. That plate number is worthless. He either swapped it or blocked it from the traffic cameras."

She let frustration show. "Stay on it. Keep checking social feeds. That's his game, after all."

He affirmed with a tired sigh. Mara lifted her radio and called out to the sheriff. "I'm giving you half my crew for the medical evacuation. We can't stay here all night. The site is secure enough as long as your team keeps gawkers behind taped boundaries."

Sheriff Thomason's reply crackled in her earpiece. "Understood. My folks will handle the rest."

Mara dropped the radio against her vest, letting the clipped acknowledgment sink in. Finch was packing his sample kit, Link was rummaging through drone data near the trailer, and Skyhook was loading a second medical kit to help the local responders. This lull offered no immediate chase. Vale had earned a head start. That reality stung, but she was not about to set off blindly with an injured crowd on her hands.

A moan rose from the far side of the clearing, where a father was cradling a trembling child. Mara hurried over, scanning for any sign of serious harm. The girl had scrapes on her arm, likely from falling as everyone scattered. The man's eyes were stricken. "I never believed any of this until I saw those spikes. We camped near the creek. Then the ground shook. Now…this?"

He gestured at the ash-covered clearing as if it were a battle-field. Mara knelt and spoke gently. "You're safe now. Sit tight while we see about your daughter's arm." She flagged the deputy distributing first-aid kits. "Let's make sure they get looked at soon."

The father's gratitude glinted behind his worried stare. Mara offered what little reassurance she could. Then she got back to her feet, heart pounding with remnants of adrenaline and anger. One cryptid contained, but the puppet master had slipped away. The forest still reeked of burning sap, and the press of onlookers reminded her that secrets never stay hidden for long. She glimpsed the remains of the carved stump, blackened and cracked around the edges. The spiral lines had melted into shapeless scars.

Finch emerged from the gloom and wiped his hands on his pants. "No further meltdown spikes. The anchor is definitely gone."

Mara exhaled. "Good job. Keep your sample sealed until we're back at the command trailer."

He nodded and trudged away, posture heavy with fatigue. Mara glanced at the remains of a half-collapsed cedar trunk that had served as partial cover earlier. She recalled crouching there with her EM-coil carbine, firing sedation rounds that barely slowed the monster. The crowd had screamed when it lunged. She had seen a swirl of bone plating and those lethal talons as it crashed into the trap zone. In the end, only thermite on the stump had forced its dissolution.

A deputy's voice cut through her memories, instructing bystanders to evacuate the grove. Mara joined him, urging folks to move along and steering them away from precarious debris. Link stepped out of the trailer, shoulders slumped. "I tried isolating Vale's radio signals. Either he disabled or replaced everything. No trail."

She gave a curt nod. "He's done this before. He'll resurface, you know that."

Link tapped the side of his laptop. "I'll keep watch for suspicious uploads. My guess is he's got fresh footage."

Mara felt tension coil in her chest. "He sure does." Her eyes shifted to the last swirl of thermite smoke drifting above the stump. "He'll spin this into his own victory."

Skyhook approached, med kit under one arm. "Have to

remind him it's only round one." She tried a thin smile. "He can run, but we'll catch up."

Mara agreed, turning to watch a group of battered social-media streamers limp past. Camera rigs still hung from their chests, capturing every shaky step. The air smelled of sweat and confusion, and it tinted the final moments of that combustible night. She lowered her gaze to a chunk of splintered cedar at her feet. A faint spiral burn was still visible along its ridges, a reminder they had disrupted Vale's plan but had not shut him down. She clenched her fists.

With slow, deliberate steps, she walked back to the stump and crouched to examine the blackened bark. Embers glowed in a few crevices. She scooped a small piece of the shredded wood into a side pouch, letting soot coat her gloves. It might have been a personal trophy or a stinging keepsake. She did not know. All she knew was that Carter Vale was gone and the farmland beyond these woods would not keep him hidden forever. Jackson and Mia were still missing. Vale did not seem to care about them or the cryptid as much as Mara had thought. Was it Vale who had captured them or were they lost on this big mountain? Even then, some clue or some trail would have been found.

A final call reached her from the triage corner, so she rose and made her way toward the battered volunteers. Medical staff needed direction, and the panic among the injured was still high. She spent the next few minutes helping calm people who had been caught in the crossfire and quietly reassuring them that the cryptid was gone.

Once the urgent care was underway, she stood beside Finch and Link near the half-collapsed command trailer. They surveyed the battered landscape of swirling ash, fallen branches, and exhausted deputies. Their expressions bore the same frustration Mara felt. She kept her voice even as she addressed them. "We came here to shut down that cryptid. And we did, no matter what Vale tries to spin. Let's get everything wrapped, then we head out."

Link tapped a few keys on his laptop. Finch sealed his sample containers. Skyhook guided the final stragglers away from the site. Mara stepped forward and gathered them in a small circle. "All right, time to disperse. Keep your eyes open for Vale. We'll debrief back at the trailer soon."

Gear in hand, they trudged away from the shattered remains of the anchor. Mara lingered a final moment, letting her gaze follow the path Vale had taken when he fled in his van. The faint tire ruts had been chewed into the muddy ground. She wanted to race after him, but she had responsibilities here. People were hurt, and the local authorities needed her team's help to secure the grove. The pursuit would have to wait.

She turned her back on the stump and joined the others. There were no illusions about how quickly Vale would vanish, so she braced herself for the next move. At least this mission had robbed him of the cryptid. She intended to make sure he never conjured another monster in these woods. Any celebration would be brief, though. She had a job to finish, and Vale's silhouette still haunted her mind.

With that resolve firmly in place, Mara signaled the group to finalize the perimeter. Tend to the wounded, collect every scrap of evidence, and dismantle the scene. She would not give Vale any more free publicity than he already had. Once everything was gathered, they could finally pull out of this ravaged grove, leaving only the blackened stump and a swirl of bitter smoke behind.

CHAPTER TWENTY-FOUR

The search for Jackson and Mia, the initial spark that ignited the entire crisis, remained unresolved, their fate uncertain despite intensified efforts from Sheriff Thomason's overwhelmed deputies and community volunteers. Skyhook meticulously oversaw the collection of charred samples from the ruined stump, its blackened remnants a stark symbol of the nightmare they had confronted. Link reported that their attempts at signal disruption had seen some success, yet Vale's digital presence had vanished, a sign of his practiced skill at slipping away once his spectacle peaked. Mara knew Vale's escape signaled that the threat continued. His methods of converting viral frenzy into tangible horrors could be repeated.

Mara pocketed a twisted piece of the scorched, spiral-marked cedar, a reminder of their recent battle and a warning of the struggles ahead. Finch, maintaining his diligence, activated automated monitoring for any resurgence of sigil-related discussions or anomalies echoing Vale's signature methods. Data gathered during the Gifford Pinchot incident would prove valuable for deciphering the intricate dynamics of belief-generated phenomena. Skyhook ensured the VTOL remained in immediate readiness, and their silent understanding was clear. The next call to action could occur at any moment. Link carefully archived terabytes of social media content, creating an extensive digital record of the hysteria Vale had sparked.

Mara settled onto the rickety stool in the SRD's mobile command trailer and noticed her reflection in the dark monitor beside her. The trailer smelled of rain-soaked gear, strong coffee, and the residue left by each exit-and-entry scramble.

She had guided the team back from the forest an hour ago, and her body trembled with adrenaline. She ran her palm over her short, damp hair and sighed. She heard them call in status updates while her mind wrestled with the fresh intel from Finch's terminal.

"Got anything promising?" she asked. She kept her voice low, unsure if she wanted an answer. Her shoulder ached from the earlier gear haul, but she tried to ignore it.

Finch glanced up. His eyes carried the exhaustion of too many nights sifting online chatter. "Depends on how you define promising. We are seeing chatter about something big in New Jersey. It is nowhere near the scale we dealt with, but the online surge is there."

She noticed the pattern of lines on Finch's screen. They looked like restless wave crests on a dark ocean. "Rule out copycats or some clickbait?"

"Doubt it." He scrolled through news clips, posts from local cryptid groups, and forum rumors. "We keep seeing references to a tall, winged figure in the Pine Barrens that has a goat-like face and horns, and people are labeling it a Jersey Devil sighting."

Mara rested her elbows on the edge of his station. "A winged cryptid after we uprooted a forest crawler. Perfect." She stared at the images, grainy photos, shaky phone frames, and bizarre sketches. The pattern of interest rose in short bursts, similar to the fluctuations that fed the Gifford Pinchot beast. "That is how it starts. Then it hits mainstream news, and everyone jumps in."

Finch nodded. "We have to remain on standby. Dr. Sato's call is incoming, so we'll see if they want us to redirect resources. We finished cleanup here, but you know how these things travel. That spiral was not the only design out there."

She looked over at the battered whiteboard and then caught herself, unsettled that the word battered surfaced in her mind. The board was marred by scribbles from part of their operation. They had mapped Gifford Pinchot sightings, pinned Carter Vale's known movements, and flagged points where crowds had swarmed. She saw new additions scrawled in green marker: "Possible NJ leads."

A beep sounded on Finch's console. Mara straightened then adjusted her comms earpiece. Dr. Sato's voice crackled through the trailer's speakers. "Team, I'm patching in from the secure facility. I trust everyone is back safely?"

Mara cleared her throat. "Yes, ma'am. Minimal injuries, all contained. Local authorities have it under control now." Her mind flicked to the forest's gloom, the swirl of phone lights and flashlights around a burned stump. She remembered the exhale that came after the cryptid dissolved. Now it felt like a memory from weeks ago instead of hours.

"That's good. We need you to be prepared for another possible assignment. Meanwhile, the local sheriff is still searching for those missing campers. If they come across new evidence, they'll forward it to me. I'll keep you in the loop."

Mara nodded, though the line was audio-only. "Understood. We're ready to assist if they find anything."

There was a brief pause. "Well done neutralizing the anchor. Remain vigilant. I've received warnings about heightened activity in the Pine Barrens. Pilots reported sightings, and local law enforcement is brushing it off as a prank. Our data shows the social feeds are building a small but steady wave of interest."

Mara edged closer to Finch's console. "Then we might need to investigate soon."

Sato's voice carried a subdued tone. "Yes, but rest if you can. I don't intend to scramble you again without reason. Link, I believe you picked up a cryptic message referencing misery under moonlight. That suggests someone is seeding all this. Vale or his associates may be fueling the talk."

Link stuck his head into the trailer, phone in hand. "Still verifying the source. The user name is an anagram of ValeSightings, but that might be a troll. Hard to say. The suspicious part is the mention of a swirl, similar to the spiral we saw." He perched on the empty seat behind Finch. "Spiral mania never ends, right?"

Mara didn't hide her grim smirk. "Feels like it's the new normal."

Dr. Sato took a moment to let them absorb the news. "Keep a watch on the data feed, Finch and Link. Mara, I'll contact you if we receive official orders for deployment. Until then, remain alert. Thank you for your hard work. We have a bigger battle ahead."

The call ended, leaving the trailer in the steady hum of server fans and overhead lights. Skyhook strolled in, flight suit unzipped halfway. "Heard we might go cross-country soon?"

"Could happen." Mara answered. She pulled a half-full water bottle from the table, took a sip, and scanned the updated post displayed on Finch's monitor. Something about hooves and leathery wings. "There's potential for a new anchor in the Pine Barrens, and I'd rather not watch it grow from a rumor into a monster. But we wait on the final go-ahead."

Skyhook's gaze shifted to Mara's anxious posture. "We have time to regroup, though, right? Let me service the VTOL so it's ready for long distance. Won't take more than an hour. If we're not launching now, I'll do it at dawn." She brushed a fleck of dried leaves from her sleeve. "Get some downtime, Bishop. You look like you ran a triathlon wearing body armor."

Mara shrugged away the tension crowding her shoulders.

"That's exactly what it felt like. I'll try to rest after I know we have this data locked."

Outside, a gust rattled the trailer's steps. She heard a flurry of debris scrape across the pavement. The day had turned into an odd gloom, as if the forest refused to let them leave. Mara rubbed the back of her neck. A quiet ache bloomed behind her eyes.

Finch turned the laptop toward her, the ARGUS interface swirling with fresh pings. He pointed at a line trending up, low on the scale but rising. "You see that? It only takes a handful of viral tweets or interesting sightings, then the wave hits mainstream. If the 'Jersey Devil' hashtag crosses a certain threshold, we might have a new cryptid on the loose."

Link scrolled through a chat feed on his phone. "People are already joking about horns and goat heads. Another fiasco waiting to happen. If Vale is behind this, he's fast."

Mara exhaled. "He invests in chaos. Doesn't matter if he's physically there or stirring the rumor from behind a keyboard." She shuddered at the memory of his van hidden among tall pines, spiral flyers taped to trunk after trunk. "I hate wondering if each new sighting is his handiwork."

She stood, opened a crate, and began stowing leftover sedation darts and a partial stack of spent magazines. The methodic clink of gear soothed her. She'd been living out of crates and duffels for years and it provided a sense of order. At least the cryptid nest they battled was gone, and the forest crowd had dispersed before nightfall. She wished that was the end of it.

Link let out a soft laugh. "Found some weird post from a user claiming they spotted a goat-faced figure in their backyard. They posted grainy footage. That's all it takes, three or four shares, a trending tag, and a spinning rumor big enough to animate something real."

Mara slotted her carbine into a foam-lined case. "Then we make sure it stays rumor. If Sato decides we're on deck, we're ready."

Skyhook tapped the door, heading out to prepare the VTOL. Finch continued typing until he locked in the final data updates from ARGUS. Mara leaned against the console. She noticed the world map pinned to the metal wall, red pushpins scattered across the country. Some marked the older anomalies they had handled, others marked rumored sightings they debunked. The Pine Barrens pin was newly added.

Fatigue tugged her inward focus again, so she stepped outside to feel the evening air. The trailer was parked next to a chain-link fence and a row of official SUVs. She heard Link rummaging around inside, double-checking the comm logs. A thin layer of cloud cover stretched overhead, tinted with bruised hues of purple. The local officials had gone home, leaving the vacant parking area to the SRD. She tried to welcome that calm, but a new tension dragged at her thoughts.

Minutes later, Finch stepped out. He rubbed his eyes and paused near her. "I wonder how long we can chase Vale if he's behind this. He always slithers away at the last second."

She nodded. "We'll corner that guy eventually. For now, we do our job." Her voice sounded hollow in her own ears. She remembered the swirl of watchers in Gifford Pinchot, with too many influenced by Vale's calls to action. This new wave showed his arsenal remained full.

Finch fumbled with his phone. "I'm setting up an automated feed watch for Pine Barrens. If we spot a steady climb in references to goat wings or spiral carvings, we'll escalate."

Her breath misted in the cooler air. She pictured another stump hidden in those thick pines, etched with new patterns. She had expected some relief after the forest creature's defeat. Instead, it felt like standing in front of one of those carnival strength-test machines. You slam the hammer down on one spot and then watch another meter climb somewhere else.

"I might run into town for a hot meal," Mara said. "We do have a few hours of downtime. The place the sheriff recommended might still be open." She paused, remembering that the sheriff was still out near Gifford Pinchot. "He said he'd contact me if they find even a trace of Jackson and Mia. I'm not overly optimistic, but we can't abandon them. They didn't ask to be part of this fiasco."

Finch rubbed the side of his nose. "Those kids were unlucky. Let's hope they're just hiding in a cabin or something." His voice fell quiet.

Mara appreciated his empathy. She felt it herself, though she locked it behind layers of routine. She still saw glimpses of the torn campsite, half-melted equipment, frantic footprints leading nowhere. That was the raw cost of these belief-fueled horrors. Real people got swallowed by them. She half-expected to wake tomorrow and hear that someone had posted a new snippet of the missing duo. Hard to say if Vale was involved directly, but it all felt connected.

She walked to the far side of the parking lot, scanning the dark silhouette of pines around them. The breeze whispered through the branches. Her boots scuffed the pavement, and she caught a faint reflection of her own posture in the side mirror of an SUV. She looked smaller than she felt. The forest had a way of humbling her. She turned back toward the trailer.

Skyhook stepped near the VTOL's open side hatch and called out, "We have enough fuel to get us anywhere on short notice. I'll sign off on these final checks, then I'm getting some actual sleep. You should, too."

"Yeah," Mara replied. She found it strange how normal their conversation sounded even though they were discussing the possibility of a new monstrous manifestation. They had faced this enough times to treat it as routine. "I'll wrap in a minute."

She ducked into the trailer once more and nodded at Finch. Link turned his gaze to the social feeds and read a comment about a so-called cryptid cultist. He shook his head, annoyed. "The chatter is insane. Some folks want to track the creature for profit, others want to chase it for clicks. They blame the government, they blame a cult, or they think it's a hoax. Meanwhile, that swirl keeps popping up."

"I hate that swirl," Mara said with a small chuckle. She reached for a pen and a scrap of paper. "When the next wave hits, we'll be ready."

Link lifted a brow. "Counting on that. At least we have a heads-up this time."

She scribbled a note to herself to check in with Sheriff Thomason first thing in the morning. Then she tossed the pen aside. The phone on Finch's console buzzed and lit up with a notification. He read it and frowned.

"Local rumors about strange prints are starting to pop up. They might be hoaxes, they might be real, and it's hard to filter," he said.

Mara didn't respond. She paced to the whiteboard and scanned the messy cluster of circles around Gifford Pinchot. That entire operation had tested them physically and mentally. She saw a single red line pointing east labeled possible Pine Barrens. It reminded her that the next threat had already begun growing in some corner of social media fed by eager watchers. She inhaled slowly.

Sleep beckoned but she couldn't rest easy. She recalled Dr. Sato's final warning that whatever they encountered next could be bigger if it gathered enough believers. They had set out to defeat a forest cryptid believed to be unstoppable and then Vale or some copycat launched a new rumor about a creature from local legend where more believers stood ready to feed it. The cycle continued.

She grabbed her jacket from a folding chair. "I'll be back in an hour or two," she said to Finch. "If anything urgent pings, patch me in."

He gave a tired nod. "Sure thing."

On her way out, she paused to observe the screen. She

watched a pattern line climb in small increments as if it were counting up to something. Her gut told her they had only a brief window before that line soared. She stepped into the night air and felt the weight of the mission thrumming behind her eyes. Vale might still be orchestrating madness, or another stooge might have picked up his methods. Either way, the spark of an unknown cryptid threatened to start another wildfire.

She lingered by the trailer steps and pinned her gaze on the partial moon overhead. Link shouted a final question but she didn't answer. She let the hush of the lot settle around her. It felt like the calm eye in a swirling storm. The brief respite might end the moment a new post went viral.

Mara walked away from the trailer and climbed into an unmarked SUV. She tapped the steering wheel. Her mind shifted between possible strategies and the simple need for a break. She switched on the engine, glimpsed the forest boundary in her rearview, and thought of the Pine Barrens. She knew that the old pine groves presented the perfect canvas for another anchor sigil. She had seen enough anchors to know how quickly they grew from rumor to terror.

We are not finished, she thought as she checked her watch. She drove toward the diner the sheriff had mentioned, determined to get a real meal before the next alarm rang. The new threat waited for them, stoking belief one share at a time. She sensed a larger confrontation on the horizon and vowed to be ready when it came.

She left the command center behind, yet it lingered in her peripheral vision like a sentinel. The map, the swirling graphs, and the repeated warnings fed the restlessness pulsing in her chest. Fatigue throbbed in her legs but she pressed onward, certain that only a short window separated them from another sleepless chase. The road stretched out before her, and each turn of the tires carried her closer to a brief reprieve. Tomorrow would bring fresh data and likely a call from Dr. Sato. She preferred to face the next cryptid with clear focus so she planned to seize whatever normalcy she could for now.

When she reached the exit, she glanced at the mirror one last time. The mobile command trailer's lights faded as distance swallowed them. She could not deny that her thoughts drifted to Carter Vale. He was a ghost in the digital realm, always surfacing with new manipulations. Mara felt the engine rumble under her hands and steeled herself. Another monstrous rumor was brewing in the Pine Barrens, and they would answer the call when it rose from shadows.

EPILOGUE

Darkness was suffocating and absolute. It pressed in on Jackson from all sides, broken only by the faint, musty odor of damp earth, stale gasoline, and something else…something metallic and faintly rotten that made his stomach churn. He lay on a hard, uneven surface, rough wooden planks he thought, and his wrists and ankles burned where the coarse rope bit into his skin with every involuntary twitch. Beside him, Mia's shallow, ragged breaths punctuated by tiny choked sobs she tried to stifle.

They were in the back of Vale's camper van or some forgotten lightless cabin deep in the woods. The air was cold and seeped through his thin jacket, raising gooseflesh on his arms. Every rustle of leaves outside, every creak of the vehicle's suspension, or the distant snap of a twig under some unseen creature's foot jolted adrenaline through him. His heart hammered against his ribs like a frantic drum in the otherwise tomblike silence of their prison.

Mia shifted and her bound shoulder brushed his. "Jackson?" she whispered. "Are you…are you awake?"

"Yeah." He breathed and tried to keep his voice from shaking. "I'm here." He strained his ears for any sign of rescue, the distant hum of a highway, the bark of a dog, or another human voice, but heard only the wind sighing through the pines, a mournful sound that mocked their isolation.

The world thought them missing, swallowed by the vast Gifford Pinchot Forest, or worse, dead and pawed by Bigfoot as the internet forums had morbidly speculated after their disastrous live stream. Only Carter Vale knew they were alive. Vale had unsettlingly calm eyes and a camera that seemed to focus solely on their terror. He was keeping it that way, and the weight of that knowledge crushed the air from Jackson's lungs.

Mia's whispered fragments of Hail Marys and pleas for deliverance formed a desperate counterpoint to the silence. Jackson remembered Vale before he left them here hours or maybe a day ago. Time had become a blur. Vale had been different, tense yet crackling with a barely suppressed manic exhilaration. He paced the small confines of the van and muttered about a "finale" and "the culmination of the narrative." His eyes gleamed with a feverish light Jackson had seen before, in movies, in the eyes of people on the brink of violence. Jackson and Mia exchanged terrified glances, understanding instinctively that something terrible was about to unfold beyond the thin metal walls of their prison.

Had it happened? Was it over? The sounds they'd heard earlier, muffled shouts, the distant, percussive thump of...explosions? Sirens, faint but unmistakable, wailing through the night. Then a preternatural silence had fallen, a quiet that felt heavier, more ominous than the preceding chaos. Had the creature, the bone-plated horror that had chased them through the moonlit forest, been defeated? Or had Vale, its architect, simply moved on to his next act, leaving them to rot in this forgotten corner of the wilderness? They had no way of knowing. Their world had shrunk to the dimensions of this lightless box, their news filtered only through the anticipated return of their captor.

Mia whimpered softly, a sound that tore at Jackson's frayed

nerves. "I keep… I keep seeing things," she whispered, her voice trembling. "In the dark. Shadows…moving."

He knew it was her mind, their minds, playing tricks. The absolute darkness was a canvas for fear. He'd seen them too, those fleeting, illusory shapes in the periphery, heard the faint, imagined growl beyond the van's door that turned out to be nothing more than the groan of a tree branch in the wind. But the rational part of his brain, the part that clung desperately to sanity, knew the real monster wasn't some spectral beast conjured from the gloom. The real monster was Carter Vale. And he could return at any moment. That fear, cold and tangible, was far more terrifying than any phantom.

Jackson found himself counting his own heartbeats, a futile attempt to impose order on the terrifying unknown. Even the nocturnal symphony of the forest, the crickets, the owls, and the rustling of small unseen things seemed to have been snuffed out, as if the woods themselves were holding their breath. Had the "finale" Vale so eagerly anticipated already played out? The quiet was a suffocating blanket, leaving them adrift in a sea of their own racing thoughts and unspoken fears.

Then a sound. Distinct. Close. Heavy footsteps crunching on gravel, approaching their confinement. Jackson's breath hitched. Mia let out a small, involuntary gasp. The metallic rattle of a lock, a protesting creak of hinges, and a sliver of weak, grey light sliced into their Stygian world, making them recoil.

Carter Vale stood silhouetted against the gloom, a looming, indistinct shape. He was disheveled, his hooded jacket spattered with mud and what looked like…ash? His breathing was heavy, labored, as if he'd been running. But it was the expression on his face as he stepped fully into the weak light filtering from the partially open door that sent a fresh wave of ice through Jackson's veins. A sinister, deeply satisfied smirk played on his lips. His eyes, usually so unnervingly calm, now held a feverish, giddy gleam. Whatever had happened out there, whatever chaos he had orchestrated, it had gone exactly according to his twisted plan.

Jackson instinctively tried to shift to put himself between Mia and their captor but the ropes held him fast. He studied Vale, noting the mud caked on his worn boots, the fine dust of soot on his shoulders and the faint scent of something burnt, like an extinguished bonfire, clinging to his clothes. These were signs of a violent, explosive climax. Mia's stomach audibly dropped. If Carter was this pleased and this invigorated it could only mean that the terror he had unleashed had achieved its horrifying purpose. They were trapped not just physically but in the orbit of his malevolent triumph.

"Well, well," Vale said, his voice a low, almost cheerful purr more menacing than a shout. "Did you two behave yourselves while I was out orchestrating the grand theatre of belief?"

His tone was polite and conversational yet carried a chilling undercurrent of malice. Jackson and Mia remained silent, their eyes wide and fixed on him, their bodies rigid with a primal fear. In that moment the supernatural horrors of the forest receded, replaced by the immediate grounded terror of the dangerous, unpredictable man who stood before them, a man who held their lives in the palm of his grimy, ink-stained hand. Carter's devious satisfaction was the only news they had from the world outside, and it was a terrifying bulletin.

As Vale took another step into their cramped prison and the weak light caught the predatory glint in his eyes, Mia's carefully constructed composure finally shattered. Fear raw and desperate clawed its way up her throat and overwhelmed everything but the need to survive.

"Please." She choked out the word as a ragged sob. Tears hot and stinging traced paths through the grime on her cheeks. "Please...let us go. We won't tell anyone. We swear. We haven't seen anything. We don't know anything." Her voice cracked, a fragile thing in the oppressive stillness. She struggled against her bonds. The movement was futile but instinctual. "Our families...they must be worried sick. We never...we never meant for any of this to happen. It was a stupid prank." She babbled as her words tumbled in a torrent of fear and desperation, a heart-wrenching appeal to any sliver of humanity that might still reside within their captor.

Jackson, though a cold dread had settled deep in his gut, forced himself to speak with a raspy but steadier voice than Mia's. He edged forward as much as the ropes would allow in a desperate attempt to shield her from Vale's looming presence. "She's right," he said, his words careful and measured as if calming a cornered, unpredictable animal. "We won't cause any trouble. We'll do whatever you want. Please don't hurt us. Let us go, and you'll never see us again."

Carter Vale listened with his head tilted slightly, the calm almost patronizing smile fixed on his lips. His eyes glinted with amusement or perhaps a detached, scientific curiosity as though he studied insects trapped in a jar. It was clear that their pleas, their tears, their desperate promises had no effect. Their words scattered into a void unheard and unheeded.

When Mia's voice broke in sobs and her question opened a raw wound in the silence, "Why? Why are you doing this to us?" Carter let his smile widen, a slow, deliberate stretching of his lips that made Jackson's skin crawl. He seemed to consider the question and savor the power he held over their fragile flickering hope. He enjoyed their fear, Jackson realized with a sickening lurch. He fed on it.

The atmosphere in the van, or whatever lightless hole they occupied, was thick with grounded psychological intensity. There were no sudden outbursts of rage from Vale, no overt threats of violence. Only his unnerving even temper and eerie composure contrasted with their raw human terror. It was the horror of absolute powerlessness, the dawning, sickening realization that their words and their lives might not matter to this man. Their desperate humanity had crashed against a wall of cold, manipulative indifference, leaving them trembling in its shadow.

Vale finally broke the silence, his voice soft and gentle, a fatherly tone that was a grotesque mockery of reassurance. "Now, now," he murmured as he stepped closer. "There's no need for hysterics. In fact, if you think about it, you two are the reason all of this…excitement…came to pass."

Jackson and Mia stared at him, stunned into silence by the audacity of his words.

"If you hadn't been out in those woods chasing your little monster stories for a few fleeting moments of internet fame, none of this would have been necessary." Vale continued in a low, confidential whisper. "You invited the narrative, my dear children. You set the stage."

He spoke as if explaining an unavoidable truth to dull-witted pupils who were being justly punished for their foolishness. The immediate brazen twisting of blame left them reeling.

He paced slowly before them, a dark predator circling cornered prey. "And you're lucky, you know. Terribly lucky. If I hadn't found you first, after your little…tumble…who knows what might have happened? That creature you so carelessly provoked…it was hungry. Or perhaps those frenzied crowds, the ones you summoned with your viral broadcast, would have torn you limb from limb in their eagerness for a scapegoat, a sacrifice to their newfound god of the forest."

Jackson's brow furrowed in confusion and dawning outrage. He knew with a certainty that chilled him to the bone that Vale was the orchestrator and puppeteer pulling the strings of this nightmare. But bound and terrified, what could he say? How could he argue against calm insidious gaslighting? Mia, he saw, was already wavering as tears of self-doubt mingled with tears of fear. Had it been their fault? Had their silly harmless prank unleashed a tidal wave of real-world horror? Carter's confident sorrowful tone made it sound disturbingly plausible.

With a cold, knowing smile, Vale leaned in, his voice dropping to an intimate murmur. "All those thousands of eyes, glued to that shaky phone screen, watching your terror unfold. Every share, every comment, every gasp of horrified delight…you were feeding it, you see. You were breathing life into the legend. You practically invited the devil in for supper." Each word was a carefully aimed dart designed to instill guilt, to shatter their remaining sense of agency. He was painting them as the villains in their own horrific story, the unwitting authors of their own torment.

Mia's heart thudded against her ribs like a trapped bird as Vale's shadow fell over her. She could smell the faint, acrid scent of smoke clinging to his clothes, the cloying sweetness of his cheap cologne. He was in control. Terrifyingly in control. Not just of their physical bodies shackled and helpless but of the narrative itself, twisting it and reshaping it to fit his monstrous agenda. Jackson met Mia's gaze across the narrow space and in her eyes he saw his own dawning comprehension reflected: Carter Vale was not a madman driven by some inexplicable obsession. He was a psychopath, a cold, calculating manipulator who reveled in the art of breaking minds as much as he reveled in birthing monsters. Their fear deepened, no longer a reaction to the unknown but a chilling certainty of the precise, cruel intelligence they were up against. The real horror, they were beginning to understand, wasn't the creature in the woods. It was the man who stood before them, his calm voice weaving a web of lies that threatened to suffocate them.

Having in his mind dismantled their pleas and reasserted his dominance, Carter Vale's demeanor shifted. The subtle menace in his voice softened and was replaced by a cheerful, businesslike resolve. He crouched, bringing his face uncomfortably close to theirs as the dim light caught the unsettling gleam in his eyes.

"Now," he said, his voice conspiratorial, "it wasn't all for naught, you understand. In fact, you two…you've become important. Integral, even, to the next chapter."

Jackson and Mia exchanged a bewildered, terrified look. Important? How? What could he possibly mean?

Vale chuckled, a dry, rasping sound. "Oh, yes. Your misadventure in the Gifford Pinchot, your dramatic 'disappearance'…it has made you minor celebrities, haven't you heard? The internet is abuzz with your story. Such a compelling narrative. Such raw, authentic fear." He paused, letting the implications hang in the stale air. "You are living proof, my dears. Survivors. Witnesses to a legend made real. And as such, you are…valuable assets." He didn't elaborate, didn't spell out the specifics of his twisted plans, but the chilling implication was clear. Their ordeal was far from over. They were props to be used and molded to fit whatever new horror he was concocting.

He straightened, a dismissive wave of his hand indicating the futility of any further resistance. "And don't trouble yourselves with thoughts of rescue. The world at large? They've already written your eulogies. Missing, presumed victims of your own reckless stunt or tragic casualties of that unfortunate…entity." He savored the word. "No one will come looking for you when you simply…reappear elsewhere under entirely different and far more interesting circumstances."

That last, thin sliver of hope, that Mara Bishop and the authorities and anyone might still be searching and might burst in and end this nightmare, crumbled to dust in Mia's gut. They were well and truly alone, tethered to this madman's ambitions, their fates entwined with his escalating obsession.

Carter Vale, now brisk, began to gather his few scattered belongings from the corners of their prison: a spare camera battery, a crumpled map, and one of his ubiquitous spiral-marked notebooks. He hummed a faint tuneless melody as if he were preparing for a pleasant journey, oblivious to or reveling in the silent, abject despair of his captives.

He paused at the door, turning back to them with that thin, knowing smile once again gracing his lips. "We'll be leaving tonight. Best get what rest you can. It's a long drive." He let the silence stretch for a beat and then delivered the final bewildering blow. "Pack your courage, kids, we're going to New Jersey."

New Jersey. The name hung in the air, alien and terrifying. Jackson's mind, already reeling, struggled to make sense of it. Why New Jersey? What could possibly be there? Mia, however, felt a jolt of icy recognition. Snippets of late-night internet browsing and articles on American folklore flashed through her memory: the Pine Barrens, the Jersey Devil, a creature of hoof and wing and bloodcurdling shriek. Her blood ran cold. Carter's devious satisfaction as he uttered the words and his gleeful antic-ipation confirmed her horrifying suspicion. This was not an escape but a relocation, the stage simply shifting.

Jackson and Mia shared a final panicked look as the heavy door of their prison creaked shut, plunging them once more into darkness. The distant rumble of the camper van's engine as it turned over was the sound of their last hope dying. They were alive, yes, but they were heading deeper into the heart of Carter Vale's twisted, unending story, their unheard screams a silent chorus to the next monstrous legend he was about to unleash upon an unsuspecting world. The red taillights of the van, had anyone been there to see, would have been swallowed by the dark, forested road, carrying them away into the vast, indifferent night.

AUTHOR NOTES

DECEMBER 8, 2025

Las Vegas, NV

First, thank you for not only reading this story, but these author notes in the back as well!

Electrons Are Breaking Physics (And I'm Taking Notes)

Physicists just discovered **quantum oscillations happening inside an insulating material**.

For those of you who didn't spend way too much time reading physics papers for "research,"(1) let me explain why this is bonkers: Insulators don't conduct electricity. That's literally what makes them insulators. Quantum oscillations are something that happens in *metals*, where electrons can move freely.

Finding quantum oscillations in an insulator is like finding fish swimming through concrete.

The researchers are calling it a **"new duality"** as materials that can behave as both metals AND insulators simultaneously.

I write science fiction, and even I'm confused.

But here's where my brain goes: How do I use this in a book?

Picture a hard sci-fi scenario. You've got a starship with a hull made of this dual-state material. Under normal conditions, it's a perfect insulator because we have no electromagnetic signature, invisible to sensors, the ultimate stealth coating. But when you need to dump heat or channel energy, you flip a switch and suddenly those same materials become conductive.

Or imagine armor that's impervious to energy weapons because it's an insulator, but can instantly become a conductor to power systems embedded in the suit.

Or, and this is where it gets really fun, a prison cell. The walls are insulating, keeping the prisoner contained, unable to interface with any electronic systems. But the guards can make those same walls conductive on demand, delivering a very motivating shock to anyone who misbehaves.

Ok, that's more my vigilante author-side coming out. I'm not saying I'm thinking about politicians right now, but I'm ... No, never mind.

The science suggests that this duality might be controllable. That we could potentially tune the transition between "solid" and "liquid" electron states. Which means switchable materials aren't just theoretical they are *now the logical next step.*

"New duality" sounds like a boss fight in a video game. "You've defeated Normal Physics. Now face... *NEW DUALITY.*"

But it's real physics. Happening now in actual labs somewhere probably close to you. No, I don't suggest you freak out. Sure, it could open a new portal into the dimension of Hell, but I'm sure you will be fine.

No... No you won't. Start screaming right now! ;-)

I love my job. I get to read about impossible discoveries and immediately start thinking about how to weaponize them, defend against them, or use them to trap fictional characters in creative ways so that even THEY want to shank my ass.

The universe keeps giving me material. I just have to write fast enough to use it before reality makes my ideas look quaint.

Like...by tomorrow.

Ad Aeternitatem,

Michael Anderle

P.S. - If any physicists are reading this and thinking "that's not exactly how it works," I apologize in advance. But also, please email me. I have questions.

P.P.S. - The fact that we're still discovering fundamental properties of matter that violate decades of assumptions is humbling AND terrifying. Definitely useful for writing fiction.

MORE STORIES with Michael newsletter HERE: https://michael.beehiiv.com/

(1) – Like me... I didn't. This is why there are scientists who write non-fiction loosely wrapped in 'fiction' wrapping paper...

And me. I write Space Opera. Don't confuse the two of us. One of these two people can MacGuyver the shit out of a paperclip and a coconut on an island...

And me.

The story continues in book two, *DEVIL'S SHARE,* coming soon to Amazon.

Legends don't die. They evolve.

The video was supposed to be a joke. Two teenagers, a dark forest, a local legend. Now they're missing, and something with wings hunts the Pine Barrens under cover of viral fame.

For Special Response Division agent Mara Bishop, what starts as a routine investigation spirals into her strangest case yet. Glowing symbols appear on forgotten structures. Believers armed with cameras and rifles flood the wilderness. *Every post, every share, every trembling witness account makes the creature grow stronger.*

Someone orchestrates the mayhem from the shadows. Someone who knows that modern terror doesn't need claws or fangs when it has WiFi and willing believers.

As the digital fever pitch builds and the body count rises,

Mara races to uncover the truth in a tinderbox landscape where one wrong move could turn fear into flame.

In an age of instant belief and viral nightmares, how do you kill a monster that lives in the feed?

Is the real threat the creature in the sky? Or the one behind the screen?

DON'T MISS OUR NEW RELEASES

Join the LMBPN email list to be notified of new releases and special promotions (which happen often) by following this link:

http://lmbpn.com/email/

CONNECT WITH MICHAEL ANDERLE

Website: lmbpn.com

Email List: michael.beehiiv.com/

Facebook: Facebook.com/LMBPNPublishing

Twitter/X: Twitter.com/MichaelAnderle

Instagram: Instagram.com/lmbpn_publishing/

Bookbub: Bookbub.com/authors/michael-anderle